Veronica Stallwood was born in London, educated abroad, and now lives in Oxford, where she has worked at the Bodleian Library and more recently as Librarian at Lincoln College. Her first crime novel, *Deathspell*, was published to great critical acclaim and became a local bestseller. She is currently working on her next book, which will be the second novel to feature Kate Ivory. When she is not writing, Veronica Stallwood enjoys going for long slow runs in the country, talking and eating with friends, and going to the opera.

Also by Veronica Stallwood

The Rainbow Sign
Oxford Blue
Oxford Knot
Deathspell
Death and the Oxford Box
Oxford Exit
Oxford Mourning

Death and the Oxford Box

Veronica Stallwood

HEADLINE

First published in 1993
by Macmillan London Limited

First published in paperback in 1994
by HEADLINE BOOK PUBLISHING

10 9 8 7 6 5 4

ISBN 0 7472 4478 2

Printed and bound in Great Britain by
Clays Ltd, St Ives plc

HEADLINE BOOK PUBLISHING
A division of Hodder Headline PLC
338 Euston Road
London NW1 3BH

With thanks for their expert assistance to
Michael Burden, Glenys Davies, Richard Gartner,
Robert McNeil, Roy Preece, and Maryanne Tubb.

Chapter One

The woman hesitated in front of 29 Redbourne Road before ringing the bell, then stepped backwards and to one side.

'Yes?' He had to come out on to the step to see who was there.

'I must talk to you about my enamel boxes.' She had a high, breathless voice, like a child's.

'*Our* boxes. I've told you before: they were a wedding present to both of us from your grandmother, so they are *our* boxes. And if I want to keep half of them, then I can do so, quite reasonably and legally. So go away.'

The February wind was sweeping up dead leaves and plastic bags and chasing them round the streets of the Oxford suburb. One plastic bag had caught unnoticed on the heel of the woman's shoe and now rustled and rattled on the tiled path.

'Please, Theo, I have to have them back. All of them. It's important. Won't you let me come in and tell you about it?'

Theo looked down with irritation at the plastic bag stuck to her shoe. He was wearing rubber gloves, as though she had interrupted him while he was doing the washing-up, and one large blue hand rested on the front door, ready to slam it shut at any moment; in the other hand he held a white linen tea towel.

'We can talk here, if you really have something to say,' he said, ignoring the wind that spattered raindrops against the windowpanes and frizzed the woman's hair around her knitted hat.

'You've got to help me out. She – Granny, that is – is coming to Oxford to see me, and she wants to talk about them – the boxes, I mean.' She blinked at him and paused as though she still expected to be invited into the house, then, disappointed, continued. 'She mentioned something about an exhibition and a sale, but her writing is so bad that I couldn't make it out. But she does want to see the collection, Theo, especially the Oxford box, that was quite plain.'

'I expect she's read about the exhibition at the V & A, *The Art of Death*. Haven't you heard about it?' The woman shook her head. 'It's raised a lot of interest in these early nineteenth-century mourning objects. And then there was the sale at Christie's last month; I hadn't realized just how sought after John Parrish's work was until I saw how much one of his fetched. This Oxford box of ours is worth a lot of money.' In his right hand, dark blue enamel gleamed in the folds of white linen.

'Don't you see that she doesn't look on them as *our* boxes? She still thinks of them as hers, and she'll be furious if she comes round to Rosamund Road and finds that half of them are missing.' She had failed to see the box, and now it had disappeared out of sight in the large blue palm.

'How old is she? Eighty-five? Eighty-six? She was obviously bright enough in her youth to invest in *objets de vertu*' – his red lips puckered into a mock kiss as they fluted the words – 'when they were the right price, but I don't expect she understands the current divorce laws. You'll just have to try to explain things to her. Aren't you supposed to be her favourite grandchild? You'll think of something, Rose.'

He started to close the door, but Rose grasped it in both hands and held it open so that he was forced to continue the conversation.

'I'm her only grandchild, but that doesn't mean she can't leave everything to her old college if she wants to. And she will, Theo, if she finds that I've let you steal her boxes.'

'Don't be ridiculous. Nobody's stolen anything. And I have no intention of giving up beautiful and valuable objects to which I have a perfectly legal right.'

Rose's eyes were watering in the cold wind, and her voice climbed even higher than before. 'But I need the money she's going to leave me, especially now . . .' She sniffed loudly and let the sentence fade away. 'I was hoping she'd let me have some capital immediately: it's the only way I'll ever be able to pay for the house in Rosamund Road, and start up my knitting business, and . . .'

'Come off it, Rose. You'll still be talking about your great plans in twenty years' time, and if I gave you the Oxford box you'd only sell it to the first plausible rogue who offered you a few pounds for it. No, it's far better that it should stay here with me, where it's properly looked after.' He had removed her hands from the door so that he was in sole command again, but Rose was pushing at his chest as though she would rush into the house and grab back what she regarded as her property. He fended her off with ease with his left hand while her treasure stayed hidden in his right.

'You've never understood about boxes,' shouted Rose. 'They're small and secretive and you never know what might be inside; that's their fascination. The money isn't important.'

'I suppose they have a certain sexual symbolism,' said Theo dismissively, 'but you are the only person naïve enough to imagine that money has nothing to do with it. We're talking about the Oxford box here: modest, blue, covetable, and now very valuable.'

'They're mine! You bastard, Theo, give them back to me!' shrieked Rose. 'You won't get away with this!'

From inside the house a young female voice called, 'What's happening, Theo?'

'Nothing,' Theo shouted over his shoulder, before turning back to Rose. 'Go away and leave us alone. And don't get any silly ideas about laying your hands on my half of the collection, will you? If you do, I'll have no hesitation in calling the police, and really, Rose, I'd hate to see you in serious trouble over them.' And he shut the door.

Chapter Two

'Theo's left me.'

Rose's words came floating back on the morning air from the group of runners in front of Kate Ivory.

'Come on!' Kate said to her companion. 'I want to hear this.' And she increased the pace so that at her side Camilla panted with the effort of keeping up with her.

'. . . with that dreadful Lynda,' Rose's high, childish voice was saying.

'I'm cold and I've had enough of this,' said Camilla. 'Let's go home.'

'We can't. Getting up at ten to six and out of the front door in the cold and dark is the worst part of the whole day. Running's easy after that. Well, *anything's* easy after that. What's wrong with you this morning?' asked Kate, in the staccato style she used when she was warming up at the beginning of a run. 'I'm the one who's bad tempered when we start out; I count on you to cheer me up and keep me running.' Camilla was a headmistress, after all, and should be good at cheering people on.

Trees and houses were emerging from the early morning gloom. The flood water rippled across the recreation ground and Kate saw the white flash of a seagull as it came in to land on top of one of the goal posts. A couple of mallard ducks floated a few feet away from her on the spot where the bonfire had blazed on the Fifth of November.

'We have five miles ahead of us, filled with the sound of Rose grumbling about Theo,' said Camilla, 'and I do not wish to hear it. I would even prefer to have a discussion about the usefulness of examinations or the prospects for the centre party in the general election.' And she slowed down so that Rose's voice became too indistinct for them to hear. 'I've often wished Rose would pick up her knitting needles and walk out on the man; so if he's left her, I'm glad. But I don't need the details.'

Around them windows glowed yellow as people switched on lights and yawned and got out of bed and looked out into the gusty morning to gauge the new day. Kate wished she was indoors in the warm, but failing that, she wanted to hear all that the Fridesley running group had to offer by way of gossip. Camilla was usually as keen as she was to listen to other runners talking about their private lives. There was something liberating about the exercise that made people pour out their troubles and their concerns as they ran. Beside her the broad white stripe that encircled Camilla's dark green torso like a lifebelt added its vertical motion to the horizontal rhythm of their feet, but Camilla offered nothing by way of conversation, and Kate had to admit that Camilla was an exception to this general unburdening. As her muscles warmed up and the oxygen found its way to her brain and feet, Kate began to feel better. She still wished she could slope off back to her comfortable house and open the packet of cinnamon-dusted doughnuts which she knew she shouldn't have bought the previous day and which she had hidden at the back of her cupboard, but she also wanted to hear more about Rose and Theo. She told herself it was her novelist's curiosity.

On the Fridesley Road the earliest commuters were already streaming towards central Oxford, their cars darker grey shapes in the grey light, dipped headlamps forming golden cones in the mist.

'We're idiots. We get up at this sodding awful hour in the morning because we don't want to let the others down,' said Camilla, 'and once we're out and running, a warm feeling of comradeship steals over us, so that these people, with whom we really have nothing much in common, feel like our oldest and dearest friends.'

'It's a great group, isn't it?' Gavin's voice joined in and his bobble-hatted head appeared next to Camilla's and just an inch or so higher. 'I owe all my running success to the Fridesley Runners.'

'Success?' muttered Camilla. 'What success?'

'Well, I'm thinking of entering the New York marathon this year,' he said, sounding hurt.

'Isn't that in November?' asked Kate, aware of the seam of her sock rubbing on her little toe and glad that she didn't have another twenty-six miles to run.

'I need time to train for it, and plan.' And he added as an afterthought, 'And to save up for the trip, of course.'

Camilla said: 'I'm feeling sick. I want to go home.'

'How many biscuits did you eat before you came out this morning?' asked Kate, without sympathy.

'Only a couple. And an oatcake. With marmalade on.'

'You know that eating before running makes you feel sick, so why do you do it?'

'I feel so empty first thing. And you drink coffee,' she added, defensively.

'With skimmed milk. It doesn't count. You'll have to give up the biscuits in future, and just fantasize about your coming breakfast, like the rest of us.'

Gavin bounded ahead of them as though demonstrating that he was already fit enough to run a marathon, and overtook Sophie and Yvonne, Rose and Penny to join Barbara Davies at the front of the group.

Rose's voice drifted back again, but still too indistinct for Kate to hear what she was saying, however hard she strained. She decided to ignore Camilla and concentrate on catching up with Rose. They would be crossing the Fridesley Road and turning left on to the towpath in a minute, and the runners would string out along the narrow path. She had to get closer to Rose and the owner of the bossy commentary voice, Penny Dale, before this happened or her manoeuvre would be too blatant. Think of it as a touch of *fartlek* training, she told herself, as she ignored the protest from her knees and forced her legs to move faster. She drew level with Sophie Baight and listened to the solid thud of her shoes on the pavement. Not a lot of spring in that step, she thought. Sophie wore dark grey uncompromising running shoes, with a lot of cushioning and a good thick midsole. They looked as though they weighed twice as much as the multicoloured ones that most of the women sported, but perhaps it was just an illusion. She wore a matching grey tracksuit that made her legs look like thick-lagged pipes, with scarlet satin shorts over the top. Sophie was running, as usual, next to her mother, Yvonne.

'It's too bloody cold to run,' moaned Sophie. 'I should have stayed at home and done half an hour on the rowing machine instead. My ears are freezing.'

'Here, darling,' said Yvonne, 'have this.' And she pulled from inside her top a hand-knitted yellow and brown hat with a large bobble and held it out to her daughter. 'Dear old Mrs Exeter knitted it for me as a thank-you present when I got her a pair of dentures that didn't click. Wasn't it sweet of her?'

Not that sweet, thought Kate. Maybe she hoped you'd wear it, Yvonne, and stop looking so impossibly perfect: it was like a caricature of one of Rose's creations, with yellow blobs that might have been flowers on a faecal brown background. Sophie put the hat on, pulling it down over her forehead. She looked like one of the seven dwarfs now; Grumpy, probably.

'Lovely, darling,' said Yvonne. 'It suits you. Running in the fresh air is so much better for you than working out on that equipment of yours.'

Kate had the odd feeling that Yvonne enjoyed making Sophie into a figure of fun. Yvonne herself floated effortlessly along, her breathing smooth and silent, her legs in their Lycra as yellow and as shiny as butter. Her dark hair was expensively cut and looked as though it was meant to fall in just that way, beaded artistically with morning mist.

'Sophie's got another wonderful new contraption for getting fit and slim, haven't you, darling? Tell Kate about it, Sophie.'

Sophie looked stubborn and stayed silent.

'It's all springs and wires,' continued Yvonne. 'I'm sure it will improve her figure no end. Eventually.'

'Shut up about it,' said Sophie.

'Oh come on, darling, I was only joking,' said Yvonne.

Sophie's feet continued their heavy *thud*, *thud* and her hands were balled into tight fists and held high, nearly bumping into her chin as each foot hit the ground. Kate made the effort to draw ahead again, Camilla staying loyally if noisily at her shoulder.

'Why do they still live together?' Kate murmured to Camilla. 'Sophie must be getting on for thirty, surely.'

'It gets to be a habit, I suppose. Less demanding than finding someone new to live with, or making it on your own. Could Sophie make it on her own, do you think? Anyway Yvonne's very well meaning, in spite of being a dentist. There must be worse people to share a house with.'

'Right, I can hear Rose now,' Kate said to Camilla, as at last they fitted in behind Rose and Penny, and she dropped the pace a little so that they stayed just behind the two other women.

'. . . that Lynda. I think it all started just before Christmas,' Rose was saying.

'I thought it started the day Rose walked down the aisle with her veil flung back and her damp little hand clutching Theo's big meaty one,' said Camilla to Kate.

'Shush, I'm listening. And he was still Keith when they got married. He renamed himself Theo when he realized that he had hit his serious upwardly mobile phase.'

Camilla made an explosive noise that sounded like a laugh, suppressed. 'You haven't missed much of the story,' she said.

Ahead of them, Rose was still wailing: 'But what should

I do?' She was dressed in a baggy black sweatshirt and even baggier cotton trousers which did nothing to make her look taller and slimmer, but only gave the world the message that she didn't wish to be visible and that on a scale of one to ten her self-esteem hadn't yet reached a positive integer. Her hair was hidden under a woollen hat decorated with flowers and leaves on a yellow background. It had earpieces which kept out the February cold and which had bright pink carnations knitted into the pattern. She was making heavy weather of the run, as her feet in their Nikes moved as far sideways as they did forwards. She could be pretty fast if she got all that effort into a forwards motion, thought Kate, just behind her.

There might have been soothing noises coming from Penny, but Camilla broke in, her voice clipped and brusque from the effort of talking and running at the same time.

'I should thank Heaven that you're released at last from the great heavy weight called Theo that you've been dragging around with you for the past seven years.'

'Honestly, Camilla,' muttered Kate, 'you are a bit hard on the girl.'

'It's time someone was,' said Camilla. 'How is she going to survive unless she looks at the facts and starts to sort out the practical details?'

They turned off the main road and the background hum of traffic lessened as they dropped down into the still, private world of the towpath.

'Live your own life,' said Camilla, getting into the swing of it. Yvonne and Sophie were close behind them, while Gavin and Barbara bobbed ahead, setting the ten-minute mile pace which was all they aspired to.

11

'Find out who you really are and what you want out of life. All you've done so far is pander to Theo's fantasies,' went on Camilla, while the trees dripped condensation on to their heads as though their branches were crowded with invisible but incontinent birds.

Rose was sniffling like a small child. 'It's easy for you to say that, Camilla. You're so competent and people listen to you. And anyway, you've got a well-paid job. No one would dream of shouting at you that you were a drag and it was no wonder that your husband had walked out on you.'

'They might shout it,' said Camilla, 'but they'd get a pretty sharp reply, I can tell you.'

'And she said that I could whistle for maintenance. That the courts didn't have time for young – well, youngish – wives who had no small children to look after. But how am I going to keep up the mortgage payments on the house with no money coming in?'

'Get yourself a job,' said Camilla. 'What qualifications have you got?'

'None, really,' said Rose. 'I only ever wanted to be married.'

'What about your knitting? Surely people would pay you to knit them hats with flowers on, or pullovers with teddy bears, or whatever the current craze is? They're your own designs, aren't they?' said Penny.

'I was hoping to get something going with my knitting, but I shall need capital, and money to live on before I start to make a profit. I was going to ask my grandmother to help, but it looks as though I'll be unlucky there too, now.'

'Start fighting back, Rose,' said Camilla, bracingly, as though addressing the junior hockey team.

'She sounds the pits, this Lynda of Theo's,' said Penny, returning to the conversation. She was wearing a bright blue jogging suit, a scarlet hat, white socks, and scarlet shoes and she had the sort of dark hair and vivid complexion that made Rose look paler and more insignificant than ever. She was also a few inches larger round the hips than she would want to be, which irritated her as she knew very well what the healthy diet consisted of, and stuck to her complex carbohydrates, her mono-unsaturated oil, her brassicas and carrots, her pulses and skimmed milk for most of the day, so that she should have been reed-slim. She had failed to register the fact, however, that in the evenings she absent-mindedly stuffed in salted crisps, peanut-butter sandwiches, and ice-cream Mars bars while she watched the television.

'She's got a brain the size of a pea, that Lynda. Take no notice of her,' said Camilla. 'And think about taking a course on self-employment down at Oxpens, so that you can make out a business plan to show your grandmother. That should convince her that you're serious about it.'

The path stood above the flooded landscape and gave them the impression that they were running over water. Magic, thought Kate, and cheered up some more. Once she had been running for twenty minutes or so she started to feel better and to see the point of all the discomfort. In fact, now she came to consider it, there was very little discomfort and her lungs were working with greater efficiency, too. Keep it up, she addressed herself, and you could be transformed, transported. She sent a silent thank you to the Fridesley Runners, in their straggling group, unaware of the warm glow of fellowship and gratitude that was spreading through her. In a short while Oxford, with its trees and spires, would appear through the dawn light, across the Meadow. It was a sight that never failed to fill her with pleasure.

'Get rid of the man,' Penny was saying. 'Go down to the supermarket and pick up a load of empty cardboard boxes. Pack up all his belongings: his striped shirts (preferably unwashed), his silk ties, his Next suits, and throw them all in. Fold them up first, if you have to. Get rid of his collection of SF books, his Batman comics, and those hideous Victorian glass vases—'

'The Victorian glassware is mine, actually,' said Rose, huffily.

'Bad luck. You'll have to keep them, I suppose. But when you've got it all together, you just hurl it all out on to the pavement. Very therapeutic. Jump about on it too, if you feel like it.'

There was something about running that brought out the most aggressive streaks in Camilla and Penny, thought Kate. Though Penny was always on the bossy side, Camilla was usually a quiet, understated person. She remembered the reserved child that she had met over twenty years ago. Millie, she had been then, but she had to be treated with more respect now that she was a headmistress. Perhaps it was because she had to be so caring and restrained at work that she let herself go like this when she was out running.

'It's too late for that,' said Rose. 'He's already taken his things.'

'We're going to have to turn right at the river,' said Penny. 'We can get past the Postle, but there's still too much water in the Meadow. We'll go round by Folly Bridge.'

'The thing is,' said Rose, once they had all agreed to Penny's suggestion, 'Theo has already been to the house while I was out doing my fortnightly Tesco's shopping. I go to the one in Abingdon,' she added, 'and it takes me at least an hour and a half, more if I stop for a cup of coffee. Theo waited until I'd left for Abingdon and then he drove up in his rent-a-van and filled it with half the furniture and all his personal effects and drove it round to Redbourne Road.'

'Which must be all of two hundred and fifty yards away,' said Camilla.

'So he's moved in with her?' said Yvonne, and again Kate caught the note of amusement in her voice.

'Yes, to Lynda's house. I never can remember the girl's surname, but you know the one I mean. Lots of blonde hair and does voice-overs for some recording studio.'

'Power shoulders and navy-patterned tights,' said Camilla. 'Gilman, or Gorman, or Kernan or something.'

'Big feet and thick ankles,' said Kate, hoping to cheer the unfortunate Rose.

'But then, who ever looks at her feet?' asked Camilla.

Their own feet clattered over the wooden bridge as they crossed from the canal to the river, calling up echoes from the lightening water and a flurry of pigeons' wings from the trees. They ran through yet more flooded meadows towards the shuttered eyes of the Peacock Inn, then turned away from Wolvercote and back towards Oxford.

'Just move your knitting machine into his study, Rose,' said Kate. 'Spread your clothes around in the wardrobe and shift the furniture about in the sitting room. More space can be very attractive. Then take Camilla's advice and work out some figures and approach your grandmother for an injection of capital into your proposed business.'

'But he's stolen her boxes!' Rose's voice rose to a shriek and every word was emphasized by the slap of her shoes on the path. 'She'll never listen to me now!'

'Boxes? What boxes?' asked Camilla. 'And what on earth have they got to do with anything?'

'Enamel boxes!' cried Rose.

'Battersea, you mean?' asked Camilla.

'The Battersea works was only in operation for six years,' said Rose, her voice unusually authoritative, 'so genuine Battersea is very rare and expensive. These are early nine-teenth century, but still pretty valuable.'

'See a solicitor,' said Camilla. 'Demand them back.'

'He's left me half the collection,' said Rose.

'Well, that's fair enough, isn't it?'

'But they belonged to my grandmother. She let me play with them if I was very good, when I was a little girl. She told me all about them and where she had got each one from. My favourite had "My Love is Pure and will Endure" on the lid, but Theo's taken it.'

'That was a bit crass of him,' said Kate.

'She gave them to us for a wedding present, so Theo reckons that half of them belong to him. But they don't. They're Granny's and mine. And she's coming to visit me in Oxford next month. She'll go spare when she finds that Theo's left me for another woman, and she'll probably have a stroke when she finds I've lost half her boxes, too. She'll say I'm hopeless and it's all my fault and she won't give me any money.'

She sounded as though she was about to burst into tears.

'Tricky one,' said Kate.

'He's even stolen the Oxford box,' said Rose, in a voice of doom. It sounded as though they should know what it was.

'Not one of the mourning boxes?' asked Yvonne, suddenly interested. 'Don't say you've got a John Parrish Camera?'

'How about telling the rest of us what you're on about?' said Camilla.

'They're called Oxford boxes because they were made at Wolvercote between 1825 and 1835 by a man called John Parrish,' said Rose. 'After that, I'm afraid that interest in enamels was lost and the works closed.'

'Why morning?' asked Camilla. 'Why not evening, say?'

'Mourning, as in death and funeral,' said Yvonne. 'A small object that you could look at that would remind you of your dear departed and of your own mortality. The Oxford boxes were rather like tourist souvenirs, but with moral overtones.'

'Unbeatable combination,' said Camilla. 'Perhaps they should bring them back for sale in the Oxford souvenir shops.'

'The Oxford works specialized in a very dark blue enamel, speckled with purple. It was known as Oxford blue, and the details of the design were picked out in gold. This box of mine is a miniature of the Radcliffe Camera,' said Rose.

'Very kitsch,' said Camilla.

'Very collectable,' said Yvonne. 'Does it have a hinged lid? A *memento mori* inscription?'

'You know about these things, Yvonne?' asked Kate.

'Just a little,' said Yvonne. 'They're well known, of

course, among collectors. And especially since that exhibition at the V & A.'

'The inscription said *Live to die, Die to live,*' said Rose. 'And then when you opened the lid, there was an ivory carving inside.'

Beside Kate, Yvonne's breathing changed tempo.

'A skull,' said Rose, and Yvonne suddenly exhaled into a near whistle.

'And the skull is still inside the box?' she asked.

'Yes. Well it was, last time I saw it.' And Rose sniffed again.

'So it's just like the one that was sold at Christie's last month for—'

'A lot of money. Yes, just like it.'

'If it were mine, I don't think I'd mind too much if the skull went missing,' said Kate, who was quite fond of small enamel boxes herself but had never got round to owning any, and wasn't too keen on dwelling on her own mortality.

'There was another inscription inside the lid, saying *Mem. Mori W.S. Ob. 6 Feb. 1831,*' said Rose, 'which means that it was made to commemorate the death of someone with those initials.'

'Not – ?' asked Camilla.

'Wrong century,' said Kate.

But, 'Middle period Parrish,' breathed Yvonne.

'He's left me "A Trifle from Tunbridge Wells".'

'Well, that's something,' said Kate.

And, 'Bad luck,' said Camilla.

Ahead of them, Gavin and Barbara had stopped to open a gate and were waiting for the rest of the group to catch up with them. Another runner was coming along the path

18

in the opposite direction and they stood aside to let him through. He was tall and thin, with a bony face and dark hair that flopped over his forehead. Lovely mover and just my type, thought Kate, irrelevantly, as he went past her.

'The development will start over there on the right, behind those willows,' Gavin was saying, as Kate went through the gate.

'It won't be over there or anywhere if we have our way,' said Yvonne. 'I'm going to make sure that Tom Grant fails in his planning appeal, if it's the last thing I do.'

'Yvonne's really got it in for Grant,' said Camilla. 'It must be difficult for Gavin, being a Councillor. Shouldn't he stay neutral?'

'He's Independent, not neutral,' said Barbara with a note of disapproval, so that Kate remembered that her husband Nick was a Tory on the same Council.

'Practise some assertiveness,' said Penny to Rose. 'Be determined about it. We're only talking about old Theo, after all. Put your foot down. Go round and demand your boxes back.'

'Especially the Oxford one,' said Yvonne, thoughtfully.

'I have,' said Rose. 'But it didn't work. He wouldn't let me into the house. He's much better at asserting himself than I am and when I left I felt more useless than ever.'

'Why don't you go round when Theo's out? Have an argument with Lynda, instead.'

'I couldn't do that, she might be rude to me again.'

'Just concentrate on her thick ankles,' said Penny, her own gleaming white above the scarlet of her shoes. Where does she find running shoes that colour? wondered Kate. She must have gone up to London and spent a lot of money.

'I couldn't face her. Really I couldn't. I'd burst into tears or something and feel a fool,' Rose was saying.

'Better than being one,' said Camilla. 'It does seem as though these boxes are the key to your survival in a nasty cold world.'

'Don't be so spineless, Rose,' said Yvonne. 'There's always a way of getting your own back if you put your mind to it. Learn to be devious.'

'On the other hand,' said Gavin, 'perhaps Theo's right. If the boxes were a wedding present to both of you, he is entitled to half the collection.'

'Oh, shut up, Gavin,' said Penny.

'So much for *l'homme nouveau*,' said Kate.

'There's nothing *nouveau* about being henpecked,' said Camilla to Kate.

'Have you noticed how henpecked men always grow beards?'

'And are five foot seven and a bit on the tubby side?'

'Shaving off the beard is the male sign of liberation.'

'Poor old Gavin.'

'But can't you come up with something creative to help Rose get her boxes back? It really looks as though she'll be in the shit with Granny if she doesn't. And then the poor cow will lose her house and any chance she had of starting up her designer knitting business.'

'Don't look at me for bright ideas at the moment,' said Kate. 'Every time my phone goes it's my agent or editor asking how the book is going and when am I going to send him a first draft, and don't I realize that if I leave a gap of more than a year between books the public will forget about me. If I get any good creative ideas in the next ten

minutes, they're going straight into my synopsis. Rose will
have to knit her own solution to her problem.' Her thoughts
strayed back to the blank sheets of paper, the untouched
notebooks, the virgin floppy disks that waited for her in
her workroom.

Then they were running the flat, smooth path along by
the canal and into Oxford. Penny checked her stopwatch
and told them they would have to push the pace up a bit if
they were going to get home at their usual time. Conversation flagged as they put more effort into their running,
passing through the empty back streets of the city, over
cobblestones and past colleges that must have looked much
the same for centuries. The smell of coffee and grilled
bacon from Lincoln College's kitchen was nearly too much
for Kate, so that she envied Camilla her early snack of
biscuits and oatcake.

Twenty minutes later they formed into a single group
again as they waited to cross the Fridesley Road and jog
the final few hundred yards back to the suburban streets
where they all lived. Kate by now was feeling elated and
full of confidence in her own physical abilities, and once
across the road she accelerated away for the pleasure that
speed gave her. The elation lasted only a couple of minutes,
however, for as she flew along her foot caught on an uneven
paving stone and her ankle turned over so that she hopped
for half a dozen steps before slowing to a very slow jog.

'And that will teach you to show off!' called Camilla as
she padded past.

'Why don't you all come back to my place for a coffee?'
asked Rose, her voice high and loud with the unaccus-
tomed suggestion.

'Just for ten minutes,' said Kate, aware of the waiting word processor and her distant, but impatient, agent, yet unwilling to snub Rose. And around her she heard the murmurs of people who would rather be drinking coffee in their own kitchens than someone else's, but who felt they should support a group member. Even Yvonne said, 'I can manage ten minutes or so. And we really must do something about that Oxford box, mustn't we, Rose?'

But Kate still didn't care for her tone of voice.

Chapter Three

They shuffled into Rose's house and stood around in the kitchen while she found mugs and instant coffee and a large saucepan for boiling water in since Theo, predictably, had taken the electric kettle. They could not fail to notice that the place felt empty and unfinished. And in spite of Penny's encouraging noises, there was nothing of the planned spaciousness of minimal chic, or any sort of chic if it came to that. Rose tended towards a Laura Ashley fussiness, and the swags and ruffles only emphasized the empty spaces where, presumably, Theo had removed some article of furniture. On every surface that did remain there was a pile of wool or a length of knitting still attached to its needles.

'Let me hand those round for you, Rose,' Yvonne said, taking a couple of mugs. 'And have you got sugar, and milk?' While this was going on, Kate wandered round looking at the charts and sketches pinned up on the walls: details of birds and flowers and leaves, translated into elongated charts for knitting on Rose's circular knitting pins.

The aroma of coffee finally overwhelmed the rising smell of sweaty tracksuits, damp running shoes, and unbrushed teeth, and they stood round the table (there were now only

23

two hard chairs instead of the original four) and looked at Rose. A tear appeared in the corner of one eye and trickled down her face.

'Granny will never forgive me,' she said. 'What am I going to do?'

'Why don't you stop whingeing about it and concentrate on getting the bloody things back, then?' said Camilla. There was a general murmur of assent.

'We're all with you, Rose,' said Penny.

'Theo warned me not to do anything silly,' said Rose. 'He was threatening to go to the police if I tried to retrieve them.'

'It wouldn't count as theft if you went round and helped yourself to your own property, would it?' said Yvonne, looking at Gavin. 'Your first duty is to look after your own interests, isn't it, Gavin?'

'That's a really good idea,' said Gavin. 'Go for it, Rose. Steal them back.'

'That's not what I meant!' exclaimed Camilla. 'And you were arguing that Theo was within his rights to keep them only a few minutes ago.'

'So sensible of you to change your mind and agree with me, Gavin,' said Yvonne.

'We'll all support you,' said Barbara behind him.

'Are we talking about breaking and entering?' asked Camilla. 'Theft? Burglary? You're all mad even to think of it.'

'Nonsense,' said Yvonne, with the smile that made Kate think of malice and manipulation. 'Rose has to get her Oxford box back, and the rest of them, of course. And I thought that you were in favour of Rose's rights, Camilla?

I was sure that you, being so liberated, would agree with us.'

Camilla, to Kate's surprise, went slightly pink in the face, and stopped arguing.

'What's up with you?' Kate asked her, with the rudeness of long-term friendship. But Camilla avoided her eyes.

'If we're talking about theft, what about Theo? He's the one who's nicked the boxes, not Rose, surely? All she'd be doing is recovering her own property,' said Penny. 'I think Yvonne is right.'

'I thought you might, dear,' said Yvonne, smiling sleekly at her.

'I couldn't do it,' said Rose shakily. 'I wouldn't know how. I'd have to break a back window or something and all the neighbours would see me. And what if Theo and Lynda were at home and caught me? And even if they didn't see me, Theo would know it was me and send the police straight round.'

'Couldn't you get hold of the front-door key?' asked Kate, who couldn't resist the temptation of solving a minor practical problem. 'You must still be in touch with Theo: why don't you nick his spare keys while he isn't looking and get one cut? Then you could go and help yourself to your boxes when he and Lynda were out.'

'Dear Kate, always coming up with such clever ideas,' said Yvonne. 'Where *do* you get them from?'

'And the neighbours wouldn't see you if you went round after dark,' said Penny. 'And it's getting dark at five o'clock after all.'

'If you chose an evening when the two of them were out . . . they do go out, don't they?' asked Gavin. He pulled out one of the remaining chairs and urged the tearful Rose to sit down on it. This was a mistake on Rose's part, thought Kate, since they now all loomed over her with their coffee mugs and steaming hair, dominating the poor girl worse than ever.

'This is a great idea, you know, Rose,' said Gavin. 'And if one of us looked after the boxes for you for a few days, it wouldn't matter if the police came round to your place.'

'That's right, Gavin,' said Yvonne. 'I knew you'd see it our way.'

'The thing to do,' said Barbara, 'is to set a date for it, then we have to plan accordingly. It will give us a focus for our efforts.'

Kate remembered that Barbara was the local organizer for some scheme for selling hideous pottery figurines to bored housewives at coffee mornings.

'February the twenty-sixth,' said Yvonne.

'Why?' asked Sophie, suddenly interrupting her mother. 'Why are we planning this at all? It's a terrible idea. It could get Rose into a lot of trouble. I think we should forget all about it.'

'Of course we must do it!' Gavin was nearly shouting, and Penny's face above her mug of coffee was quite frightened.

'And if we're going to do it,' said Camilla, slowly, looking at Yvonne as she spoke, 'I suppose that the twenty-sixth is as good a day as any.'

'Just right,' said Penny. 'Far enough ahead to plan properly, but not so far that we put it off and forget about it. Go out there and fight for your rights, Rose.'

'Oh no!' wailed Rose, taking off her woolly hat and crumpling it up in her hands before mopping her damp eyes. 'Poor Theo! I couldn't do it to him then! That's his birthday. He liked to celebrate, and in the evening we always went out for an Indian meal at the Mogul Star. It was *our* place. For seven years I had a chicken dansak and he had a beef vindaloo. He really enjoyed a hot curry.' She started to cry again. 'And now he'll take *her*! He couldn't, could he? Not to *our* place?'

'I expect he could,' said Sophie tactlessly. 'Men don't think about things like that the way women do. They just think "Where's the best beef vindaloo in town?" and go off to the Mogul Star, never thinking that it was your special place.'

'Right, that's it,' said Penny, putting her empty coffee mug in the sink and turning on the cold tap, then looking to Yvonne as if for approval. 'February the twenty-sixth. Theo and Lynda will be off for their Indian meal, their minds on candlelight, curry, and romance, leaving the field clear for Rose to break into Lynda's house and reclaim her boxes. All we need now is to work out the finer details of the plan, but that's the outline, isn't it?' She looked around at the group, who, apart from Yvonne, who was still looking pleased with herself, were shocked into silence by what they had brought about. It was, thought Kate, so much easier to urge a friend to take her life into her own hands and act in a positive manner than it was to find yourself involved in some criminal activity, however justified you thought it was.

'We can't do it,' said Sophie. 'Why are we even thinking about stealing things?'

'Not stealing, liberating,' said Yvonne. 'Reclaiming, perhaps.'

'But what if we're caught?' asked Rose.

'We won't be. Our great advantage is that we're not the sort of people who commit crimes,' said Barbara.

'You're right,' said Kate, who had thought about this before. 'All that slang the police use, it helps them put people into pigeon-holes. We're not in the villains' pigeon-hole. We're the sort of people who get their belongings nicked, not the ones who go out after dark nicking things from other people. If we tell them we didn't do it, they'll believe us.'

'On the other hand, they might choose to believe Theo,' said Sophie.

'I don't want to be questioned by the police!' shrieked Camilla. 'What would my governors say?'

'We'll make quite sure your governors never hear anything scandalous about you, don't worry,' said Yvonne. 'We all know how important your reputation is, Camilla, and it's quite safe with us. And the important thing is that we're a group and we act as one. When one of our number is in trouble, it's up to the rest of us to rally round. Kate, you're so good with ideas, why don't you work on it?'

Kate, who did feel the warm glow of comradeship when she was out running, and who couldn't resist developing a new idea, said, 'Maybe it needs a refinement or two, but I think we have the outline of something usable here.'

'Where does Theo keep the boxes?' asked Penny. 'In a cabinet or locked in a drawer?'

'I don't know, but I expect he'll have them out somewhere on display. He'd like to show them off.'

'Especially the Oxford mourning box,' said Yvonne. 'Anyone would.'

'We'll find out,' put in Barbara. 'And we'll need details of how many there are, and how big. Can you slip them into your pockets, or will you need some sort of bag to carry them in?'

Beside Kate, Camilla was fuming and her face was growing pink, but she still wasn't arguing with the others. Kate could feel the tension building inside her friend and pulled her out of the room, shouting: 'Goodbye and thanks for the coffee,' and, 'See you all tomorrow,' as she went. As they left she could hear Barbara and Penny still bullying Rose.

'They're mad,' said Camilla. 'They'll end up in prison if they go on like that.'

'Come on, Millie,' said Kate. 'Forget you're a headmistress for the moment. Can't you feel the buzz? This is letting everybody know they're alive. It's like entering for a marathon and then realizing you've got to go out there and run twenty-six miles: terrifying, but exciting, too. Can't you feel the adrenalin pumping round all the dull corners of your body? And I don't see how Rose is going to survive unless someone helps her with a large sum of money. She just isn't one of life's winners.'

But as she put her weight on her turned ankle it produced a stabbing pain that reminded her that life can always find a way to trip you up when you least expect it. And she had, too, the feeling that the scene had been manipulated by one person. She remembered the way Yvonne referred to 'slight discomfort' before inflicting real pain, and wondered whether that was why she distrusted the woman. Behind them, Rose's door banged shut again, and Yvonne and Sophie walked down Rosamund Road towards the recreation ground. Kate could hear Sophie talking angrily to her mother, and the sound of Yvonne's laughter in reply.

Chapter Four

Kate and Camilla crossed the Fridesley Road and turned into Waverley Lane, their tracksuits cold and clammy with sweat. It was another three or four hundred yards before the lane realized the rural promise of its name by filling its borders with hawthorn hedges and meandering up to the river. Here at the Fridesley Road end they walked past narrow-fronted terraced houses that had none of the comfortably middle-class feel of Rosamund Road. Camilla lived in a small detached house further up the lane, while Kate had bought a two-bedroomed terraced house in Agatha Street. She had considered herself lucky to afford anything at all so close to the centre of Oxford, but she did wonder sometimes whether all the noise she had to put up with was really worth it. The house next door to hers contained three children, and the sounds of slamming doors, thumps, and yells came clearly through the thin communal walls. In summer the children shouted and played in the street with skateboards and bicycles while in winter they shouted and kicked footballs around before going indoors to turn up the volume on the television and slam a few more doors.

Kate was limping by the time they reached Josephine Street where she would turn off to the right.

'Has it started to swell?' asked Camilla.

'A bit. I must deal firmly with it straight away or I won't be able to run for a few days.'

'Ice,' said Camilla. 'Or rice. Rest, ice, compression, and elevation.'

'I keep a special pack of frozen peas in the freezer just for the purpose,' said Kate. 'As a matter of fact I had to replace it recently because I gave the old one to Andrew for supper one evening by mistake. The peas tasted a bit odd, but he seems to have survived.'

'You'd better try Tubigrip for the ankle.'

'I'll hobble up to the chemist.'

'I've got some at home, it's nearer for you and you're welcome to borrow it.'

'Thanks.'

'And why don't you come round this afternoon for tea? Give yourself a break from the VDU: I've got no meetings and no parents visiting and I'm coming home at four. So how about five o'clock?'

'Fine. Thanks.' Kate was aware that this was an unusual invitation from Camilla and she wondered if she would explain her odd behaviour.

In Camilla's neat house, Kate waited in the hallway while Camilla went to fetch the bandage from upstairs. Her ankle was really aching now and she was longing for a pot of her own filter coffee to take away the taste of Rose's weak instant. And she would treat herself to a croissant for breakfast. Or even one of the doughnuts. She would start the diet again tomorrow. And anyway, she was always hearing runners going on about how they could eat anything without putting on weight.

Camilla had reached the top of the stairs when the phone started to ring.

'The Tubigrip's in the small left-hand drawer in the chest next to the wardrobe in my bedroom,' she said. 'Could you get it while I answer this?' Kate made her way slowly up the stairs as Camilla answered the phone. Kate noticed her voice, low and different from the brisk Camilla she knew. Oh well, it was none of her business if she had a man on the end of her phone or in her life.

She found the drawer, and the Tubigrip. Downstairs, Camilla's voice was still murmuring in an intimate way and Kate felt she would be intruding if she went down immediately. Next to the chest of drawers, the wardrobe door stood ajar, and Kate idly pulled it open and looked inside. She wished that she could be half as organized. Her own wardrobe was a jumble of bright colours and oddments mixed with the shoes at the bottom, where belts had fallen off dresses and rarely worn blouses had slipped off their hangers. But Camilla's wardrobe was packed with suits and jackets and skirts, all colour co-ordinated, many still in plastic wrappers from the cleaners. Towards the left were some slightly less formal clothes, but still much smarter than anything Kate owned. But there, nestling at the end of the row, was something different. She knew she shouldn't be prying like this. It was an unforgivable invasion of Camilla's privacy, but she had to look at it.

She pushed a couple of silk dresses to one side so that she could see it properly. The dress was soft and pink and made of many yards of chiffon. The small top was beaded and there was a long scarf draped round the shoulders, over the hanger. Kate tried to imagine Camilla wearing it: Camilla with her round, lightly freckled face and gingery gold hair that needed a decent cut, her pale, greenish-blue eyes; most of all Kate tried to imagine Camilla's rounded hips and bosom in this odd dress. Kate touched it, moved it a little to the right on the hanging rail, then, guiltily, pushed it back again. It whispered expensively at her as it stirred and gave off faint breaths of *Mystère*. Yet it was not a fashionable dress. It could have been designed and made any time after nineteen-sixty. But it was hardly a dress for a headmistress to wear to a sherry party with her governors. Then, hearing that Camilla's telephone conversation was ending, she closed the wardrobe door so that Camilla would not guess what she had been doing, and went downstairs with the packet of elastic bandage.

Camilla was just putting the receiver back and there was a slight flush on her cheeks – which might, after all, have come from their recent exercise – and a foolish smile on her lips, which probably hadn't.

'Oh, good, you found it then.'

'Yes. Thanks very much. I'll pack the ankle with frozen peas and strap it up with this. I expect it will be cured by the time I come round this afternoon.' It wasn't, she thought, looking with new eyes at Camilla, that she had an unattractive face: it was intelligent and alert and belonged to a woman who was only, after all, thirty-three, but it was not the sort of face that went with pink chiffon, sequins, and a very low neckline.

'This afternoon?' Camilla sounded puzzled.

'You invited me for tea, remember?'

'Yes, of course. So I did. Five o'clock.' She appeared to do a rapid sum involving timetables in her head. 'Yes. That will be fine. I'll see you then.'

'We'll talk about how to get back Rose's boxes.'

'It's mad. The whole world is going mad.'

'But if you really didn't think it was a good idea, why didn't you argue? Why didn't you stand up to Yvonne? And why didn't Gavin or Penny, if it comes to that?'

'Maybe we'll talk about it this afternoon.'

And Kate had the impression that Camilla was not only talking about Rose's boxes and the scheme to retrieve them.

As she limped to her own small house in Agatha Street, she thought how running changed her perspectives: after twenty minutes on the road everything she ever wanted to do seemed within her reach. When she ran alone she used to fantasize about running a marathon, and as she ran through the paths of Fridesley, the countryside would change until she was surrounded by other runners in the London or New York race. She couldn't stop and walk because the crowds lining the roads were cheering her on. She flew. She overtook other people. This exhilaration lasted for an hour or two, before she emerged into the ordinary world, still grasping a couple of valuable ideas for whatever book she was working on.

And now she had to change gear back to her working life. She had to return to the Napoleonic Wars and the plight of her heroine, trapped penniless and alone in France. Writing had a lot in common with running, she thought, as she turned into Agatha Street. She couldn't imagine getting further than a few hundred yards when she bought her first pair of running shoes, any more than she could imagine writing ninety thousand words when she started on her first novel. But she had built up her distance over the months until she could contemplate ten or fifteen miles on a good day. And she had managed the ninety thousand words of a novel some eight times now.

At five o'clock Kate walked the few hundred yards to Camilla's house. There was a smell of baking scones and the sound of an unmusical person singing happily as Camilla opened the door.

'How is it?' asked Camilla, showing Kate into the sitting-room. Kate extended a foot and showed her the ankle encased in white elasticated bandage.

'Improving by the minute,' she said. 'And it's got to be all right for tomorrow morning's run. For one thing, we have the annual race coming up soon, and for another, there's no way I want to miss out on the Great Box Theft.'

Camilla made a face. 'I could do without that sort of nonsense, myself. I'm having a difficult enough time with my governors over the Friends of Fridesley Fields as it is.'

'I'd have thought they would all approve of that: isn't everyone supposed to be in favour of the environment these days? Aren't we supposed to be fighting for our green belts against the encroachments of the wicked exploiters?'

'That's all perfectly acceptable as long as we stick to protecting fritillaries or riding our bicycles instead of driving motor cars. But as soon as I hit a parent – or, even worse, a governor – in his pocket and hurt him, then I have to start reading the small print in my contract very carefully.'

'It can't be that bad, surely?'

'One of the governors has a financial interest. He hasn't come out into the open about it, but I think he stands to lose a lot of money if the scheme doesn't go through. He's the one making most noise at the moment, but there were a couple more who were unenthusiastic about my appointment. They thought I should be either older and uglier, or safely and respectably married. I'm on a year's probation, and they're watching me pretty carefully, I can tell you. One foot wrong and I'm out.'

'But they'll never manage to get a road across those fields.'

'There are techniques for doing it. It will be expensive, but Grant and his colleagues can raise the money. Our best luck so far has been the floods: no one could do anything at all on those fields at the moment. I think they're a couple of feet under water in parts. But when the flood water has dropped again they'll start arguing that it was an exceptional year and the land can be drained and a road driven through. There are enormous sums of money at stake here, and people get very touchy indeed if they think that their percentage is at risk. It's time you returned from the nineteenth century and noticed what's happening here on your own doorstep.'

'You're almost persuading me to start wearing one of Rose's pullovers as a statement of my position.'

'Very pretty pullovers they are, too.'

'But she shouldn't have added the acronym for Friends of Fridesley Fields on the back like that.'

'And she still can't see what's funny about it.'

And they both giggled like the schoolgirls they had once

been and buttered another couple of scones. Kate decided to confront the other problem.

'If you're so concerned about keeping your reputation clean during your probationary period, why didn't you fight harder against the scheme to steal back Rose's boxes? I mean, for me it's fun, a challenge to come up with a viable plan. It's like working out the plot of a book without having to write the ninety thousand words afterwards. I don't see how else Rose is going to get hold of the money to start her business and, anyway, no one's going to fire me if I get caught – not that I think we'll get caught. But why didn't you argue against it? Is it group loyalty? I know we've seen each other through the cold, dark winter mornings and up hills and along muddy tracks with wet feet and sleet in our eyes, and that makes us members of a clan. I understand how people can do something when they're in a crowd that they wouldn't contemplate on their own. But even so, I don't understand why you didn't fight harder against us. The way you put it, it's your career at stake if we get caught.' Kate piled strawberry jam on to her third scone. They really were very good.

'It's not that simple,' said Camilla, pouring more rosehip tea for them both.

'Yvonne was forcing the pace, wasn't she?' said Kate, remembering the scene that morning. 'But why did you give in? Has she threatened your root canals? Offered to replace all your fillings? What is it with that woman? I know she dominates the unfortunate Sophie, but she seems to have all the rest of you rolling on to your backs and waving your paws in the air when she whistles. Why don't you tell me what's bothering you?'

'What makes you think that anything is bothering me?'

'There's the way you casually and out of the blue invited me back to tea: you with your crowded schedule and non-existent social life during term time.'

'Well, we hadn't had a chat for ages.'

'Rubbish. We chat five times a week when we go running. And there's the way you've made a couple of dozen scones and scoffed eight of them with strawberry jam and whipped double cream, in spite of being on a diet.'

'Well, you've just done the same.'

'Three, I've eaten three. But I'm not the disciplined Miss Rogers, am I? If I'm on a diet, everyone knows that after two or three days I'll go home and bake a cake or some pies and eat them all, but you . . . No, Camilla, it's definitely out of character. So what's wrong?'

'I do need your advice. But you'll have to give me time to get round to it in my own way.'

'Have the last scone and cream to get your courage up. And it's a good thing you haven't taken to the gin bottle, or you really would be in trouble by now.'

'I don't know where to begin, Kate. It's all a bit embarrassing.'

'What have you done? Taken up ballroom dancing?' said Kate, then regretted her flippancy when she saw the expression on Camilla's face.

Camilla opened her mouth to reply, but before she could speak she was interrupted by a peal at the front-door bell. 'That might be a friend of mine,' she said carefully. 'I was expecting someone, but rather later than this.'

'Shouldn't you open the door?' said Kate.

'Yes,' said Camilla, sounding as if she meant 'No', and

she walked slowly through the hall as a second and longer peal sounded.

There were noises of greeting and much murmuring. Kate picked up the tea cups and crumb-littered plates and took them out to the kitchen. Then she took out the jam and the empty dish that had contained whipped cream. As she returned to the sitting room for the second time, Camilla came in from the hall, leading someone by the hand.

'Kate,' she said. 'This is Carey. Carey Stanton. And Carey, this is Kate Ivory.'

Carey Stanton was very good looking, very attractive, and very young. He was the sort of young man who would turn heads when he entered a room without apparently being aware of the effect he was creating. He wasn't particularly tall, but his eyes were a dark and velvety brown, with equally dark lashes; his hair, in contrast, was brightly blond and cut long on top so that it parted just off-centre and fell in two wings to frame his forehead, while the back and sides were close-cropped. He had narrow features and the sort of suntan that in winter is acquired only by the very idle or the very rich. His clothes had a thirties look to them like a leading player in a movie of an E. M. Forster novel – except that he was wearing an elegant ceramic earring in one ear. Kate realized that she had been staring at him for just a shade too long.

'Dear Kate,' he said. 'It is delightful to meet you at last. Camilla has spoken of you so often that I feel I've known you for ages.' And he drooped a graceful arm around Camilla's shoulders, while his brown eyes held Kate's.

Stupid bitch, Kate told herself, you know better than to fall for youthful charm, even if Camilla doesn't. But she had to admit that he had a particularly disarming smile, and an actor's charisma, which were getting in the way of her judgement.

'I'm so glad we've met, too,' she said, smiling foolishly. 'But I'm afraid that I have to get back to work now.'

They pressed her to stay, but she knew she wasn't wanted. She wondered for a moment why the glorious Carey had picked on Camilla, who was ordinary-looking if sharp-brained, but reminded herself that there was no accounting for physical attraction. She felt shut out of their world: she knew they wished to be on their own and do whatever it was that they did together. For a brief, disloyal moment she remembered how dull Andrew, the man in her own life, could be sometimes. Camilla and Carey followed her to the door, his arm still lightly touching Camilla's shoulder. Camilla, her friend of twenty years, looked like a stranger.

And what would the straitlaced governors of the Amy Robsart School for Girls make of that? she asked herself as she walked down the road, and couldn't help wondering whether Camilla at that very moment wasn't slipping into something pink and diaphanous and embroidered with sequins to play games with the oddly disturbing Carey Stanton. And what had Yvonne got to do with any of it?

Kate sat in her darkly womblike workroom and switched on her word processor. She read through her morning's work and made a few corrections. Concentrate, she told herself fiercely, and stop longing for an improbably attractive man to walk into your life and transform it into a garden of sensual delights. Boulogne, 1803, provided little comfort and all her ideas struck her as stodgy.

Next morning she would run further and faster and send

the oxygen pumping into her brain so that it spewed up a whole pageful of usable ideas. Tomorrow, on the other hand, she reminded herself, she would find herself involved in making plans for breaking and entering Lynda and Theo's house and stealing his perfectly legally acquired collection of valuable early nineteenth-century enamel boxes. She brightened: that could be fun.

She knew she should talk it over with Andrew. If she gave him a ring he would tell her she was being ridiculous even to consider stealing back Rose's boxes: he was good at curbing her sillier ideas. She would cook him a large meal and they would eat it while he talked her round to his point of view. Her life would go on in its old, sensible way. She saw Carey and Camilla laughing at her as they waltzed through her house, and she left the telephone receiver on its rest.

Chapter Five

Next morning was dry, but it must have rained during the night for the flood water glimmered higher than ever and seagulls floated two feet above the land which the Fridesley Development Association had earmarked for its expensive complex.

The Fridesley Running Group ('and there's another minefield of an acronym for Rose to knit if she's not careful,' as Camilla had remarked to Kate) were warming up in Rosamund Road next to the barrier that led into the recreation field. Kate and Camilla jogged to the end of the street and back to keep warm, for although it was unusually mild for the time of year, the first grey light was only just starting to creep into the sky.

'It's time you took your nose away from your monitor and noticed what was going on at the end of the lane,' Camilla was saying.

'So tell me what I should know about the Fridesley Fields development,' said Kate, who knew there was no stopping Camilla in pedagogic mode. 'I thought the developer had had his scheme turned down. Isn't that the end of it?'

'He's appealed, and the Friends are putting together a

case to oppose him. The Council have to take into account the likely increase in the traffic and the appearance of the surroundings, as well as the effect on public transport and services, and that's where we hope to win our case. It's not very interesting to the general public, but they'd notice the changes soon enough if Grant won.'

'Don't they have to hold a public inquiry?'

'Not necessarily. The Secretary of State can send along an inspector to visit the site, and can look at all the evidence and make his decision. But we're pushing for a local inquiry so that we get as much publicity as possible.'

'But should we automatically oppose all development?'

'That's not—'

But to Kate's relief, as they reached the rest of the group Gavin called out to them: 'Can you give us an update on the group race?'

'It's all under control,' said Kate, and made a mental note to phone for the permissions they needed as soon as she got home.

At last Rose's door opened and Rose came out, and they set off, led by Penny. What would we do without her? wondered Kate. Probably find ourselves jogging through North Oxford and up the bypass to Bicester before we realized that we were lost.

'We'll have to run the same route as yesterday,' said Penny, 'or we might have to swim instead of jog.' There was weak laughter from the group, then Penny was lecturing them all about repetitions and hill work and increasing their pace, and how about entering for a marathon later in the year?

'I'm entering for the New York,' said Gavin loudly, in

case someone had missed the fact.

Penny made them sound like a proper running club with members competing with the élite in the National Championships, but in fact she was as incompetent as the rest of them, with her ten-minute miles improving to nine-and-a-half on a good morning, and a short sprint bringing her down to seven-and-a-half. And it was only the running group's own annual race that they would be competing in: just under a dozen miles of tracks through the neighbouring woods and fields. We all have our running fantasies, thought Kate.

They ran in silence for the first few minutes while sleepy brains and tired legs got used to the idea that they were off on another five-mile outing. Yvonne broke the silence.

'I saw Lynda – isn't that the girl's name? – coming home with Theo yesterday,' she said, with the same relish that she took in drilling a major cavity for a nervous patient with sensitive teeth. 'And Lynda was wearing such a pretty woolly hat, patterned with leaves and with what looked like daffodils on the earpieces. It looked lovely on that blonde hair of hers. One of yours was it, Rose?'

There was a loud wail from Rose. 'But that's the hat I knitted for Theo! How could he give it to that woman!'

'Easily, I should think,' said Camilla quietly to Kate. 'Any man would think twice about wearing a hat decorated with daffodils. And why does Rose waste her energy in worrying about a hat, which doesn't matter, instead of devising how she's going to eat next month, which does?'

'I think we should return to our plan for getting Rose's boxes back,' cut in Penny before Yvonne could make another unfortunate remark.

'Since they seem determined,' muttered Camilla, 'use that creative brain of yours to come up with some foolproof scheme so that we don't all end up in our solicitors' offices explaining what we were doing on the night of the twenty-sixth.'

'Now, I like the idea of getting hold of a key to Lynda's house so that Rose doesn't have to break in,' said Penny, as they waited to cross the Fridesley Road. 'You'll have to think of an excuse to go round there, Rose, and borrow the key while Theo isn't looking.'

'No,' said Rose. 'You don't know what you're asking. Theo was horrible to me last time I saw him, and he certainly wasn't letting me inside the house.'

There was a short hiatus as they all jogged across the main road and then re-formed the group to turn left down on to the towpath.

'If there's no quick and legal way to get Rose's boxes back in time for her grandmother's visit, we're just going to have to do something sneaky, you know. She could always give them back again, after Granny's taken the inventory,' said Kate to Camilla. 'Where does Theo keep his keys, Rose? Does he dump them down on the hall table like every other man I've known, together with his small change?'

'On the hall table,' said Rose, 'and he puts his keys and his small change down as soon as he walks in through the front door in the evening and before he kisses me – *her*, that is – on the cheek and asks what's for supper.'

'The man of fixed habits. I bet he still does the same at Lynda's,' said Camilla.

'So we make some excuse to go round to Lynda's and visit them,' said Kate. 'Not in the evening, because we need the shops to be open. It will have to be a Saturday morning. In fact it will have to be this Saturday morning. Tomorrow. We need to go round and borrow something from Theo, or Lynda, and then return it shortly afterwards, before Theo needs his keys again. Hmm.'

'Is this how you think up those far-fetched plots of yours?' asked Camilla. 'I've often wondered.'

'Quiet. I'm nearly there.'

For some minutes the only sounds were the thudding of shoes and the puffing and grunting of runners as they all waited for Kate to come up with an idea.

'Did you divide up all the cassettes and CDs?' Kate asked Rose.

'I've got all my cassettes, but Theo's taken the CDs. I do miss the Mozart. I got them when I went to the Fridesley Musical Appreciation evenings at the Community Centre, but Theo thought they were really classy and so he took them with him. He said that since I wouldn't have a CD player I wouldn't be needing them anyway.'

'That's our line, then. You've acquired a CD player—'

'But I haven't, Kate.'

'I'm the one going round to Theo's, am I?' Kate asked rhetorically. 'Yes? Then I'm just going to have to lie a little bit. So I go round to Theo and Lynda's on Saturday morning, and demand your Mozart discs back. While Theo's fetching them—'

'Suppose he refuses?' said Camilla.

'I'll have to improvise, won't I?'

'And just suppose you get into the house for long enough to pocket Theo's keys, how are you going to return them without raising his suspicions?'

'Stop being so negative, Camilla. This is easy: I go back

twenty minutes later, saying that I took a disc that Rose considers is his, and being a fairminded person, she wishes to return it. OK?'

'I quite fancy his Dire Straits,' said Rose, thoughtfully.

'Fine, I'll try to get it for you.'

She waited a moment or two for someone to argue, or volunteer to go round to Theo's in her place, but they all seemed content to leave it to her.

'Come on Rose. Let's show the others how to run, shall we?' And she accelerated away from the group, down the towpath towards the metallic grey surface of the flooded meadow. She could hear Rose's large feet padding along behind her, and the lighter, faster pace that belonged to Yvonne. The heavy breathing must come from Sophie, trying hard to keep up with her mother. As they reached the gate at the end of the path, she found herself looking out for the man who had been out running the previous morning, but he must have taken another route or gone out at a different time.

'Well,' said Camilla, as she and Kate made their way back to Waverley Lane after the run, 'I'm really glad to hear that you think you know what you're doing. And once you've got the key cut – *if* you get the key cut, that is – what then? Have you thought out the rest of the plan, or are you making it up as you go along?'

'I've got the whole thing worked out. Trust me.'

'One of your first drafts? Lots of bright ideas and a bit short on accurate detail?'

'Final draft, Camilla. Checked, typed, and proof-read. Since we've all agreed that Rose has got to get her boxes back I'm going to make sure that she doesn't get caught doing it. And don't pretend you don't know about helping people when they need it. Remember the time I was ten and you let me wear the pink dress?'

'When you were the cherry-blossom fairy. I'd forgotten that.'

'I haven't, Millie. But you don't have to get involved in this scheme to help Rose.'

'I'm in trouble if I don't go along with it, and I'm probably in just as much trouble if I do. So I'm relying on you to come up with a watertight scheme. And I suppose if Rose gives the boxes back afterwards, it won't be so bad.'

'I shouldn't rely on that. I expect she can be just as stubborn as Theo when she wants.'

Saturday morning was again unseasonably warm. The daffodil stems stood a foot high in Fridesley's front gardens, with buds ready to open. Purple crocuses were already blooming and the snowdrops were past their best. After a leisurely bath, Kate sprayed herself with *Ivoire*.

She walked to the bottom of Rosamund Road, through the barrier at the end and along the tarmac path at the top of the recreation field, with the water lapping gently at the grass only a foot or so away and nudging the empty drink tins and plastic debris on to the narrow grass verge. She passed the end of Wheatfield Road, and called 'Good morning' to Valerie Binns as she unloaded two small children and two musical instruments out of her Morris Minor, and walked to the corner of Redbourne Road where she saw the big window of Yvonne's studio looking out over the field towards the willows and alders on the far

side. Then, feeling a surge of exhilaration, she turned into
Redbourne Road and walked up to Number 29.

'How did it go?'

Rose was on the telephone, sounding anxious.

'Fine. I now have one key to Lynda's house, courtesy of
the lad with the dreadful acne and four earrings at the DIY
place.' Kate had drunk a celebratory glass or two of white
wine and was feeling expansive. 'And I've rubbed it with a
2B pencil to make sure it works easily. Oh, and I've got half
a dozen Mozart CDs for you, too. I'm afraid Theo wouldn't
let go of anything else.'

'Thanks, Kate. I'm just starting to think that things might
turn out all right, after all.'

'Of course they will, Rose.' Kate felt complete confidence
in her powers of invention. 'And I saw your boxes in the
display case: the Oxford box was in the middle.'

And now, she thought when Rose had thanked her again
and she had finally rung off, we can get on with the main
part of the plan: the theft of the boxes.

Chapter Six

Fridesley Runners met on the following Monday. It was another mild, blowy morning with the crocuses glowing pale in the lamplight and a greasy skin of moisture on the pavement.

'I've planned a route that's a mile shorter than usual,' said Penny, after everyone had congratulated Kate on getting the key to Theo's house. 'So we'll take it at a slightly faster pace.' There were murmurings at this break in their routine and rumblings of dissent at the idea of moving faster than usual. Penny raised her voice to continue: 'That means that we'll be back nearly fifteen minutes early and we can meet at my place afterwards for a planning session to recover Rose's boxes and help her to put her case to her grandmother. Barbara and I have made some notes.'

As they set off, Kate thought that Penny had brought a strange man with her, but when she took another look at him she realized that it was Gavin, but without his beard. It was just as well that it was winter rather than summer, she thought. At least the pallor of the lower half of his face matched the winter paleness of the parts that had been exposed to the elements. And he didn't have the weak chin

51

that was the traditional reason for growing a beard; that's a stubborn mouth, she thought.

'How did the key stealing go?' Camilla asked Kate as they set off.

'We didn't steal it, we borrowed it. And it went fine, and even if Rose never gets her boxes back, at least she's got half a dozen Mozart CDs for consolation.'

'And nothing to play them on.'

'You want us to steal back the CD player now?'

'I don't want you to steal anything.'

There is still something on Camilla's mind, thought Kate as they started to increase the pace, following Penny up the lamplit streets of Fridesley and towards the centre of Oxford. But there was no spare oxygen for talking as Penny led them at an increasingly brisk pace round a flat, fast route that took them through empty streets and past silent colleges that made Kate think of the centuries before William Morris built his factory out at Cowley and filled Oxford with motor cars. They ran over the cobblestones of Radcliffe Square, under the looming bulk of the Camera with the plume of white vapour curling out from a heating duct. It looked as dark as Rose's mourning box, and for a moment Kate saw its dome swinging open from the balustrade while the black eye sockets of an ivory skull peered out at her above the pediment. *Die to live*? It wasn't her own philosophy. Then they were running along the narrow lane where the television company parked their trailers when they were making the Inspector Morse films, and turning left into the Turl.

'What do you think it means, *Live to die, Die to live*?' Sophie asked suddenly, her voice close behind Kate's shoulder. The Radcliffe Camera, oppressively large for its surroundings, must have had the same effect on her as on Kate. 'It's a funny sort of saying, isn't it?'

'I suppose it means that you should live every day by the rules, and keep the thought of dying well always with you,' said Kate, slowly. 'And believe that death is the gateway to eternal life. If you get the preliminary living bit right, that is.'

'It could become a touch obsessive, don't you think,' said Camilla, 'if you took it too literally? Would you ever be able to take a day off and have fun? Or do something naughty without feeling guilty?'

'I think the point of the mourning object was to stand around and remind you, simply by being there, that one day you would die and be judged and you'd better keep your nose clean,' said Kate.

'It's odd, though,' said Sophie, 'but when you think about it, you can make those words mean all sorts of different things, can't you?'

'But all of them glum,' said Kate, who had had enough of this conversation, and wanted to think of something cheerful.

The sun had still not risen when they got back to Fridesley and Penny opened her front door and ushered them all into the kitchen of her house.

Penny believed in delegation. Kate and Camilla were told to make and hand out the coffee while Penny organized the meeting and Barbara took notes. She'll be distributing an agenda in a moment, thought Kate, but Penny got straight down to business.

'Now, we've got the key to Lynda's house, right?'

'Right.'

'And do we know exactly where the boxes are?' asked Barbara.

Kate described the cabinet where the boxes were kept while Barbara noted it down.

'How many? How big? How much do they weigh?'

'Isn't this overkill?' Camilla murmured to Kate.

'I'm not really sure I can go through with this,' said Rose.

'If you're hoping that one of us will volunteer to do it for you, forget it,' said Camilla. 'This is something you're going to have to do for yourself, Rose. Think of it as the first step on the stony and uphill road to independence.'

Penny interrupted her. 'Of course you're going to do it. We haven't got this far just so that you can give up now. The next point to decide is how you're going to get into the house without being recognized.'

'She must wear a disguise,' said Yvonne.

'How about black biker leathers?' asked Gavin. 'Big black gauntlets, black helmet with visor down, black boots.'

'Are we indulging in our favourite erotic fantasy, do you think?' said Kate to Camilla.

'They'd have to be enormous black boots,' said Rose, ruefully.

'Don't worry,' said Penny. 'Lots of people have big feet: think of Lynda's.'

'That's it,' said Kate. 'We dress her up as Lynda. No one would wonder why she was going into the house if they thought it was Lynda, would they?'

'But I don't look anything like her! No one would ever take me for her.'

'Actually,' said Kate, looking at her with a dispassionate

eye, 'you're not at all unalike. You're only about an inch shorter, and with higher heels no one would notice. And if you looked taller, you'd look slimmer, too.'

'And then there's your enormous feet,' said Camilla, 'just like Lynda's. You'd be mistaken for her on that alone.'

'It will be dark,' said Barbara. 'And by the time the vandals have been at the streetlamps there really isn't a lot of light down these side streets. We only need a general impression.'

'Hair,' said Gavin. 'Lynda has this long, thick curly blonde hair. Lots and lots of it. It hangs down over her shoulders and she tosses it around a lot.'

'Wear a wig,' said Sophie.

'I haven't got a wig,' said Rose.

'There's a long blonde wig in our drama department at school,' said Sophie. 'We could trim it and curl it so that it looked like Lynda's.'

'That's *my* drama department in *my* school,' snapped Camilla. 'And I don't want the Amy Robsart dragged into this affair.'

'Don't be so mean.' This was Yvonne's amused voice. 'We're only asking to borrow a wig for an evening, Camilla. We don't expect you to dress up in it and prance around Fridesley wearing tulle and sequins.'

Camilla went pink. 'Very well,' she said stiffly. 'I will provide a blonde wig for this ridiculous charade.'

'Didn't someone say that Lynda had been wearing one of Rose's knitted hats?' said Barbara.

'Pink bobble on top, flowers on the earpieces, ties under the chin,' said Gavin.

'Well, well,' said Kate. 'Penny will have to rope our

Gavin a little more firmly to the kitchen sink if she's not going to lose him.'

'You've got another one of those hats, haven't you, Rose, that you could wear?'

'I think it's got different colour flowers on, but it's got a pink bobble to match Theo's.'

'What else does she wear that's easily recognizable?' rapped out Penny.

'Scarlet duvet jacket,' said Gavin, failing to take the hint.

'Well, at least the school drama department can't provide one of those,' said Camilla. 'Someone else will have to volunteer. How about you, Yvonne?'

'Not my style,' said Yvonne. 'Can't you help, Barbara?'

'My sister's got one,' said Barbara, reluctantly. 'I suppose she'd lend it to me for the evening if I asked her.'

'So that's it,' said Penny. 'Rose wears Camilla's wig, her own knitted hat, high heels—'

'High-heeled black boots,' said Gavin, unwisely. 'Shiny ones. Tight fitting.'

Yvonne laughed.

'Tarty boots,' translated Penny, through gritted teeth. 'Have you got that, Barbara? Now, Rose, what time will Theo and Lynda leave for the Indian restaurant? Does he book a table in advance?'

'No, he hated the idea that something might come up and make him late. I can't tell you exactly,' said Rose. 'But between seven-twenty and seven-forty, I should think.'

'Could you have lived for seven years with a man of such predictable habits?' Kate asked Camilla.

'I think the pink rosebud mouth and the beer gut would have got to me before the habits,' said Camilla, almost back on her old form. 'Also the hairy hands.'

'Pay attention, please,' said Penny. 'We still have two points to cover: firstly, we need observers to report when Theo and Lynda have left the house. And secondly, if Theo really does go to the police we need to establish an alibi for everyone so that if questions *are* asked, then none of us, and especially Rose, will be involved.'

'Pity to waste all this planning on a set of enamel boxes,' said Kate to Camilla. 'We could have taken out a bank or a building society and made it really worth while.'

'Don't suggest it. Penny is likely to take you seriously. She wouldn't think about the legality, she would just see it as a challenge to her organizing abilities.'

'And Yvonne would encourage her,' said Kate, thoughtfully, 'because she enjoys making people do what she tells them.'

'So,' Penny was saying. 'I want everyone at Rose's house by ten to seven on the evening of Wednesday the twenty-sixth of February. You're all to wear dark tracksuits, woolly hats, and running shoes. We want to look as much alike as possible so that anyone who sees us will be confused as to how many of us there are and where we were and when.'

'Will anyone notice and care that much?' asked Kate.

'No, of course not. But it would be a shame to spoil her fun,' said Camilla.

'And we'll put some music on—'

'Mozart on the non-existent CD player?'

'Barbara will bring her cassette player and speakers,' said Penny. 'And I'll bring some aerobics music. When we're not out observing we'll all do an aerobics session. That ought to convince the neighbours that we were here all evening.'

'That should convince the neighbours that we're all quite barmy and obviously planning something illegal,' said Camilla, gloomily, when they had left Penny's house and were making their way back to the other side of the Fridesley Road. 'I know this is going to end in tears, Kate.'

'If you disapprove of the whole thing so much, why are you agreeing to help?'

'I suppose it's gone too far to back out now. And I'd be letting people down if I said I wanted no more to do with it.'

'You don't sound very convincing. The old Millie would have gone in there fighting until she had got her own way. What's stopping you? I know that something is.'

'I don't want to talk about it.'

'Is it anything to do with Carey?'

'How did we get on to that? I haven't said a thing.'

'That's what I mean.'

Kate left her and turned right into Agatha Street, thinking about the scene in Penny's kitchen. Although a part of her agreed with Camilla that it was unwise to get involved in something illegal, another was elated and wanted to see it through. She started humming as she turned the corner and went up the path to her front door. As she walked through the front door, Fridesley disappeared and she moved back to Boulogne and her heroine. She just hoped that the neighbours would stay quiet for long enough for her to get her ideas on to her word processor.

Her phone rang at lunchtime: it was Andrew.

'I never find you in these days, Kate. Isn't it time we met up for an evening of food, wine, and conversation?'

'I'm afraid I'm awfully busy just at the moment, Andrew.'

She knew that after a couple of glasses of wine she wouldn't be able to resist the temptation to tell him all about their scheme and he would try to talk her out of it.

There was a silence at the other end of the line.

'How about Thursday next week?' she said: it would all be over by then.

'I'll take you somewhere new and expensive, with delicious food,' he said.

'Sounds wonderful,' said Kate. She only wished it sounded as exciting as stealing Rose's boxes.

Chapter Seven

During the next few days the group laboured up hills at a pace that left fingers of pain digging into the fronts of Kate's thighs. But when she complained, Penny said that they should be properly fit for their endeavours on the following Wednesday, and anyway, what about the annual group race?

Sophie turned up one morning with the blonde wig from the drama department from the Amy Robsart and in spite of Camilla's objections, Barbara said that she would trim and set it so that it looked just like Lynda's hair. Barbara reported that her sister would let her have the red duvet jacket at the weekend, and Rose said that she had seen just the right pair of boots, reduced to £35, and she would buy them on Saturday, charging them to Theo's Access account.

'Well, that has a sort of poetic justice to it, I suppose,' said Camilla, as they set off through the cold morning air and a rising wind. The wind blew all that week, although the temperature was still high for February and the flood waters lapped the edges of Fridesley Fields. Panic came on Saturday, when Rose reported that Lynda had been sighted with a new hairstyle: the blonde hair no longer fluttered in tendrils around her shoulders but had been cut very short at the back and left long on top.

'No problem,' said Barbara, and set about the blonde wig again with scissors and rollers.

'That's all very well,' said Camilla, 'but we'll have Ophelia looking like a choirboy in our next school production.'

'I'm sure the audience will love it,' said Kate.

Camilla hugged her white lifebelt to herself even harder.

And then it was at last Wednesday, and a cold and gusting day after a noisy night when dustbin lids flew around the side passages of the houses, and car doors were whipped out of clumsy hands and slammed back on to bodywork. The afternoon added torrential rain and umbrellas pulled inside out by a capricious wind. One by one the runners dressed in dark tracksuits and running shoes and put on hats that they pulled low over their foreheads, and hid hands in gloves. Kate took one last tour of her house, securing windows and locking doors as they rattled in the increasing wind. The radio was giving warnings of structural damage, but she couldn't think of anything more to do to protect her house from the elements. She made sure her bicycle was locked in its shed and her dustbin lid secured with a heavy stone, then she looked around for any other loose objects that might be carried away by the wind. Her cream Peugeot swayed slightly but looked solid enough to withstand anything.

Once she had turned the corner into the Fridesley Road, the wind tore at her face and dragged at the odd strands of hair that escaped from her hat, plastering them across her face and into her mouth. Her feet splashed in puddles and the unpruned branches of a hedge whipped at her face. She turned thankfully into Rose's gate.

The others, too, were arriving: damp, windblown, nervous about what they were about to take part in and jittery as cats in the wild weather.

Penny put some strongly rhythmic music on the big black radio-cassette player and encouraged them all to jump up and down and make a lot of noise. Kate noticed that Camilla was there, although in a subdued mood, but Gavin was missing.

'No Gavin?' she asked Penny. 'I thought he was keen to help.'

'He had some Council business to catch up on, but he'll be along in the next quarter of an hour.'

'And Yvonne? Isn't she coming?'

'She had to go out to a meeting,' said Sophie. 'The County Dental Association, I think.'

'That was a bit sudden, wasn't it?' said Penny.

'At least,' said Kate, 'there won't be many people out in this weather, noticing Theo and Lynda leaving and someone quite different letting themselves into the house.'

'Rose won't look different at all,' said Penny. 'Quite indistinguishable from Lynda, in fact. Lynda's been wearing that red duvet jacket every day, everyone must have noticed it. And I think she likes to show off that hat Rose knitted, too. Unless someone comes right up to her and stares into her face, everyone who sees her will assume that it's Lynda.'

'Isn't it time we started round the block, checking on whether they've left or not?' asked Sophie, her dark hair in rats' tails round her face, her stubby, freckled nose pink with excitement or an approaching cold.

'I've got the list here,' said Barbara. 'You're first, Penny.'

Penny set off to the accompaniment of a chorus of dustbin lids rolling down Rosamund Road. As soon as she had left, the others jumped about to the music while Barbara did some loud counting to cheer them on their way for a couple of minutes.

'I'm off now,' said Barbara. 'Here, Kate, you hold the list and the stopwatch. You should be able to manage this sort of thing all right.'

And so the rest of them jumped and raised and lifted as loudly as they could, and took their turn at going out into the storm that raged over Fridesley. At some time Gavin turned up and took his place in the rota.

This part of the plan is a real pain, thought Kate, wishing that she had Camilla to grumble to, but Camilla must have been out running the streets. They seemed to have been jumping around for hours when Penny returned with her report.

'The lights are on in Lynda's house and I can see movements behind the blinds. There are still lights on upstairs, too, so I suppose one or other of them is getting changed.'

'Maybe they're—' Sophie started to say, but was stopped by Penny, saying, 'Your turn to go out, Kate. Give me the stopwatch and the list. Gavin, you get ready to leave next. And Camilla. Where's Camilla?' She was in her element.

Oh, bugger the ones who've bunked off, thought Kate as she set off into the teeth of the boisterous, unpredictable wind. How many times are the rest of us going to have to run round this bloody block?

She pushed her way through the resisting air along Rosamund Road with her head down, then turned into the comparative calm of the tarmac path at the bottom. Cars were rocking as they stood parked in the road, and she jumped as the Binns's bicycles, chained in a heap by their back door in Wheatfield Road, fell over with a crash. Further up the narrow street, Mrs Graybel was struggling with a boulder that she had prised out of her rockery, anchoring her dustbin lid to its dustbin and the dustbin to the ground. Beside her, the black-leather-clad figure of her son, helmet shiny in the rain, vizor down over his uncommunicative face, was revving the engine of his bright green motorbike and filling the narrow street with blue fumes and growling noise. As she watched, he gunned his engine once more and set off up the street away from her. Mrs Graybel's voice wailed loudly but ineffectually after him. Round the corner into Redbourne Road went Kate, slowly in the teeth of the gale and against the cold rain that was hurling itself into her eyes. Some of her hair had come loose and dripped in wet strands across her forehead. She told herself to concentrate on what was happening in the houses ahead.

On her left, the lights from Yvonne's studio windows spilled out on to the flooded recreation ground. But hadn't Sophie said that she had left to go to a meeting? If you were going to tell white lies you should make sure that you wouldn't be found out. Ahead of her a tile came crashing down from a roof, shattering and scattering fragments across the pavement. In the garden opposite, two indistinguishable figures were struggling with what looked like fencing and a washing line: the Gatlock sisters. But it was Theo and Lynda who should concern her. Number 29. The curtains were pulled shut in the upstairs windows, but Kate could see that lights were on in the room above the front door, and also behind the frosted glass of the window on the side of the house. Even above the noise of the wind and the rain she heard the water gurgling down from the pipes: someone had just finished their bath. She must report back to the others. It looked as though Theo and Lynda would be leaving soon. As she slowed down outside the house to note the details, she thought she heard their phone ringing, and she moved on. She padded past the Gatlocks'. Their side door was open and Mr Gatlock's voice was giving out a stream of instructions to Elma and Betty. They were still struggling with what looked like a few hundred yards of rope, and doing something complicated and incomprehensible, their bodies bent over and their large square rumps, turned towards Kate, dark, wet tweed flapping around their sturdy legs, in the light from the kitchen. They cried like curlews to each other, offering instruction and imprecation, as far as she could hear. She slipped past as quietly as she could, guilty at not stopping to offer help.

It was a slow, wet jog back to Rose's house, with the rain soaking into her cotton trousers so that they clung to her legs and flapped around her ankles. But she dutifully reported back to the others and joined the group who were now into a Jane Fonda routine in Rose's half-empty sitting room. Sod this, thought Kate, as she swung her arms, nipping her bosom in a painful way as she crossed her elbows. I hope those enamel boxes are going to be worth it. What was the thing called? The Oxford Death Box? Rose was welcome to it. Then she was down on the floor and doing complicated and painful things with her legs, refusing to go for the burn however hard she was urged to do so. Maybe it only took ten minutes, but it seemed like an eternity before it was her turn to leave the room and go round the block again.

This time, when she got to the corner of Redbourne Road she saw that the light was out in Yvonne's studio; perhaps she had gone to her meeting after all. The lights were off upstairs in Lynda's house, but on downstairs, and Theo's car was still outside. Ahead of her, on the opposite side of the road, another figure approached from Fridesley Road, hat pulled down hard against the rain, shoulders hunched in a dark anorak. As he or she passed under the streetlamp she saw the gleam of pale hair, or maybe it was just the effect of the sodium lamp. There was something about the way the figure moved that might have been familiar, but impossible to tell in this weather who it was without peering under that anorak hood. Then she bent her own head down into the wind and finished her tour of the block; she didn't want to stop and talk to anyone. She jogged on.

It was only a few minutes after she reached Rose's house, as she bent forwards, trying to keep her back in a straight line, that Sophie returned with news for them all: she had seen Theo and Lynda departing, not in Theo's BMW but on foot, and Lynda was wearing the red duvet jacket and the flowered woolly hat to protect her new flashy haircut. (Not of course that Sophie put it quite like that, but that was how Kate described it to Camilla, later.) Sophie's sallow face was flushed with excitement, her green eyes watering from the cold air, her dispirited hair still sticking to her scalp, and she joined in with enthusiasm as they fixed the wig on Rose's head and topped it with the second woolly hat.

'That's it,' said Penny, as Barbara flicked at strands of blonde wig. 'Bright red lipstick, now, Rose.'

'Stand up straight and push your chest forward,' said Gavin.

It was true, thought Kate, half-closing her eyes and squinting at Rose, she did look quite a lot like Lynda really, if you couldn't see the detail. And in the storm that was blowing outside, no one was likely to notice detail, even if all the streetlights were working, which, as she had seen herself when she was running round the block, they weren't.

'I've got to do it, haven't I?' said Rose. 'I have to remind myself about the things I want to do with Granny's money and get on with it. If I just grit my teeth and get through this evening, I'll be all right. And I don't have to meet Theo and talk to him.'

'We can't promise you that there'll never be another problem in your life,' said Kate, 'but it could solve some of the immediate ones for you.'

'Off you go now, Rose,' said Penny, as Rose hesitated on the doorstep. 'Everything's OK. You look just like Lynda, and Lynda and Theo have gone off for a long evening of curry eating. You've got the key. You've got a bag to put the boxes in?'

'They'll fit in my pockets,' said Rose, waggling her mittened hands around in the pockets of the red duvet jacket. 'And I've got a pair of thin plastic gloves like they wear at the clinic inside my mittens so that I don't leave any fingerprints.'

'You're getting a proper criminal mentality,' said Penny without a hint of irony.

'I saw it on the telly last week,' said Rose.

At last Rose was persuaded to leave the shelter of the hallway and she disappeared down the street as the rest of them watched.

'She looks like a burglar,' said Barbara, watching the skulking, non-assertive figure.

'No time to waste,' said Penny, putting the cassette back on. 'Shall we go back to the beginning of thighs? Or would you like to work on your abdominals?'

'I'd like a large gin and tonic while I'm waiting for Rose,' said Kate.

'Stop being disruptive,' said Camilla. 'You're always saying that writing wrecks your figure, so you should be grateful for the exercise.'

'Well, I'm not. I'm hating it.'

'Camilla, it's your turn to go round the block this time,' said Penny.

'But we know they've left for the restaurant,' protested Kate.

'We have to keep an eye on the house in case something unexpected happens. And Gavin, you get ready to go out two minutes after her. When I went out the first time I saw Lynda come out of her house, you know.'

'Why didn't you mention it before?' asked Camilla.

'It didn't seem important. She just popped over the road to Yvonne's house, and straight back again.'

'I didn't know they knew each other,' said Camilla.

'Everybody in this place knows Yvonne, I don't suppose it means anything,' said Kate. 'And if you really don't want to go out, Camilla, I'll go round for you.'

But Camilla had left Kate to clench and lift and circle and pivot and disappeared again. Kate hoped that it would indeed show in the reduced size of her hips the next morning. And then, at last, after another eternity of jumping and leg swinging and arm lifting, there was a rattling of the front door, and Rose was back.

'Have you got them?'

'They're here,' said Rose, pulling small enamel boxes from her pockets and placing them carefully on the kitchen table.

'Don't stop yet,' shouted Penny, as they all crowded round to look. 'We've got to establish a proper alibi for the evening. Keep at it, girls—'

Kate winced and looked round for Camilla to sympathize with her, but she couldn't see her in the cluster of tracksuit-clad figures. She and Gavin were still out, she assumed.

'Barbara, you keep taking the class, and I'll make sure Rose gets out of those clothes and that wig. Oh, that's a pretty one, Rose: "Think deeply, speak gently".'

'Yes,' said Rose. 'But the Oxford box wasn't there. I don't know what Theo's done with it, but it was missing. There was an empty space in the middle of the display, as though he'd only just taken it out. I've got all the others, though.'

'That's odd,' said Kate. 'Do you think he's sold it?'

'Not without publicity,' said Rose. 'Do you think I'll ever get it back?'

'I don't think I'd mind not having anything that morbid in my house,' said Kate. 'Will your grandmother notice it's missing?'

'I expect so. I'll have to invent some story to explain its

disappearance. At least it'll be easier than talking away half a dozen of them.'

And so they carried on with their music and their aerobics class. And later Gavin brought in a bottle of cold white wine, and they found glasses and toasted Rose and the boxes in the kitchen, then pulled on hats and gloves and talked about getting back to their own houses, though no one felt like leaving the warm, bright room and going out again into the gale and rain of that Fridesley evening.

'I ought to be going,' said Kate to Rose. 'I like to start work early when I'm writing a first draft.'

'Do you think the police will be round in the morning?' asked Rose.

'He'll be lucky if he gets a constable round by lunchtime,' said Kate. 'There are much worse things than that happening every night in this city. He'll just claim on his insurance, especially since he's still got the blue Camera, and everyone will forget about it. It's over, Rose, put it behind you.'

Chapter Eight

Kate was woken next morning by the phone ringing. Outside her window the Fridesley sky was dark grey and dripping with moisture and she had the impression that the storm had only just died down and she had only recently fallen asleep.

'Kate, it's Penny,' said the voice on the phone as she struggled into consciousness. 'Look, I've just had the police round, asking questions.'

'Already? They took three days when I had my car stolen last year, and then they weren't very helpful.'

'Well, you'd better believe me.'

'What did they say?'

'They were stone-faced plainclothes men. All they would say was that they were investigating a crime and had I seen or heard anything yesterday evening.'

'What did you say?'

'I stuck to our story: we were all at Rose's house, jumping up and down to music and we didn't see or hear anything with the noise we were making. I'm just ringing round everyone to make sure that they all tell the same story, OK?'

'I don't really like it, but we'll have to, now, won't we? I wonder what Theo said or did to the police to get this sort of treatment out of them?'

'Will you get hold of Camilla and tell her to keep to the same line? It will save me a call. I'll get on to as many of the others as I can.'

'All right. As soon as I've got myself round a mug of coffee.'

'There's no time to lose, Kate, they seem keen to get this thing sorted out. It wasn't Jim Giles on his bike, you know, but two young men with short haircuts that I'd never seen before. They didn't smile once and they wouldn't even have a cup of tea. This is important, Kate. You won't forget, will you?'

Penny sounded so upset that Kate rang Camilla straight away, but there was no reply, so she abandoned the idea of catching up on her sleep and put the kettle on for some coffee, instead. And then someone was knocking at her door, ringing her doorbell, shouting through her letter box. She left the kitchen and went to open it. It was Camilla, in her green tracksuit, hugging the white circle of the lifebelt to herself as though she was drowning. She dragged off her woollen hat. Her face had the drained look of someone who has had no sleep.

'Important, huh?' said Kate, leading the way into the kitchen, wondering why Camilla wasn't wearing grey flannel, carrying a briefcase, on her way to school. Camilla didn't bother to reply, but stood in the kitchen staring at Kate, as though she had forgotten how to speak.

Kate poured boiling water on to ground coffee and carried the cafetière across to the table.

'What is it? You'd better tell me about it.'

Camilla pulled strands of wool from the bobble on her hat. Kate found biscuits and put them out on a plate to distract her.

'She was dead when I found her,' said Camilla, then shut up again. Kate poured coffee and thought about brandy.

'Found who?' she asked.

'She must have been dead, mustn't she? There wasn't that much blood, but she couldn't have been alive.' She sipped at her coffee, still not looking at Kate.

Kate stopped herself from shaking her friend into coherence. 'Sit down. Tell me. Who was dead?' Her own breathing was doing something peculiar. 'Where? When?'

'Yvonne. I went round there last night to get my things. But she was dead.'

'What was it? A heart attack?' But Camilla had said something about blood. Alarm bells were ringing inside her head and she thought about Penny's phone call. 'Did you call an ambulance, or the police?'

'No. I couldn't.'

'You're making no sense at all, Camilla. You've got to tell me about it. Well, you've got to tell someone, by the look of you.'

'Get dressed, can you? We have to go out. I can't stay in here. I can't breathe.'

'Don't be a fool. Just sit down and tell me what's happened.'

Camilla looked round as if the walls would start moving in towards her and crush her. 'I can't stay here, I have to go,' she said. 'I shouldn't have come. It was a mistake.'

Kate stopped arguing. 'Give me two minutes,' she

shouted, and raced upstairs to put on the tracksuit and trainers that were laid out on her bedroom chair, ready for her next early-morning run. She splashed water over her face and scrubbed briefly at her teeth, which at least gave her the impression of normality. Camilla was still destroying the bobble of her hat when she went back into the kitchen.

Kate took the back door key from the hook and led the way out. It was one of those mornings when night creeps imperceptibly into day without ever becoming fully light. Around them orange lights glowed in windows and the sun was buried so deep in cloud that it was impossible to tell where the east was. The street was empty. They turned towards the city centre. Kate waited a long time for Camilla to speak.

'Life is unfair, isn't it?' she said, eventually.

'I knew that by the time I was three,' said Kate. 'I also know that you are finding it difficult to confide in a friend. But you've got to, so tell me about Yvonne.'

'It's cold. Do you want to start running? Would we feel better, do you think?'

Kate didn't say that the only thing that would make her feel better was an end to this nightmare, a hot bath, and another couple of hours' sleep.

'Start at the beginning. Where did you find her?'

'In her studio.'

'When? What were you doing there?'

'Yesterday evening. While Rose was getting her boxes back, I suppose, or maybe just after that. I don't know. I can't tell you why I was there.' Each answer came after a long pause, as though Camilla had to think hard before putting her thoughts into words.

'You said something about collecting your things. What things?'

'I can't tell you that, either.'

Kate stopped running and grabbed Camilla's arm so that she slewed round to face her.

'What the hell are we doing, Camilla? Why did you come round to my place instead of going to the police? If you don't want me to go down to St Aldate's with you, why did you tell me anything about it?'

'She'd been murdered, Kate. I could see that. And I can't go to the police. They'd think I did it. They'd ask too many questions. Just like you're doing.'

'They'd be worse, Camilla, much, much worse if you behaved like this. Believe me, they wouldn't have my patience.' And yes, Camilla, she thought, they'd certainly assume that you did it. I'm even beginning to think that way myself.

They had reached Parks Road. A figure loomed out of the murk ahead of them and they fell silent as he approached. It was a tall, dark-haired man in a black tracksuit. Kate waited impatiently for him to move out of hearing. It was the man they had seen at the end of the towpath: this was a small town. She watched over her shoulder as he ran down the pavement behind them and turned into the grey stone gateway of Leicester College. As soon as he had disappeared, they jogged north again and Camilla sighed and at last spoke.

'No one was watching me, so I slipped out of Rose's house and down the road. Sophie had said that Yvonne was going out to a meeting. I went carefully because I didn't want anyone to see me and wonder what I was doing. I needn't have worried, though. No one was out of doors: the weather was awful by then. I let myself in and went up to Yvonne's studio. I saw the curtains were closed, and I couldn't see any lights and I assumed that she had left for her meeting. I went in through the back door and past the waiting room and surgery, and then pushed open the door to the studio. I was nervous, but I knew I had to do what I was doing: it was just as important as Rose's theft. I'd brought a pencil torch, so I could see immediately in front of me, but even without the lights I knew something was wrong. It was the smell.'

'What sort of smell?' asked Kate.

'You know when you go into the Covered Market, just after they've delivered a load of beef carcasses? I hate going into the butcher's when they're hanging up on those hooks. I imagine they're going to drip great slow gobs of blood on to my head. And they smell of blood and dead flesh. A hot, metallic sort of smell. Well, that's what Yvonne's studio smelled like. Dead meat. Death.'

Camilla paused, and they padded on through the Parks, running round the path by the side of the Clarendon Laboratory. At least she's talking now and when we've completed this circuit, we'll be facing back towards Fridesley, thought Kate. I can get to a telephone and call St Aldate's police station and hand over responsibility to someone else.

'The thick blue velvet curtains were pulled, so I could turn the light on without anyone noticing from the street. And then I saw her. Yvonne. She had fallen backwards, her arms lifted as though to protect her head. And there were photographs, as though someone had flung them down. Some were black and white, most were in colour, and all of them were torn and crumpled. Some of them were smeared with blood. There were broken images of arms and legs and torsos, next to the . . . next to her. I knew she was dead: there wasn't much blood, but her head was the wrong shape, and I could see these white fragments that must have been bone. And there was the way she was lying. But I wasn't sick. I knew I mustn't be sick. They can tell so much from things like that, can't they?'

'I believe so.' Kate looked round behind them. There was no one else out running within hearing distance that she could see. No one to overhear this awful story.

'How long did you stay? How could you bear to be in that room?'

'I held my breath. I was only there for a couple of minutes, doing what I had to do. I couldn't face going back to Rose's and I've been at home, wondering what to do, ever since. I couldn't go to the police, so I waited till I thought you'd be awake and then I came round. I had to talk to someone about it.'

'You found me up because I'd just been woken by a phone call. Penny rang to say that she'd had the police in, asking questions. We both assumed it was about the enamel boxes, but Sophie must have reported Yvonne's death when she got home.'

'What sort of questions were they asking?'

'Basic stuff about last night: who was where and whether they heard or saw anything. Penny thought they were asking about the boxes, so she gave the agreed story: we were all at Rose's place, jumping up and down to music, training for the club race, and we were so busy and making so much noise that we saw and heard nothing. She was ringing to tell me so that we all stuck to the same story. I was supposed to pass the message on to you.'

'That's all right, then. We'll be all right if everyone does what they agreed.'

There was a bench just ahead of them and Kate slowed to a walk. 'We're going to sit down and talk about this. You can't expect a group of people to tell lies to the police during a murder investigation, Camilla. We're not dealing with Rose's boxes. I noticed you were absent for a time during the evening, and I expect some of the others did, too. The best thing for you to do is to go to the police yourself, before they come to you.'

'I can't. Believe me, Kate, I can't.' And Camilla started to cry, sitting there in the grey light, with broken-off twigs and branches around her on the ground and a clump of flattened daffodil buds nudging her feet. Tears brimmed and coursed until she was sobbing and gulping, bending over like a child and hiding her wet, puffy face in her arms. She was not a person who welcomed touching, but Kate put out an awkward hand and rested it on her shoulder, just so that she should know that there was someone there.

Eventually Camilla sat up and rummaged in her pockets. 'Sod it, no handkerchief,' she said, and pulled out the hem of her T-shirt and wiped her face on it. Her eyes were bloodshot and her skin looked raw, as though several layers had been removed, leaving her exposed and vulnerable, but she sniffed one final time and stood up.

'I knew that crying was a mistake,' she said, and the effort to sound like the usual Camilla was evident in her voice. 'Once I started, I would lose control of myself.'

'For God's sake, you're allowed to cry!'

But Camilla said: 'It won't happen again. Come on, we must go back now.'

They walked in silence for a time. Then Kate said:

'How did you get into Yvonne's house, by the way?'

'I took your idea and used their spare key. I knew they kept it under a flower pot in the garden because I saw Sophie get it out one day while I was in the surgery waiting room.' She sounded like herself again, and only the red blotches around her eyes gave away her recent fit of weeping.

'So you'd planned your visit to Yvonne,' said Kate slowly. 'Why?'

'I can't tell you. You've just got to trust me, Kate.'

They should go straight to the police and tell them everything, but Kate couldn't do it. Not now. And she knew the question that Camilla wouldn't ask her and she answered it anyway.

'Yes,' she said. 'I'll help you.'

Years ago, when she was ten, and had needed help herself, Camilla had given it. Now she could repay the debt.

'I'm getting cold,' said Kate. 'Shall we start moving again?'

They were leaving the sodden back streets of North Oxford, where the pavements and roadways were strewn with broken branches, spring flowers were beaten into the ground, and gardens had a despoiled air. They ran through the centre of Oxford and only slowed to a walk when they were in Fridesley again, and had to pick their way over more suburban wreckage. Kate's running shoes and socks were soaked and her tracksuit was splashed with mud to the knees.

'I've been thinking,' said Kate, eventually. 'It's too much of a coincidence that there was another criminal plot being worked out on the same night, so it must have been one of us, doing what you did, using the same plan, but to kill Yvonne rather than steal Rose's boxes.'

'It's possible, I suppose, but I don't want to think about it.'

'Isn't it the most likely solution? We knew Yvonne, so why shouldn't we know her killer? Don't you remember that scene in Rose's kitchen when we decided to steal her boxes from Theo? All sorts of odd, unspoken things were going on. We should tell the police about it.'

'No! We can't! I can't! Don't ask me why. I can't tell you. Can't you find out who did it, Kate? You know all the people who were there. You'd do it much better than the police.'

'This is rubbish, Camilla. It's no job for an amateur: we have to leave it to the professionals.' But even as she spoke she recognized the impossibility of explaining to a policeman the stresses and unspoken threats that had reverberated round Rose's kitchen.

'You said you'd help me.'

They stood in the storm-strewn suburban street and stared at each other.

'Yes, I did, didn't I?'

'Just think about it for a while: maybe you'll start to get some ideas. And promise you won't tell anyone about my visit to Yvonne's house.'

'All right,' said Kate, reluctantly. 'For the time being. Because we're friends, and because I remember what you did for me, I'll leave it for twenty-four hours. I'll think over everything that happened and see if anything occurs to me. I can't promise any more than that.' And what was she supposed to do if she worked out who the murderer was?

Camilla, allowing her emotions to show for the second time that day, stood in the street and hugged her.

'And if I'm right about its being one of us who killed her,' said Kate, after a moment, 'there'll soon be an urgent phone call from someone else who doesn't want the police involved.'

Chapter Nine

Camilla Rogers had been a quiet, podgy child when Kate first met her. While the rest of the girls in the class had had hair that flopped in their eyes, Camilla's had been tightly plaited and tied with navy-blue ribbons. When their skirts had been short, Camilla's had been too long, until the fashions changed and Camilla's stayed just below knee-length while theirs descended towards their ankles. Kate knew now that Camilla had been an unexpected arrival, surprising a couple who had married in their forties and assumed that parenthood was not for them. At the time she had felt sorry for someone who so obviously didn't fit in, and though she was a year or so younger, she had befriended Camilla, introduced her to some of the more amusing facts of life, and named her Millie.

Then Kate's father was found to have cancer. For months she was excluded from the knowledge of his illness, and, baffled, she had known only that there was something dreadful that was being kept from her.

Meanwhile, rehearsals started for the concert put on by the dancing school Kate and Millie attended. Perhaps their teacher had noticed what a dreary life Millie led with her middle-aged parents, adherents of some fundamentalist sect that apparently forbade any form of pleasure. Whatever the reason, she gave Millie the part of the cherry-blossom fairy and the pink net dress that went with it. This was the first time that Millie had had the chance to wear anything that wasn't grey or navy or beige. After the first fitting, she wasn't allowed to wear it until the dress rehearsal, but Millie made some excuse to look at her costume every time they went to the class.

When Kate's father died, Millie knew what she had to do: she gave Kate the most precious thing she had. She had to argue with Mrs Wood, who ran the dancing school, but she was an obstinate child and she won. Kate got the part of the cherry-blossom fairy. The costume itself didn't thrill her the way it had Millie, with its satin bodice, its layered net skirt, and bunches of silk flowers, but she recognized, through her haze of misery, what her friend had given up for her. She and Millie had stayed friends ever since.

'Shouldn't you be writing?' asked Camilla.

They were back in Kate's kitchen, sitting at the table, drinking coffee, failing to eat cold toast. Kate had stopped caring that her feet were wet and that she wanted a hot bath.

'How can I concentrate on the actions of a group of imaginary people in 1803 when all this is happening here and now? I'd go mad if I just tried to ignore it. There are nightmare pictures and scrambled thoughts jumping around inside my head, and I have to sort them out.'

'Yes. That's why I had to come round and talk to you. I couldn't keep it inside me any more.'

'But you haven't really unburdened yourself, have you? You've just given me fragments of the story and locked the rest away.'

'You said you'd help me.'

'I said I'd give you twenty-four hours, and during that time I'll do some thinking.'

'You could find out who killed Yvonne: we must know enough between us to sort out what happened.'

'But I didn't know her that well. I knew her as a dentist, as a runner, and I've seen her public act as a mother. There must have been a lot more to her than that. Where did she come from? She's been here in Fridesley for what? Ten years?'

'Nearer fourteen,' said Camilla.

'Where did she live before that, and what happened to Mr Baight, whoever he was?'

'I think she came from the West Country somewhere. And I got the impression that she was a widow and that she moved to Oxford when her husband, Sophie's father that is, died.'

'Did she have any special men friends, lovers or whatever? She was an attractive woman, after all.'

Camilla started to say, 'Not everyone's sex mad, you know,' but the phone rang and Kate left her and went to answer it. She looked thoughtful when she returned to the kitchen table.

'That's the first of them: Barbara, just ringing to make sure that we were all going to stick to the same story, after all, we didn't want to involve the police in our silly affairs, did we? What do you think? Is she the guilty one? And if so, why on earth did she want Yvonne dead?'

'It's difficult to see her as a murderer, certainly,' said Camilla. 'I suppose a lot of people just don't want to get involved in something nasty. And then there are the boxes...'

'Getting back to Yvonne, then. She must have been discreet about her love life, though, because I've never heard any gossip about her.'

'So you didn't hear about the vicar of King Charles the Martyr?' Kate lifted her eyebrows. 'It only lasted a few months and then he was moved on to a parish on the other side of Liverpool. And perhaps they were only discussing the Church jumble sale during their late-night sessions, after all. I have the impression that we learned nothing of Yvonne's private life unless she wanted us to.'

'And there's been no one else in fourteen years or so? I can't believe it.'

'Well, gossip says she turned sour when some man let her down.'

'Her husband, do you think?'

'I'm only guessing, but maybe she came to Oxford to be near another man.'

Kate got up to make more coffee and was interrupted again by the phone.

'Gavin,' she said when she returned to the kitchen. 'Much the same argument as Barbara, but this time I had to remember, too, his position as a Councillor and how awkward it would be for him if any hint of our burgling activities leaked out.'

'Again, it might be genuine,' said Camilla.

'Or not,' said Kate. 'Interesting, though, don't you think?' She yawned and stretched and remembered her cold, damp feet. 'I think you should go home and change and get into school now: the more normal your behaviour, the better. You don't want people to notice that you turned up on the morning after Yvonne's murder looking white-faced and peculiar. And I'll be thinking about the possibilities. You could be right: we might well know more about it than the police do.'

'I'll put some makeup on,' said Camilla. 'And I had no appointments until eleven-thirty. I'll invent some dull excuse for being late, don't worry. It was my deputy's turn for taking Assembly, anyway.'

Yes, thought Kate. You've got all those messy emotions under control again. No one would know what you'd been through in the past few hours. And how much have you hidden from me?

'I wonder what time she was killed,' she said, as they made their way to the door, 'if she was killed. Are you quite sure it wasn't an accident or suicide?'

'I couldn't see a weapon lying there,' said Camilla. 'And I don't see how you could thump yourself hard enough over the head to kill, do you?'

Kate opened the front door. The street was strewn with oddments of twigs and branches, with broken tiles and metal bits that had been ripped off motor cars. Blunt instruments every one of them, she thought, and many of them could surely be lethal. The twisted mudguard from some-one's bicycle, painted a dark blue, lay in the gutter.

There was another coincidence: the Oxford mourning box had disappeared last night, too. She had forgotten about it, with the news of the murder driving it out of her mind.

She went upstairs to the bathroom and turned the taps on. If she could manage to stay awake in the hot water, she would start thinking things out in the bath. The way to learn to live with violent death was to work through it, to face it and put all the pieces together into a pattern until as much of it as possible made sense.

She squirted foaming bath oil into the water and watched the bubbles forming into white mounds. Her starting point must be Yvonne herself: there had to be things in her life that Kate knew nothing about that explained why someone had bludgeoned her to death. She lay back in the water, her arms folded behind her head. As she had told Camilla, she knew Yvonne as a dentist, as a fellow runner, but after that her life was a mystery. It would be like the research she did on a character before starting to write a book, only this time she couldn't invent the details, she would have to go out and find them from the people who had known Yvonne. And as the bubbles started growing cold around her knees, she admitted to herself that she was serious about finding Yvonne's murderer. Problems demanded to be solved, mysteries unravelled. She wouldn't be able to travel back to 1803 and sit down contentedly at her word processor again until she had found the answers.

And what about Camilla? By the time she left Kate's house she had her emotions under control. But suppose she had been bottling feelings up until they erupted, not into the fit of weeping she had seen in the Parks, but into violence and murder? She couldn't push the thought away. Unless the murderer was found, she would never, deep inside, be able to trust her friend completely again. There would always be this question between them: did she do it?

She sat up and pulled out the plug.

Tonight she was supposed to see Andrew. She needed someone to share her nightmares with, but she didn't think Andrew was the right person. If she spilled out everything that was on her mind, in her usual way, Andrew would steamroller her into giving up, and would drive her down to St Aldate's in his red Sierra and escort her through the door of the police station. No, she would put him off until tomorrow night: by then it would all be over.

Before she had finished dressing, the phone rang again. This time it was Rose, sounding flustered and worried, and hoping that Kate was going to stick to the agreed story about last night's activities. After all, she said, it wasn't as if the murder could have anything to do with any of *them*, was it?

Chapter Ten

Kate was glad she'd had a bath, washed her hair, and changed into something more respectable when, a couple of hours later, the front door bell rang and she opened the door to find two polite, clean, short-haired young men on her doorstep. When she had looked at their warrant cards she invited them in and asked them to sit down.

They asked her if she had seen or heard anything untoward the previous evening. She told them, quite truthfully, that she had secured her house and loose belongings and turned, head to wind, and jogged round to Rose's house in Rosamund Road. Less truthfully, she told them that she had spent the entire evening exercising to a Jane Fonda tape. She managed to produce a stiff muscle or two and told them about the club race that would be taking place in three weeks' time. She omitted to tell them about her run round the block to spy on Theo and Lynda. The weather had been so awful, the night so dark, the company at Rose's so stimulating that no, she had noticed nothing, she was very sorry, Officer. And anything more she could do to help, just to let her know. It was dreadful the way so many cars were stolen in Oxford and . . . this was about stolen cars, wasn't it? And then they asked her whether she knew Yvonne Baight, and she had said, Who, the dentist? Well, of course I know her, she does my teeth and we belong to the same running group. Why? Has something happened to her? She is all right, isn't she, Officer? But they said that a statement would be made later that day by their superior, and meanwhile thank you for your co-operation, Miss Ivory, and anything else that occurs to you, any little thing, please to let us know. And they gave her a telephone number to ring in case she thought of something.

She showed them out, and they thanked her again, and although she couldn't see where they might have doubted her story, she was left with the impression that they were not wholly satisfied with her and that she would be seeing them again. Well, she had promised Camilla twenty-four hours' grace. After that she would be more forthcoming with visiting policemen. Then she went to clear her mantelpiece.

When she was working on the recalcitrant corner of a plot, Kate found it useful to occupy herself with a simple domestic chore: while her hands were busy, her mind was free to work on the problem. She had a collection of small, eclectic objects jostling their way along the mantelpiece in her sitting room, oddments that she had been given or sent or that she had seen, liked, and bought: postcards, paperweights, spoons, pottery and wood figures, a porcelain box, a scent bottle, a tiny square of embroidered silk, and now she scooped them up and took them out to the kitchen to dust or wash as appropriate. As she squirted Fairy Liquid into warm water, she started to go back over the previous evening's events.

She had been in the neighbourhood, at about the time when Yvonne was killed. A smell of warm raw meat, Camilla had said. She gagged. She picked up a blue pottery hedgehog and wiped it over with the sponge. Why wouldn't Camilla tell her why she was in Yvonne's house that evening? Why should she want to hide it, even from her best friend, unless it was something major, like murder? She took an old toothbrush and scrubbed at the silver lily on her scent bottle. She had to admit it: it was the most likely solution. But what about Penny? Or Gavin? Or Rose herself, for that matter? Weren't they just as credible as killers? Camilla had entered Yvonne's house believing her to be out at a meeting, so if she had encountered her unexpectedly, the killing would have been unpremeditated. But Gavin, on the other hand, had been absent from the room when Sophie made her announcement. If he called round at Yvonne's – for whatever reason – it was because he expected to find her at home during the first part of the evening.

Kate plunged her green glass paperweight into the warm water; it was smooth and heavy in her hand and she imagined lifting it up and bringing it down, *hard*, on someone's head. Yvonne's head. She closed her eyes to shut out the picture, put the paperweight to dry on the draining board and set to work on two inoffensive shell spoons. Then she saw again a figure hurrying along Redbourne Road with its collar up, its hair covered, its face unrecognizable under the streetlights, but something familiar about it, nevertheless. Thoughtfully, she washed the first of the Staffordshire cats.

By the time she had dusted or washed and dried all

the objects and placed them in a new, carefully casual, arrangement on the mantelpiece, she was starting to sort the evening out into a rough chronological order. When she had finished she went to telephone Andrew.

Andrew worked at the Bodleian, Oxford University's library with its six million items, its eighty miles of shelving packed with priceless treasures and yellowing Mills & Boons. After a short argument, he settled for a twenty-four-hour delay in their meeting, food from Marks and Spencer and a bottle (or two) provided by himself, rather than the expensive restaurant he had had in mind for that evening.

Kate was cleaning her house when her doorbell rang again. She was afraid that it was going to be the two policemen back but it was Penny. She pushed into Kate's small hallway. Her usually bouncy dark hair looked subdued, and she was frowning.

'Look, Kate, we've been thinking about last night.' She stopped. 'You've heard about Yvonne, of course?' Kate nodded. 'Well, we've all got to keep out of it, haven't we? I mean, we don't want anyone to think that we were doing anything unlawful yesterday evening.'

'Stealing boxes, you mean?'

'It's obviously got nothing to do with this dreadful murder, and it would only confuse the police investigation if they found out about it. I mean, people like us just don't get involved in murders, do they?' The words 'not nice' hovered in the air but remained unspoken.

'You want us to keep our mouths shut, stick with the original story?'

'Gavin and I think it would definitely be the best thing.'

'Yes, Gavin rang me about it this morning, too.' Penny looked put out for a moment. 'But suppose one of us is involved?' continued Kate. 'Shouldn't the police know?'

'Of course it's got nothing to do with us! What possible reason have any of us got for killing her? Really, Kate, what on earth put an idea like that into your head?'

'All right, Penny. I agree with you, we have to keep quiet about last night. Just for the moment, anyway, while we see how things develop. But you won't mind if I go round and ask a few questions, just to reassure myself that none of us has any involvement with Yvonne's death?'

'Whatever for? I can't think that it's necessary, Kate. Just because you're a novelist, you don't have to poke your nose into our affairs, you know. We don't want to find ourselves as characters in your next book.'

'If you all want me to lie about last night, against my better judgement, you're going to have to humour me on this. There are inconsistencies that need to be sorted out, odd things that have happened and are unexplained. How can I be sure that these things are irrelevant and that one of us didn't kill Yvonne unless I find out for myself? Just a few questions, Penny. They won't do any harm. And then you can rely on me to be totally discreet about our burgling efforts.'

'It was just a small domestic incident, Kate, between Theo and Rose. Nothing at all to do with the police.'

'Have you spoken to the others?'

'Yes, of course. Barbara saw our point of view, and so did Rose.'

'What about Sophie?'

'No, I didn't speak to her. A policewoman answered the phone and said she was under sedation and in no state to speak to me or anyone else. She sounded cross about it. The poor child must be devastated, and in no state to make decisions: I think we should act in everyone's best interest in the mean time, Kate. Yvonne was obviously killed by an intruder. The trouble with you is you've got too much imagination, you want to turn everything into a good story.'

'I promise I won't say anything for the moment,' said Kate. 'But if it looks as though we know something that might help the police catch Yvonne's murderer, I shall have to reconsider.'

I'm moving further away from a sensible position every time I talk to one of them, she thought. But I suppose if it keeps Camilla off the hook, and persuades them to co-operate with me, I'll go along with it. And the awful thing is that since they are all so determined to keep away from the police, any one of them could have done it. She was glad that she had put Andrew off for that evening: she just wanted to get on with the job of looking for Yvonne's killer.

First, she made lists. She listed all those people who were party to the box-stealing plan, and then realized that she would have to widen it to include their partners. She had to put on her Walkman to blot out the noise of her neighbour's taste in music, so she played her *Graceland* tape while she tried to compose a list of possible motives for the murder.

Money? Revenge? Because she was a brutal dentist?

But that last, flippant suggestion seemed no more unlikely than the first two.

When it came to money, everything pointed towards the

Fridesley development scheme that Yvonne had opposed with such vigour. Kate looked through the notes she had received from the Friends of Fridesley Fields. She had joined the Friends when it was formed, but she had taken little part in its activities, as she had been busy with the final revision of her previous book. Now she looked at the County Structure Plan and the Local Plan and its variations over the years, and saw the loophole that the would-be developers had exploited: the small area of land that fell just outside the Green Belt, partly built on and partly low-grade agricultural land, called Fridesley Fields. The developers argued that they had acquired or would shortly acquire the few run-down houses that stood there, and that their own new buildings would be hidden in a hollow and screened from the centre of Oxford by trees and hedges. They would provide recreational facilities, indoor and outdoor; they would bring an access road, and jobs. Nevertheless, their first application had been turned down, and now a slightly improved scheme had been put forward, and the fear was that this time it would be approved and another wild piece of Oxford would be built on and taken away from the local people who had considered it their own, for walking over, for exercising their dogs, for summer lovemaking. The man behind the scheme was called Tom Grant, and he was rich, influential, and ruthless. But, interesting as it was, her study didn't produce an obvious suspect, or a reason for Yvonne's death. She would have to go round to the neighbours and ask them whether they had seen anything on the night of the murder. It was where the police had started their investigation, after all, and they were the professionals.

She needed a reason for knocking on doors, and as she had spent so much time researching the development scheme, it seemed a good idea to pretend that she was investigating attitudes to it.

She went down to the local library and asked for the electoral register for Redbourne Road. It would look better if she knew people's names when she knocked at their doors, less as though she was offering free samples of washing powder, more as though she was canvassing for something.

She felt better after all this effort: she was starting to take control, to impose order on the chaos of events. In the evening she cooked herself a meal, and realized it was her first of the day.

Chapter Eleven

Kate woke next morning with stiff muscles, a thick head, and the knowledge that something appalling had happened. She drank a glass of orange juice and a pint of coffee and decided against eating anything solid. The sink was piled with yesterday's dishes and she was still slowly washing them up and thinking through the events of the past two days when her doorbell rang.

It was one of the policemen who had visited her yesterday. Or at least, he looked just like them, with his grey suit, white shirt, and dark tie. He wasn't very tall – five foot nine or ten, perhaps – but he had the build of someone who worked out regularly with weights. He also had rather pleasant grey eyes, short, sandy-red hair, and the fair, freckled skin that goes with it. Kate took a closer look at his warrant card this time: his name was Paul Taylor and he was a detective sergeant. He didn't look very friendly. Kate put him down as neutral, but armed. He sat on her small sofa while she took the armchair at right-angles to it.

'Have you thought of anything relevant to tell us since yesterday, Miss Ivory?' he asked.

Were there grey-suited young men on sofas all over

Fridesley at this moment asking the same question, being lied to by Fridesley Runners? Kate smiled sincerely and looked Detective Sergeant Taylor in the eye. 'I'm afraid not,' she said.

He sat back on the sofa and spoke in a careful, non-accusing voice. 'People withhold information from the police for all sorts of reasons, not all of them important, or criminal. Some people feel that it isn't quite nice to get involved, that somehow some of the mud will stick to them. And with a crime like murder there is a reluctance to admit that it could happen to anyone like us. Ridiculous, really, don't you think?' He paused, but Kate just went on smiling blandly at him. 'But as an intelligent and educated woman, you wouldn't believe anything like that, would you?'

'Of course not,' said Kate.

'And then again, other people think they should protect their friends, that it isn't very nice to tell tales on people. Childish, wouldn't you say?'

'Very,' said Kate, remembering what happened when she was ten years old.

'And then, it's an odd thing about blackmail,' said Detective Sergeant Taylor, rising to his feet and wandering across to the fireplace.

'Is that what we were talking about?' asked Kate, who now had to twist round to look at him.

He ignored the interruption and aligned her Staffordshire pottery cat with her Oxfam snail on the mantelpiece. 'Yes, it's funny the way the mildest of people have things they want to hide from the rest of the world.'

'Most people put it down to Eve and the apple,' said Kate, watching as he straightened her carved wooden pear and nudged the silver Art Nouveau scent bottle back into line. 'The feeling of shame, I mean.'

'But in a murder investigation, people should keep a sense of what is important and what isn't.'

He reached into an inside pocket and brought out a brown envelope, about eight inches by five.

'After all,' he said, 'there is a murderer loose out there, and until we know who he or she is, we can't guess who else is at risk, can we?'

He opened the envelope and took out eight or ten photographs. Kate saw they were in colour and matt, not glossy. He handed them to her. Did they smell of dead meat, or was that just her imagination?

'Bearing in mind what I've been saying, I wonder whether you can recognize any of the people in these photos, Miss Ivory?'

It wasn't easy. For one thing, you couldn't see any of their faces. There were plenty of close-ups of other portions of male and female anatomy, but not necessarily parts that you would see in a normal social situation. In one background, although out of focus, she recognized her favourite poster of a red canna lily. Then Kate looked at one of the photos and paused. She knew that if she wanted to fool this policeman she should pass over it as quickly as the others, but she couldn't help herself. One of the characters in this particular scene was wearing a dress: pink, trailing chiffon, sequinned, beaded. She had seen it before. She didn't recognize the hand and arm that also appeared in the picture, but they belonged to someone young and male and she could guess. She went slowly through the remainder, looking carefully at each one, trying to spend as long as she had on the picture of the woman in the pink dress. She handed them back to the detective and shook her head.

'We believe that there are three different women in these pictures,' he said, 'but probably only one man. We are very concerned to interview him as soon as possible. And the women, of course. We would be as discreet as we always are in these cases, if any of them came forward and helped us in our enquiries.'

'You think one of them's me!' she screamed, seeing at last where he was leading.

'Not necessarily,' he said, keeping his voice neutral. 'But if—'

'You're thinking that just because I write books for a living, I must be a tart! And I suppose you're sniffing around looking for illegal substances while I'm talking. And have you counted the empty gin bottles in my dustbin? Questioned the neighbours about the number of men who visit in the evenings? Well, let me tell you that I spend most of my time at a word processor, and the rest of it either catching up on some exercise – conventional, mostly vertical, exercise – or sitting in a library researching the next book. You lot are so predictable!'

'What lot would that be?' asked Paul Taylor, mildly. 'The sexist, racist policemen who push women around with one hand while turning to page three with the other? The fascist pigs? The male conspirators who have kept women on their knees for the past five thousand years?'

'Yes, well . . .' said Kate.

'You think I ask intrusive questions for fun? For kicks? Get it straight: we want to catch this bastard, and we need all the help we can get. So please, think about it again, and if you know anything, phone us.'

For a moment, Kate was tempted to tell him all she knew, including the identity of the woman in the pink dress, but then she saw that he had lined up every one of the small objects in her carefully casual arrangement on the mantelpiece so that now they marched along in a straight procession, separated by a regulation one-centimetre space. No, he wouldn't understand. And he and his single-track colleagues would never unravel the tangled skein of Yvonne's life and find her murderer. It really was up to her.

As soon as Detective Sergeant Taylor had left, she telephoned Camilla. She didn't care if it was inconvenient, she had to speak to her.

'Why the hell didn't you tell me?' she shouted into the phone when she was finally put through. 'The woman was blackmailing you, wasn't she? That's what you went to see her about. You wanted your pictures back. Didn't you, Camilla?'

'Yes,' said Camilla slowly. 'And I succeeded. No one need ever know about it now.'

'Wrong. And wrong again.'

There was a short silence, then: 'Oh my God! No.' Another silence, while Kate still waited. 'Oh, shit! I can't talk here and now.'

'When? Lunchtime?'

'All right. Your place, five past one.' And she put the phone down.

'You've got to tell me about the blackmail,' said Kate. 'Don't you see, blackmailers get killed. Their victims get tired of being bled white and they turn on them. They have little to lose, after all.'

'She wasn't interested in money,' said Camilla.

'What then?'

'Power, I suppose. She liked to get people to do what she wanted, preferably against their will, against their character. It amused her. She probably pulled the wings off butterflies for all I know. She had a distorted sense of humour.'

'You weren't the only one, you realize. There were two other women in those photos.'

'Didn't you recognize them?'

'No. And I wouldn't have recognized you if it hadn't been for the dress. Who was the man? Carey?'

'There hasn't been anyone else.'

'Well, the police think he was in the pictures with the other two women, too. They are very anxious to discover his identity and interview him.'

'He's hardly the type to go down to the police station and volunteer to help with enquiries. I don't think I've anything to fear there.'

'Where did she get the photos from?'

'I don't know. I know that photography's her hobby, so maybe she used one of those long-distance lenses that they photograph sunbathing royalty with.'

'And why did you give in to her? Why didn't you, of all people, stand up to her and tell her to go to hell?' (Oh God, she thought, maybe you did just that, and then helped her on her way.)

'I had to. I couldn't risk the governors finding out about me and Carey, not until after the end of the summer term, when I would have some job security, so I did what she wanted. But when she pushed us all to steal back Rose's boxes, I saw how I could get free. I'd use the same plan to steal back the pictures she had of us.'

'But you can't shock people these days by telling them that an unmarried couple are sleeping together, even if they're wearing funny clothes and even when one of them is a headmistress. It's not news.'

'There's the fact that I met Carey through one of my pupils. He's Helena Stanton's brother. Their parents are usually too busy to come to school functions, and Carey is very fond of his sister, so he turns up instead. And he came to talk to me when we found she was going to parties and using Ecstasy. That was the beginning of it: I agreed to deal with the matter without going to the police, and Carey took me out for an Italian meal to say thank you.' She frowned at the toes of her polished brown shoes. 'We went in my car, and I paid for the meal, as a matter of fact. But that's when it started. I was wrong to go out with him, wasn't I?'

'Unwise.'

'I can't understand how I came to miss some of the pictures. She was very methodical. There was a filing cabinet and a folder with my name on. I'd seen her put the key in the top drawer of her desk the last time I was there, but I didn't need the key after all: the cabinet was already unlocked. I took the file and stuffed it inside my tracksuit top. Everyone was looking damp and lumpy, so no one noticed.'

'What about negatives?'

'They were in a little envelope, labelled with my name and the date they were taken. And I was wearing gloves, of course.'

'You said there were photographs all over the floor, around the body.'

'Yes. It's odd that, isn't it?'

'Not if another of her victims had been there before you and lost their temper. But I expect that's where the police got their photos from.'

'I didn't see any of me there, but I only had a small torch and I didn't stay to search.' She closed her eyes for a moment and swayed backwards and forwards in her chair. 'Oh God! It was horrible! You're not going to give me away, are you, Kate?'

'I said I'd give you twenty-four hours, and that was before I knew about all this. What else are you hiding from me? How can I possibly trust you?'

Camilla sighed and went back to staring at her shoes. 'For the same reason that I have to trust and believe you. It could have been you in one of those other photos; you could have killed Yvonne as easily as me. But I don't, I can't, believe that you did. Why not? Because we've known each other for over twenty years, because we're friends, and because without that trust our whole lives would fall into fragments. We'd be cut adrift, never knowing what was solid land and what was quicksand.'

'That's sentimental, overwritten garbage.' Kate grinned suddenly at Camilla. 'But true, of course.'

'So what happens now?'

'I have to find out who killed Yvonne. Our lives are on hold until we know who did it. You must help me, by telling me everything you know. For real, this time, Millie: holding nothing back. And I'd better get to the answer before the police track down the actors in Yvonne's porno pics and give the story to the tabloids.' She realized that she had been fiddling for the past few minutes with the objects on her mantelpiece, rather like the young detective, only now she had moved some of them out of line. She looked back at Camilla. 'It wasn't me in any of those photos. Carey's a very attractive young man, but the only time I met him was at your house that once. Yvonne wasn't blackmailing me. I didn't go to her house that evening, and I didn't kill her.' She balanced a china box on its side with its lid open and moved a silver thimble half an inch forward. That was an improvement.

'I'd better tell you about Carey and me,' said Camilla. 'Do you remember my home and my parents? My parents are dead now, but even so I still wake up sometimes and expect my feet to encounter cold, slimy lino when I get out of bed, and to see the words *Thou, Lord, seest me* on the wall. After they died, I went out and bought myself a dress. I know that the woman in the shop thought I was mad: I went in in my grey flannel and navy barathea and came out with a bag full of pink chiffon and sequins. But I never dared to wear it in public. I didn't escape from the grey porridge that they made of my life until I met Carey. It was at the school fête. He was standing in the hot sun, spooning strawberry ice cream into his mouth. He has a rather dark, pointed tongue and he lifted each spoonful with its little mound of ice cream and looked at it, as though he was about to undergo a great erotic experience, savouring the taste in imagination before swallowing the reality. And I knew that this was someone who knew all about the joyful parts of life that I'd missed out on. We looked at one another. He registered my existence, I registered his. He was twenty-one; I was thirty-two, going on fifty-five. Nothing happened.

'It was a few days later that the trouble with Helena erupted and he came to see me. You may think he was just using me, but really, there was more to it than that. He liked playing games, I know, but there was an attraction on both sides there, Kate, whatever you think. And I believe he enjoyed seeing me change from this staid, middle-aged woman to someone younger, prettier, who could enjoy . . . things. You see, I still can't say those words out loud. And we did have fun. He made me laugh, and I amused him, too.

'MDMA. Ecstasy. E.

'Then I got the first phone call from Yvonne, asking me to go round and see her.

'I felt uneasy as I knocked on her door. I tried to put it down to the fact that I was nervous about going to the dentist. But that was it: someone was about to prod at nerves, rather than offer me a sherry and talk about the public enquiry over the Fields. She kept me on edge for twenty minutes before she showed me the photographs.

'To begin with, she just wanted my active support over the opposition to Grant's scheme. I didn't really mind, though I would rather have kept a lower profile since not all the Amy Robsart parents agreed with our views. From time to time after that she would invite me over for a drink, just to tease, I think. I sat there for half an hour or more, wondering what demands she would make, but there would be nothing. I used to imagine the sound of her laughter following me down the road and across to Waverley Lane. And just when I thought that I had nothing to worry about, came the plan to steal back Rose's boxes. Now, I can see that it is vitally important to Rose to get her hands on them, but I didn't see why a group of respectable professional people should involve themselves in theft to achieve it. Why should we put our jobs on the line for Rose? I know all that stuff about camaraderie and group loyalty, but this was taking it too far. Then Yvonne started hinting, and threatening, and laughing all the while. It seemed simpler to go along with it than to oppose her and risk exposure. I have another five months to go before I'm confirmed as headmistress.

'And I wasn't the only one, was I? Gavin and Penny looked terrified of contradicting her. And what about Barbara? Maybe the phone calls you've been getting are what they seem, but on the other hand, maybe I wasn't Yvonne's only blackmail victim among the Fridesley Runners.'

'So I've been elected sleuth, have I?' asked Kate.

'Come on, you know you'd be furious if I suggested someone else. You're longing to give it a go.'

'Yes, you're right about that. I write novels because I want to explore people's lives and motives, and the chance to do it for real is irresistible. I'm also scared: what happens if and when I find the murderer? I don't fancy a confrontation. I'm as much a coward as the next person when it comes to getting hurt.'

'No confrontations, Kate. When you find the killer, we both go to the police and tell them everything.'

It didn't work out like that in fiction, but maybe real life was different. Or again, maybe not.

Chapter Twelve

Kate emerged from her door that afternoon, clipboard in hand, home-made identity badge pinned to the lapel of a plain, dark coat, her bright hair hidden under a woollen hat, thick black tights and comfortable boots on her feet.

There was not a lot of activity in Redbourne Road: just a uniformed constable standing outside the door of Yvonne's house, and a few people staring at it, moving on, and being replaced by other, similar watchers. Nevertheless, Kate decided to start at the other end of the road: she did not want anyone in authority wondering what she was doing with her clipboard, or looking too closely at her home-made identity badge; neither did she want to bump into Detective Sergeant Paul Taylor and answer any more of his questions.

She nerved herself to approach the first front door and ring the bell. The houses at this end of Redbourne Road were small, late-Victorian terraces, with a bay window on the ground floor and only three or four feet of front garden to separate them from the pavement. Number one had grey paintwork and a well-kept front patch, and two occupants called Flint, according to the electoral register. Kate rang the bell and waited for a moment, but all that happened was that a woman threw up an upstairs window, leaned out and asked 'Yes?'

'Mrs Flint?'

'If you want my husband, he's not in, and anyway, he never votes,' and she went back in and slammed the window down again. Only the slight swaying of a grey curtain proved that she had ever existed. Kate watched it for a moment, wondered whether all her calls would be that unproductive, and moved on to the next house.

Here there were flowered Austrian blinds, window-boxes with snowdrops and daffodil shoots, and occupants with two different surnames. She knocked with the brass dolphin doorknocker. No one in. At this rate she would be home again by teatime with the whole area covered, but with no useful information.

At number five there was no doorbell and Kate had to rattle the letterbox. There was a shuffling sound behind the door and then it opened a few inches, letting out a hot cloud of Friar's Balsam with an end-note of cat litter-tray. A woman with scant white hair and a face grown sexless with age looked up at Kate. A cat came howling in from the garden, shot between her legs and pushed its way through the narrow gap into the house, while the woman's expression grew less friendly. 'Well,' she said, 'what is it you want? I haven't got all day to stand here.'

'Friends of Fridesley Fields,' said Kate. 'I'm conducting a survey of attitudes, Mrs Exeter.'

'Attitudes?' muttered the woman, opening the door wider to let more of the hot, smelly air pour over Kate. 'And what are they when they're at home? Questions, always asking questions, you people. Why don't you ever have any answers, then?' She shuffled behind Kate, showing her into the back room. The air in here was stifling and many other more subtle but still unpleasant odours filled her nostrils. 'Mind the cat there and you'd better sit down in here. Move me knitting off that chair, will you? And I don't suppose you want a cup of tea. You'd be a coffee drinker, by the look of you.'

Kate moved knitting, sat down on maroon cut moquette, arranged her feet so that they weren't disturbing a saucer of furry grey cat food, and refused tea, coffee, and anything else that she would have to eat or drink. She consulted the first sheet of paper on her clipboard. It was blank. 5 Redbourne Road, she wrote at the top. Mrs Exeter.

'I'm Kate Ivory,' she started.

'Oh yes,' said Mrs Exeter, investigating one of her ears with a mauve finger. Pale blue eyes stared at Kate. 'You're the one who writes the books, aren't you?'

Kate nodded.

'They had one of yours down the mobile, but I didn't read it. I like something a bit spicier, myself.'

'Yes, well, it takes all tastes, doesn't it?' said Kate, wondering how she was going to get on to the subject of murder. Outside the window a dustbin lid went bowling down the pavement and clattered to a halt against the wing of a Ford Escort. 'Did you manage all right in the storm the night before last?' she asked. 'Did you get any damage?'

'The night of the murder, you mean? Nothing but questions, there've been, ever since it happened. Nice boys, nice clean shirts, but they wouldn't stay to tea.'

'I suppose they asked you whether you'd seen anything.'

'Seen anything, heard anything, noticed anything strange. Mr Gatlock lent me a big stone from his rockery for the lid of me dustbin, and then I pulled me curtains closed, switched on me fire, and just hoped the telly wouldn't go off in the storm.' She put out a heavily veined hand and caressed the head of an ugly tabby cat. 'They don't like that stormy weather, so we sat it out in here together.' Again the blue gaze was turned on Kate. 'And I thought you said you wanted to ask questions about the Fields. One of the Friends, aren't you?'

'Yes, yes. That's me,' said Kate. 'So what's your view on the Development Plan, Mrs Exeter?'

'Shouldn't be allowed, that's what. Hasn't that man got enough money already? And I don't like them hippy types, but even so, he shouldn't do it.'

Kate wrote 'shouldn't be allowed' on the pad on her clipboard, and 'Hippies? What hippies?' underneath it. Perhaps Yvonne had been murdered by hippies high on Ecstasy, but if they really were hippies, left over from the sixties, they must qualify for their concessionary bus passes by now.

'You go and talk to that lot down the Postle if you want to know about it,' said Mrs Exeter, 'if there are any of them left by now, and if they'll let you near. That's one thing about that Mrs Baight, whatever people might say about her, she was on their side. Don't you listen to no gossip: she was strong for the Friends and stood up to the money men. I shouldn't put it past them to get rid of her for good.'

Kate scribbled 'Go down to the Postle' on her pad. Maybe some of the other neighbours would tell her more about it.

'Do you know who the money men are?' she asked.

'They hide in their big houses,' said Mrs Exeter, 'but we know the people they use. Representing local interests, they tell us when they want our votes, but they're after what they can make out of it.' She stopped and pointed at her cats. 'They're all you can trust these days. You can't believe in people any more.'

Kate stood up, ready to leave, just as Mrs Exeter said, 'Are you sure about that cup of tea, now?' Kate was getting used to the smell, but she didn't like to think what was growing in the kitchen.

'That's really kind of you, but no,' she said. As she left the room, the cats jostled round her legs as though determined to leave their hairs all over her black tights.

Outside in the street the clouds had disappeared from the sky and the brisk breeze was clearing the puddles from the streets. It was an exhilarating afternoon and Kate wished that she could leave the narrow streets of Fridesley and stride out across the Fields, leaving murder and blackmail and doubts about her best friend behind her. She could put on her running shoes and go for a long jog. Lost in this dream, she nearly missed Mrs Exeter's last query.

'Wasn't it you wearing the hat?'

'I don't think so,' said Kate, wondering what she was on about. Mrs Exeter shook her head and closed the door.

The next two houses were tarted up, but empty. It obviously took two incomes to buy and improve Fridesley property these days. Kate added a doodle of a couple of daisies in the corner of her pad while she waited in vain for expensively furnished doors to open. Mrs Singh was at home, but preoccupied with a baby and a toddler, and she asked Kate to come back when her son returned from school. She was nearly half-way down the street now and the next houses were built a little later, were of red brick, and were taller, semi-detached, and had wooden gates into their back gardens.

She rang at the last terraced house, having little hope now of ever finding anyone at home with anything useful to say. But the door opened abruptly and she was sucked into the house on a cloud of steam from boiling potatoes, while predatory flowers rioted over the carpet and snapped at her ankles. The walls were thick with pink and blue roses, and when Kate went into the front room, she was met by another, more unusual smell overlying that of boiling vegetables. The room held a large sofa, two squashy arm-chairs covered in a shiny tartan pattern, and a 24-inch television set and video recorder on a chrome stand; there was a black tower music centre and two speakers in another corner. And then, on a table that ran the length of one whole wall, there were cages of fluffy yellow birds, and two parrots, like bookends, one at either end on a perch. One was grey, the other green and red. The grey parrot sat staring stolidly at the opposite wall, but the green and red one flapped its wings at her and swung on its perch. And now that she looked, she realized that the frames all over the walls did not contain pictures of pairs of children in school jerseys and big smiles, but were, too, photographs of more parrots. All of them, real and photographic, stared at her.

She turned to look at the women who had let her into the house. Beak nosed, broad hipped, grey haired, with matching hand-knitted cardigans, they could have been sisters.

'Mrs Price? Mrs Reeny?' she asked.

'Miss,' they answered simultaneously, and stared at her as unblinkingly as the parrots.

'I'm Kate Ivory and I'm conducting a survey of attitudes to the Fridesley Fields development plan,' she said.

'I thought you were the one who wrote those books,' said Miss Price, or perhaps Miss Reeny.

'We read one last year and we wondered where you get your ideas from,' said Miss Reeny (or Miss Price).

'Oh, here and there,' said Kate, watching the green and red parrot swinging on its perch. 'I try to keep my eyes open for good ideas.'

'You'll have to watch what you say, Price,' said Miss Reeny, solving one of Kate's problems. 'You'll find yourself in her next book.'

'Not with that murder going on,' said Miss Price. 'I reckon she'll be writing about that, not about two dull old things like us.'

They were all sitting now, so deep in the soft chairs that Kate wondered how she would ever be able to get out.

'Dreadful, isn't it?' said Kate encouragingly. 'However could such a thing happen in a neighbourhood like this, and to such a pleasant woman?'

'I don't know about pleasant,' said Miss Price. 'If you'd ever had her working on your root canals, you'd consider murder yourself. "This might cause a little discomfort," was her favourite phrase, before she put her drill in your mouth and aimed at a nerve. I wouldn't have gone for a swift blow to the head, though. I'd have thought up something slower and more painful.'

Kate was warming to the Misses Price and Reeny. These had been her own feelings when Yvonne Baight had got out her collection of spiky instruments and scraped at Kate's high-quality glued-on plaque. Yes, 'You have to expect a little discomfort,' had been the phrase she had used when Kate reacted to the pain by jerking a spluttering pump out of her mouth and on to the shining vinyl floor.

'Is that how she died?' she asked, interested to find out how they knew.

'So they say,' answered Miss Reeny, leaving Kate to wonder who 'they' were. 'And there was more to that woman than met the eye. So careful to keep her reputation squeaky-clean, but we saw him, calling round at all hours.'

'Saw who?' asked Kate.

'I'm not saying,' said Miss Reeny. 'I'm not one to gossip, am I, Price? And why did he stop visiting her, that's what I'd like to know.'

'And it was only right to tell that policeman about seeing the woman from next door going over to Mrs Baight's. What was she doing, running over the road in the rain, calling in at meal time?'

Kate wondered what to write down on her clipboard, and settled for a large question mark and a third daisy.

'But she was a great one for the Friends of Fridesley Fields, Reeny. You mustn't forget that when you're bitching about her,' said Miss Price. 'Like you, Miss Ivory. That is why you're here, isn't it?'

Kate nodded vigorously, hastily scribbled down 'Friends of Fridesley Fields' and 'very enthusiastic' on her pad.

'She got the window stickers printed,' said Miss Price. 'And the posters when we had the Bonfire Party in November. And gave us some really nice things for the Christmas jumble sale. She was quite determined that that man wasn't going to get his hands on our fields and build his dreadful complex on it.'

'He's got to be stopped,' said Miss Reeny. 'There've been complaints to the police and to the Environment Minister, but he's above the law, with all that money of his.'

They sat and gazed at Kate, and the two parrots on their perches echoed the stare. Kate felt that she was expected to achieve something miraculous, right at this minute, and she didn't want to start explaining about planning applications and public inquiries. She looked down at her clipboard, then back at the Misses Reeny and Price. They had stopped talking and were waiting for her to leave. She would get no more gold nuggets of information from them today, so she slipped forward on the glossy surface of the chair and pushed herself up until she could get to her feet. The two women rose with her.

'You've been so helpful,' she said, 'but I mustn't take up any more of your time. It is good to know that we have such keen supporters.'

As she left the house she wondered about the potatoes: they must have disintegrated into their water by now, and yet it was still early for an evening meal.

The next house on that side of the road was the first of the larger houses, and it was the one that Lynda and Theo lived in, the house that the runners had checked out only the previous night. It was some thirty yards from Yvonne's, and yet there seemed to be more activity there than at Number 36, Yvonne and Sophie's house. A police car was parked outside. And then as she watched, the front door opened and a tall, dark-suited figure came out, followed by Lynda and a woman police officer who had her hand on

Lynda's arm, and another tall, anonymous figure behind her. Lynda was pale, her face without its usual layer of make-up. She was wearing the red duvet coat and Rose's flowered hat. And then, behind them on the steps she saw Theo: Theo looking middle-aged and unshaven and bewildered. He stood watching as the policemen piled into the two cars and drove off with Lynda in the back of one of them. Two pairs of hard eyes noted Kate as she stood there on the pavement, only a few yards away, and watched. She found that her mouth was open, and she closed it.

Theo looked for a long time at the empty roadway, rubbing at his arms as though he was cold. Then he saw Kate.

'Oh, hallo,' he said vaguely, as though he realized that he ought to recognize her. 'I don't understand it. They've taken Lynda away to ask her some more questions.'

Kate walked up the steps and joined him in front of the door. 'Why would they have done that, Theo?' she asked.

'Someone saw her going into Yvonne's house yesterday evening and reported it to the police. They couldn't remember exactly what time it was, and the restaurant where we were eating didn't know what time we arrived, so the police are saying that it could have been Lynda who went over the road and murdered Yvonne. But why on earth would she have done that?'

'And why did she go to see her?' asked Kate.

'That's the odd thing. I didn't know that they were friends, but Yvonne phoned and asked her to go over and see her. And she told Lynda to take my Oxford mourning box with her – a little blue enamelled thing that I was rather fond of. Why should she have done that? She didn't bring it back and now all the rest of my enamel boxes have disappeared too, but Lynda says she doesn't know anything about them. I just don't know what to believe.'

'It's very puzzling,' said Kate. 'But you're getting cold, Theo. Why don't you go back inside and get hold of a solicitor for Lynda; she's going to need one by the sound of it.'

'You think I should?' Theo went indoors and shut the door.

That horrible blue box again, thought Kate. Why would Lynda take it over to Yvonne when she asked for it? She remembered the interest Yvonne had shown in it when they were talking about Rose's enamel boxes, and how amused she had been at the idea of stealing them back. Well, she would have found their elaborate plan funny, wouldn't she, when all she had to do to acquire the box was make one brief phone call? And if Lynda, too, was being blackmailed she would go running across the road when Yvonne called her. Remember that what Yvonne wanted was power, not money. She did it for kicks, Camilla had said.

Kate turned and started back towards Agatha Street. It was possible that Lynda had killed Yvonne. All the woman's victims must be suspects and it looked as though Lynda could be one of them.

It was seven o'clock that evening when Andrew reached Kate's front door. He had managed to find a place to park his Ford Sierra among the Escorts and 2CVs and Morris Minors that rusted their lives away in Agatha Street, and now he held out a bottle of Sancerre, at drinking temperature, and went to put a second bottle in the fridge and fetch glasses while Kate found her efficient corkscrew.

He was not a very tall man, so that she felt she had to wear flat shoes in his presence, and though he was still slim, it was a soft build rather than a wiry or muscular one, and she knew that by the time he hit forty-five, in a couple of years' time, the effects of the eating, drinking, and failing to take enough exercise might start to show on his face and figure. Since he was invariably well dressed, she had changed out of her sweatshirt and jeans and was wearing a black skirt and long pink top, had put on swinging earrings and applied lipstick. Even so, there was something very restful about Andrew's company, and he was quite good looking if you liked red hair. He had boyish features and slightly protuberant pale blue eyes, all overlaid with a pleasant, willing-to-please expression. She hoped he would still feel as comfortable after she had told him her story. She would pour them both a drink before starting on it.

'I can't believe that you really got yourself involved in this daft scheme to steal Rose's boxes,' he said, when she told him the first part.

'Well I did. And what were we supposed to do? Wait until Rose had her house repossessed, and was unemployed and unemployable before we thought about doing something? There's nothing I can do to change it now, and it wasn't entirely my fault: everyone else was so enthusiastic that it was difficult to be the only one arguing against it.' She heard herself explaining too much and wished she could stop.

'Why didn't you tell me about it before it happened?'

'Because I knew you would disapprove of the scheme, just the way you're doing at this moment.'

'You have to admit it was pretty bloody stupid.'

'Yes, all right. But it was also funny and exciting, and it reminded me that I was young and alive and didn't always have to do the right thing.' She could tell by his silence that he didn't like that, and she poured him out another glass of wine to make up for her unkindness.

'There's more, and worse, Andrew,' she said, and plunged into the story of the murder and blackmail.

Andrew listened and then sat without speaking.

'You do understand why I have to find out who killed her, don't you?'

'No, Kate, I don't.'

'I hoped you would. I thought you'd understood about friendship and loyalty.'

'But why does it have to be you? Why can't you leave it all to the police? It's madness to do anything else.'

'That's the way I felt at first.' She glanced at the casual scatter of small ornaments along the mantelpiece. 'But if you'd met them you'd realize how impossible it would be to explain the subtleties of what was happening. They would leap to the conclusion that since Camilla was there, and was being blackmailed, she must have done it. I told Camilla I would give her twenty-four hours' grace before talking to the police, but I'm not going to speak to them at all. The others would probably deny everything, so I'd sound like a mad woman.'

'Oh, don't exaggerate!' said Andrew.

'Exaggerate? Detective Sergeant Taylor thought I was being blackmailed! He thought I was one of the women in the photographs! He'd jump to the conclusion that Camilla and I were in it together. That's it: case closed.'

'Now you're being melodramatic.' He looked at her in silence for a moment. 'No, I don't think you killed her,' he said finally. 'You wouldn't have done it that way. And if she'd been blackmailing you, I'd have heard about it long before this.' He passed his plate across and Kate filled it with more food.

'Kate, this is a really bad idea,' he said. 'I don't want you to go through with it.' He speared a small new potato, shiny with butter, and popped it, whole, into his mouth. 'But I'm sure you don't want your decisions made for you by me,' he said, indistinctly.

'I'm glad you understand,' said Kate, and poured them both another glass of wine.

By the time they had eaten the meal, Andrew had recovered his good humour, as she knew he would: he lacked the stamina to sustain a really good argument.

'How do you know I won't go straight to St Aldate's police station myself after dinner and tell them what you've told me?'

'That's a very fragrant Sancerre we're drinking,' said Kate. 'They wouldn't believe you if the rest of us denied it. And anyway, you know you're dying to give me some advice on how to be a sleuth.' She spooned more mangetout peas and flaked almonds on to his plate.

'Have you thought who else was being blackmailed?' he asked, when they were on the last glass in the first bottle of wine. 'As you've already noticed,' he said, as he opened the second bottle, 'if Yvonne was killed by one of your little group, they would be keen to keep their activities from the police. Can we eliminate anyone? Which of you has gone down to make a statement and do their civic duty?'

'A good question,' said Kate. 'No one, as far as I can tell. And that, of course, includes me. I don't know about Sophie yet: her doctor and solicitor were stopping her from saying anything yesterday, but things may have changed today.'

'If she'd told them about the recovery of the boxes, you'd have heard from them before this. I'd have been bailing you out by now.'

'If no one's telling the police about it, I really must find out where they all were when, and what they saw. But the way people were talking this afternoon made me think that the others could be right: the boxes have nothing to do with it, the answer lies in the development plan and Yvonne's opposition to it. The men behind it are ruthless, Andrew, and I have to find out more about them and what they've been doing.'

'Can you speak to Sophie yet?'

'I'll give her a ring tomorrow. She should be able to fill me in on some background. And there's another thing: as I left the parrot house – Oh, didn't I tell you about the parrots? Well, never mind – I saw the police taking Lynda away, and it looked as though she'd just been arrested, though Theo said they were going to ask her some more questions. He was standing in the open front door, watching her, his expression incredulous. And he was hugging himself the way women do when they feel they can't cope.'

'You could be letting your imagination run away with you here. Perhaps they were taking her down to the station to look at mug shots.'

'You didn't see them. It looked really heavy. Theo said she'd been seen going into Yvonne's house that evening.'

'Did he know why she went?'

'To take Yvonne his Oxford mourning box.'

'Well, if Lynda did kill Yvonne, it will let all of you off the hook, won't it?'

'But suppose it was something we did that landed her in the shit?'

Andrew frowned. He didn't like it when she used language like that. 'I suppose you'd better carry on finding out what happened, Kate.'

She noticed that he had passed imperceptibly from allout opposition to a mellow acceptance of her plan to investigate Yvonne's murder. If she wasn't careful, in a minute he'd be telling her how to do it.

They turned on the television to catch the local bulletin after the national news, and there was Yvonne's face staring at them, and the outside of the house on the corner of Redbourne Road, and a tired-faced, flat-voiced senior policeman saying that the police were pursuing their enquiries and had several lines they were investigating at the moment and would be grateful for any help from the public, if they had been out and about on such a stormy night, as to what they had seen, and when.

Kate couldn't imagine trying to tell that prosaic face about curtains that first of all were, and then weren't, drawn, of the strange undercurrents in a group of friends, of gossip about lovers and opposition to the development of a swampy piece of ground. The item was over in a minute or so and they were shown computer graphics of the next day's weather, and she switched off.

'I have to work tomorrow morning, but give me a ring if you need me,' said Andrew, getting up to leave.

It wasn't late, but he seemed happy to go back to his own

place. Perhaps it was because the wine had run out, perhaps because he realized she wanted her own company.

She rang Camilla before she went to bed.

'I've made a start,' said Kate, 'and I'm going to see it through.'

'Are you sure? The answer is likely to involve someone we know. Are you prepared for that?'

'I have to find the answer.' Kate put the phone down. Had they been threatening one another, or just stating their positions? She was too tired to work it out.

Chapter Thirteen

Next morning, Kate rang Sophie, stumbling through condolences. Sophie sounded awful, as though she had been crying for days and was still confused about what had happened. Kate didn't think she would get any useful information from her, but she persuaded Sophie to agree to let her visit the next day. When she rang off, she felt mean and manipulative, but convinced herself it was in Sophie's own interest.

Then she prepared for another session on the doorknockers of Fridesley. Trousers, she thought, that green fake-fur jacket she had bought years ago and had meant to donate to Oxfam, scarf, bright red lipstick. She pushed her hands through her hair so that it stood up in the casual way that her hairdresser had charged her a fortune to achieve, and practised a friendly smile in the mirror. As she pulled a face at her reflection, the doorbell rang. It was Camilla.

'I'm not interrupting anything, am I?' she said, walking into the kitchen. 'But this morning I thought I'd better destroy that file I'd taken from Yvonne's place on Wednesday night, just in case the police came and searched my house.' She stopped and stared at Kate. 'What on earth are

you wearing? That thing wouldn't even make an acceptable hearthrug.'

'Never mind. Get on with the story.'

'And that lipstick doesn't suit you, either.'

'Shut up, Millie.'

Camilla was scrabbling in her handbag. 'I hadn't looked
at it since Wednesday night, and I found this.' She pulled a
piece of paper from her bag. 'It must have got caught in the
folder: it didn't belong with my stuff. It didn't mean anything to me, but then I thought I'd better hand it on to you,
just in case it was relevant.'

Kate looked at it. Ordinary recycled typing paper. The
local council letterhead. It was an agenda for a planning
committee meeting. One item was circled in blue ink, and
under all the official language, Kate recognized that it
referred to the Postle. There was a list of names written in
the right-hand margin, with G. Dale among them. Underneath the list was a message in the same hand: 'Tom – this
lot are in the bag. N.D.'

'Thanks, Millie,' she said slowly.

It still wasn't enough to take to the police, even if she
could have explained how she had got hold of it. It only
made sense in conjunction with the other gossip she had
heard around Fridesley. Councillors were being bought by
Grant, or his agent, and Yvonne had found out about it, had
got hold of this piece of paper, and was blackmailing Gavin.

Gavin, she thought, as she offered her visitor a cup of
coffee, was being pulled in two directions by two ruthless
people. The parrot ladies had hinted at corrupt councillors,
and Gavin, presumably, was one of them. He was being
paid to push through the development scheme by Grant, or

perhaps by 'N.D.', and he was also being blackmailed by Yvonne into opposing it. How had he resolved his problem? Nice, upright, kind-hearted Gavin, early-morning companion on their runs. Had he gone along with their scheme to steal the boxes, and then sloped off to Yvonne's place and hit her over the head with a blunt instrument?

She realized at last that Camilla was refusing coffee, and switched the kettle off again.

'I can see you were just going out,' Camilla was saying, 'though God knows where, in that outfit. So I'll push off back home. OK?'

Kate nodded vaguely and closed the front door behind her. I have to ask more questions, she thought, and picked up her clipboard, her biro, and her gloves and set off again, in the opposite direction from her previous expedition, towards the canal, Peter's stream, and the Postle.

The houses on this side of the Fridesley Road were smaller than those in Redbourne Road. In Agatha Street, where Kate lived, the houses had been done up: people weren't well off, but they cared about their outside paintwork and their front gardens; they washed their cars and cut their grass on Sunday mornings where a generation ago they would have gone to the service at the church of King Charles the Martyr.

She could see the waters of the flooded Fields glinting through the thin bare branches of the willows and alders as she walked down the narrow road. There was nothing welcoming about any of these houses and there was little sign of habitation, apart from the skeletons of rusted bicycles that lounged in their gardens.

At the end of the street, the road turned away to the

right, and this was the part known as the Postle, a swampy piece of ground, with mean houses on one side of it, facing the canal, only the narrow width of the road separating them from the dark green water. At one end was a small footbridge and weir, with the Peter's stream below it, carrying away the excess water from the canal, so that the houses on the Postle no longer flooded, as they used to, every February.

Someone, once, had tried to make something of them, and two of the eight houses still had bright paintwork and tidy gardens and window boxes. They weren't quite up to the level of the Austrian blinds of Redbourne Road, but they had certainly been cared for until recently. But now Kate could see how only two of them showed signs of occupation. The others had their windows and doors boarded up and the desolate air of houses that had not been occupied for some time. This was the row of houses that would be demolished if Fridesley Development Scheme was carried out. She had read that the houses were all derelict and ready for demolition, but seeing them now, she judged that the dereliction was quite recent. She approached one of the two houses that still appeared to be inhabited.

The door opened as she came up to it, but not so widely that she could see who stood there behind it. She had a glimpse of a hunched, bent figure and white hair, an eye shining in the dark behind the crack of the door.

'What you want?' It was a woman's voice and unfriendly.

'I'm asking about attitudes to the development scheme,' said Kate.

'I'm not talking to no one.' The chain was up on the door.

'Bugger off. And your friends and all. You let it happen, now you make out it was nothing to do with you. But what about us and what that bastard did to us, eh?'

'Which bastard?' shouted Kate as the chain rattled and the door started to close. 'What did he do?'

'Just bugger off out of here,' came the muffled voice through the letter box.

'Did he have a dark beard?' tried Kate.

'Won't get nothing out that silly old cow,' said someone behind her. Kate turned round. He was standing just behind the gate of the only other occupied house in the row. This house had a makeshift air about it, and old, peeling stickers in the window saying 'No Poll Tax Here', although the poll tax had been abolished over a year ago. Two mongrels with a lot of German shepherd about them appeared from the back of the house and glared at Kate over the low, crumbling wall at the front. She stopped moving forwards. These dogs did not look like obedient, disciplined, sociable animals. They looked as though they would take out one of her ankles at the slightest provocation.

Kate tried to forget the dogs and her nervousness and concentrate on the man, though he wasn't much of an improvement with his matted hair and his clothes the colour of dirt itself. Kate felt overdressed in her Oxfam outfit.

'Yes?' he said. 'Dogs don't like strangers.'

Kate held on to her clipboard and dropped her accent a couple of notches. 'I just wanted to ask a few questions.'

The young man scowled at her and one of the dogs started to growl, drawing back its lips and showing its teeth. 'They don't like questions, either.'

'Could I have your name?' she asked hopefully.

'Jude. They call me Jude.' Well, they would, thought Kate. 'What about you?'

'Kate. They call me Kate.' And that's what's on my birth certificate and my National Insurance card, and it's even what my mother calls me. But you, Jude, I wonder what you started out as. 'I'm trying to find out what people think about this development scheme.' She had said it so often that this time she believed it herself. It even sounded plausible.

Jude's face was brown with a mixture of suntan and grime, his matted hair drawn back with a black tie. His clothes fitted him tightly and had their own, aggressive style. He wore boots, laced up his legs to just below the knee, and a leather bracelet on one wrist.

'We were wondering what you thought about the development scheme here on the Postle,' she repeated.

'It's crap,' said Jude.

Just the other side of the Postle, through the willow trees, across the canal, stood the city of Oxford, one of the most civilized places in the whole country, if not the whole world. She could nearly see its grey buildings crouching in the mist, hear choristers singing in chapel and cathedral, feel the gravel in front of the Sheldonian under her feet. But here on the Postle she was back in another country, living life according to a different set of rules. Anything could happen here.

A woman had appeared as silently as Jude and stood just a little behind him. She was dressed, on this cold February day, in cotton clothes, a headband, and sandals. She had a filthy baby on her hip and another couple of the mangy, dull-coated dogs at her heels. The baby started to grizzle.

'Shut it, Lilith,' said Jude. 'This lady wants to hear about what we think about the development scheme, Beck. What we going to tell her?'

'It's a load of crap,' said Beck. 'It's about making money for people who already have too much. They just got rid of the people who lived here any way they knew how. They didn't give a shit for what they wanted, did they? Just tried every trick they knew, and sod the compensation.'

'But who?' asked Kate. 'Who did it?'

'They say it was that wanker Davies, and one of his mates,' said Jude. 'But who's he work for, then?'

'Who's he work for?' repeated Kate.

'That bastard Grant, if you ask me,' said Jude, and two of the dogs started growling. 'He knows what he wants to do with this place, and he's going ahead with it as soon as he's got us to move.' He spat on the ground. 'But we're not going. Or if we do, it's on our terms. There'll be some surprises for Grant if we move on, I can tell you. He'll get more than he bargained for when he takes this house over.'

He had very dark eyes, not quite in focus, and now he brought a flat tin out of his back pocket and started to roll a thin cigarette. He took a couple of drags on it, then passed it across to Beck.

'Give us something for the dog food,' he said to Kate, abruptly. She hadn't brought a handbag with her, but she dug in the pocket of her nasty green fur jacket and came up with a couple of pound coins.

'How's this?'

'Is that all you've got?'

'Yes.'

'It'll have to do, then.'

Beck muttered, 'Mean cow,' then turned round and wandered round to the back of the house as silently as she had appeared. Kate saw that Jude wasn't going to say any more, and she mumbled some sort of closing comment before turning back to the road away from the Postle.

'What's that jacket made from then?' Jude's voice followed her down the road away from the Postle. 'Green monkeys?' He laughed and the dogs started to bark in sympathy.

Sod that, thought Kate. I'm sure there are other things I should have learned from that man, but I can't go on with it. I feel uncomfortable here. I don't belong. The thoughts were like a hand in the middle of her back, pushing her fast down the road away from the Postle. When she turned left into Waverley Lane she felt better. There were new houses here, expensive ones, with gardens tidied for the winter and about to burst into spring bloom. The few cars that were on the road or parked in driveways were expensive, too. The front door of one of them opened and a woman got out.

'What you on then?' she asked Kate. 'I seen you, with your clipboard and your questions, creeping round the place, staring through windows, watching us.'

She was dressed in a most peculiar way for the time of day: gold lamé top with wide shoulders, tight black Lycra skirt that ended above mid-thigh, black tights, spike-heeled shoes. Her eyes were pale, her hair was golden, and she wore a lot of makeup. Tart? wondered Kate. Was this Oxford's red-light district? She hadn't thought up to now that Oxford had such a thing or would know what to do when it got there.

A large dog appeared behind the woman, well groomed this time, but still as bad tempered as the ones she had met on the Postle. 'I'm just investigating attitudes to the development scheme,' said Kate.

'Why? It's all decided, isn't it? Those buggers on the Postle aren't going to hold out much longer. One last surprise party and they'll move on. Even that stupid bitch who bleats on about living there since her wedding day, she can't last out without electricity and water. Water in the taps, that is. There's plenty of the stuff everywhere else.'

'You mean someone's forcing them out?'

'Look, they've been offered money, haven't they? When they offered me money to leave Sudden Cottage I accepted it fast enough, I can tell you. Glad enough to leave the place, anyway, with all them snobs looking down their noses at me and my lifestyle. People should love animals, shouldn't they? Not complain about them. We're all God's creatures, I say.' A couple of cats appeared from the open door and ambled down the path to stare at Kate. One of them was heavily pregnant. 'But if that lot up at the Postle want to do it the hard way,' her informant was saying, 'that's up to them. They can't say they weren't warned.'

Warned by whom? wondered Kate, as a picture of a couple of short-haired men with muscles bulging through Armani suits came into her mind.

'There must be a lot of money at stake,' said Kate.

'You what?'

'Any idea who they are?' asked Kate, hopefully. 'The men who stand to make all the money. Are they local?'

'Some are,' said the woman, but at that moment they were interrupted by a Mercedes turning through the gates and coming to a halt in front of the garage doors.

'What's this, Kay?' asked the man who got out of it. 'Not answering any questions, are you?' He turned to Kate. 'What is it this week, soap powder, coffee granules, or what?' He was big, Kate thought, and broad, and his eyes weren't as casual as his words. She was sure he could see right through to her interest in Fridesley development scheme, and even to her investigation of Yvonne's murder. She hoped there were no blunt instruments lying around, because he looked as though he might use one on her if she gave the wrong answers to his questions. She tried a simper and a brainless little woman expression and hoped that they came out right. They felt pretty stupid from the inside.

'I'm just asking about attitudes to the Fridesley development scheme,' she trotted out. 'No free samples, I'm afraid, just some very simple questions.'

'Get off, you buggers,' said the man. The cats had climbed on to the warm bonnet of the car, in the way of cats, and were leaving muddy pawprints all over the shining bodywork. He pushed them back on to the ground and they walked a few yards off, then sat and started to groom themselves. 'Just you clock this,' he said to Kate. 'We're in favour of the scheme round here. All of us. It's going to bring work and public transport and a new road. It's going to raise the tone of the place when that useless lot are moved off the Postle, and that means our houses are worth more, right? What have you got to set against that, you and your friends? Some rare kind of thistle? Some stupid bloody bird that no one ever sees?' He turned to Kay. 'You go back indoors and stop sounding off your mouth to strangers. And you,' he said to Kate, 'stop listening to troublemakers. Revenge, that's all it was with that woman. She was just trying to get her own back. You'd better get off home to your yogurt and your muesli and your unleaded petrol, and leave the rest of us to run the real world.'

Kate, being an intelligent woman, clutched her clipboard to her furry green bosom and left. What the hell was he going on about?

She was just coming up to Josephine Street when she met Carey. She had a feeling that he had a room somewhere thereabouts.

'Katie darling,' he said, 'how lovely to bump into you like this.'

'Plain Kate will do,' snapped Kate, taking out her bad temper on him.

'Definitely not plain,' said Carey, walking very close to her and invading her space. She wished he wasn't so good looking in his flimsy way. He brought something out of his pocket and started simple juggling. Showing off, thought Kate, still in a bad temper. He was using three socks, folded and tucked into neat packets.

'What a shame I wasn't born into a circus family,' he said. 'They would have been proud of me, don't you think, instead of setting academic hurdles for me to leap over and withholding their approval when I failed to live up to their standards.' Then he smiled brilliantly at her and started doing something fancy with the socks, as a variation. 'I love magic and magicians, don't you? Yes,' he said, not waiting for her reply, 'you must do, with those books you write. Something cunning, something flashy, that's what I like. We're two of a kind, Katie my darling.'

'We're not,' said Kate, 'definitely not.'

141

Carey threw something dark blue and shining up into the air, caught it one-handed behind his back and replaced it with another folded sock before Kate could be sure what she had seen. 'Live to live,' he said, then he leant across and pulled a twopenny coin from behind her right ear. She laughed.

'There you are,' he said. 'Same technique as a writer: get the punter's attention on your right hand while you do something tricky with the left.' Like murderers, too, thought Kate, turning to look at him. The low clouds had kept the day as dark as evening and the streetlamps were on, making their faces a livid colour, shining on the almost imperceptible rain that was falling. Carey hitched up the collar of his jacket and the next streetlamp caught the bright colour of his hair, turning it to orange. She remembered then.

'It was you, wasn't it?'

'What are you accusing me of, beloved? In which of my sins have you found me out?'

'On Wednesday night. In Redbourne Road. I saw someone coming towards me on the other side of the road. The figure was vaguely familiar, but I couldn't recognize him. Now I do. It was you. In this light I recognize you.'

'Caught in your trap, am I? And what were you doing out in Redbourne Road on the night of a murder, Katie dear? I thought that you and your friends were all incarcerated in Rose Smith's front room, toning your lovely thigh muscles with Jane Fonda.'

'How did you know about that?'

'Doesn't everyone? This place is a village, Kate.'

'But you, what were you doing, Carey?'

'Visiting a very naughty friend,' said Carey, 'who was prepared to do lovely, naughty things all evening.'

'But Camilla doesn't live in Redbourne Road,' said Kate before she could think and stop herself.

'No, she doesn't, does she?' Carey threw three socks up in the air, caught them one at a time and pushed them into the pocket of his jacket. 'Three's my lucky number,' he said, pushing open the gate of a small terraced house. 'All the best things come in threes, I find.' He unlocked the front door, smiled at Kate. 'One more clue,' he said. 'If you're really wandering round and sleuthing in earnest, I should go and ask the delightful little Miss Binns what she saw on Wednesday evening. If you can get past her dragon mother, that is.'

'What? Who?' Kate found herself asking. But Carey had disappeared inside. A brass number 3 was on the gate. Is that what he was talking about? Kate doubted it. Did he mean that deaths came in threes? Was she next on his list? And who was the delightful Miss Binns? Damn Carey and his mysteries: he did it on purpose to annoy her. She walked slowly back to Agatha Street and her own small, restful house.

The wind was rising again, blowing rain and wet hair into her face. The buddleia that she should have cut back in November was swaying and rocking and nodding its dead black flowerheads at her as she let herself in.

She must ring Sophie again, she thought, even if it did seem crass of her.

After Sophie had answered, and Kate had gone through the awkward routine of apologizing for disturbing her again so soon, she asked her question.

'The Oxford box?' said Sophie in a puzzled voice. 'No, Kate. Why on earth should Yvonne have it? It's not here. What made you think it would be?'

Kate extricated herself from the conversation and replaced the receiver. Then she rang Andrew.

'Can we have lunch, Andrew?'

'You're worried? Why not? Your company is always a pleasure. How about the Crypt at five past one?'

Chapter Fourteen

Kate went down the steps into the low lighting of the Crypt to find that Andrew had just arrived and ordered a bottle of pinot blanc. They took the bottle with them round the corner into the restaurant and sat on either side of a candle-lit table.

'Smoked salmon, I think, Max,' said Andrew, 'followed by chicken and chestnut pie. Same for you?' Kate nodded. They drank a glass of their wine and chatted about the latest gossip at the Bodleian. Kate reminded herself that he wasn't callous, it was just that he hadn't known Yvonne and couldn't be expected to care about her death the way she did.

'Right,' he said, as the wine started to produce a warm glow in the empty space above her early breakfast. 'By the look of you, you need to eat something before you start to tell me about your morning.'

Plates of smoked salmon, prawns, and brown bread and butter appeared in front of them. Kate found that she was hungry and began to eat. The restaurant was filling up.

'I've found a new motive for the murder,' said Kate.

Andrew ate his last prawn, said 'Hmm?' and started on

145

the smoked salmon. He has lips as precisely limned and as red as dahlia petals, thought Kate, only glad that this fanciful thought could not be read by Andrew.

'I have three more people who might have wanted her dead,' she said, while the waitress removed their plates and Andrew poured them each another glass of wine.

'I think this is all about major corruption in the local council,' said Kate, as Andrew sniffed and sipped.

At the next table a man was choking over his soup, and Kate realized that the wine was having its usual effect of making her voice too loud. She must learn to lower it when she was talking in public.

'Oh dear,' said Andrew at last. 'I do believe you're off on one of your romantic plot-lines again.'

'Rubbish,' said Kate. 'There's a letter on Council headed paper, and if you read it in conjunction with what I've been hearing from people in Fridesley, you can only come to one conclusion.'

She had raised her voice again in the way that embarrassed him, and he glanced round the room to see whether any of the other lunchers had noticed. A tall, dark man at the next table had raised his head from his steak and was looking at them. He and Andrew nodded at each other in acknowledgement. The rest of the room was pretending not to listen.

'You know him?' asked Kate. The man looked vaguely familiar. Maybe she had met him in a different context.

'One of the young Fellows from Leicester,' said Andrew, dismissively. Kate guessed that the young Fellow was doing better in his career than Andrew was, and was probably around ten years younger. The Leicester don smiled briefly at Kate before returning to his meal. He had the well-defined look of someone who exercises regularly, and as she pictured him in a black tracksuit, she thought he might just be her ubiquitous runner, though she couldn't be sure.

'It's all just gossip, isn't it?' said Andrew, pursing his dahlia lips and stabbing his fork into the puffed pastry lid of his pie.

'Isn't that what detecting is about? Listening to gossip, drawing conclusions, and then looking for concrete evidence?'

'You know, Kate, you are being very indiscreet. Don't you realize that everyone in this room has been listening in to what you've been saying? And most of it has been wild supposition, hasn't it?'

'And what about the Oxford box?' she said, ignoring Andrew's last remarks, and still refusing to lower her voice.

'This blue-enamelled copper mourning object, produced at Wolvercote by John Parrish in around 1830?' asked Andrew.

'Have you seen it?'

'I've seen one like it.' Andrew chewed lengthily and swallowed; he drank half a glass of wine. 'They are seriously collected, I believe. What was the *memento mori* message on the pediment?'

'*Live to die, Die to live,*' said Kate.

'Very nice.'

'Lynda picked up Theo's Oxford box when Yvonne told her to, and walked across Redbourne Road with it. As far as we know, she gave it to Yvonne.'

'Is it still there in the house?'

'Sophie says it isn't. But I thought I might have seen it since.'

'Where? Who's got it?'

'I can't be sure. It wouldn't be fair to accuse someone.'

'If you find out who has the box now, you'll probably find your murderer.'

That had occurred to her, too. Maybe Carey had picked it up in Yvonne's house, maybe Camilla had and then given it to him. Carey, Camilla, Gavin. They were all strong candidates for Yvonne's murderer, and she didn't want to believe in any of them. She couldn't approve of Carey, but she saw why Camilla found him attractive. And she didn't look forward to telling Camilla that her lover might be a killer. And then again, suppose that Carey had been there when Camilla let herself in. Camilla, or Carey, on their own might not have killed Yvonne, but what about the two of them acting together? And what about Jude's two bastards, Davies and Grant? Or even Gavin?

Andrew waved away her protests about her diet with, 'You're going to need your strength this afternoon, my dear,' and ordered coffees and apple and cinnamon cake for them both. Kate ate hers in a ladylike way, with a fork, to make up for her previous behaviour, since Andrew was paying.

She felt the young don from Leicester looking at her as he got up to leave.

'Do you think he heard what we were talking about?' she whispered to Andrew.

'Everyone in this part of the restaurant could hear you,' said Andrew, and called for the bill.

Outside in the Cornmarket the rain was falling on the umbrellas of dispirited shoppers and the cold bare wrists of student cyclists. A young man was playing Bach on his violin, reflecting the improved standard of busking during

University terms. Kate fished in her bag for her purse.

'You shouldn't encourage them,' said Andrew, and he turned towards Broad Street and the Bodleian. Kate dropped a larger coin than she had previously intended into the busker's hat before walking the couple of hundred yards with him. In front of St Michael's church sat a group of beggars, much more threatening these, with their unkempt hair and pack of wild mongrels, and calling more aggressively for money. One of them played a tin whistle, his dog curled up next to him, its brown muzzle resting on his knee. Kate thought she saw Jude and Beck, but she couldn't be sure.

She and Andrew turned into the civilized expanse of Broad Street and walked towards the Bodleian. Even in the grey drizzle it was impressive, with its spiky pinnacles and the huge glass windows of its reading rooms.

On the cobblestones in front of the Clarendon Building a film crew had set up a pavement café with striped parasols over the tables and laughing customers in summer dresses. Behind the café stood a flower stall full of gold and white dahlias.

'It's some publicity film,' said Andrew. 'Bringing in more foreign tourists.'

'Won't they be surprised to find no pavement café here when they arrive?' she asked. Enormous lights provided counterfeit sunshine, but the short-sleeved customers looked blue and miserable.

Kate left Andrew in front of the Sheldonian as unsynchronized clocks chimed two o'clock around them and she walked past the heads of the Roman emperors, and paused on the pavement, looking for a gap in the traffic to make it across to Blackwell's bookshop. She would just pop in for a moment to see what was new in the fiction section before she turned left and walked back towards the railway station. She needed a walk after lunch with Andrew, and she could pick up the towpath by the canal and go back to Fridesley the long, but pretty, way.

Someone was standing beside her, ready to take his chance with the Broad Street traffic: it was the don from Leicester, the one who looked like a runner.

He looked as though he was about to speak to her, but at that moment she saw a small space between a bicycle and a delivery van and raced for the Bodleian roadway. He must have changed his mind about speaking when he got to the other side of the road because he walked past her and went in through the inconspicuous side door into Leicester, just on the other side of the White Horse pub. Blackwell's and its latest novels lost their appeal and she turned left towards the railway station and the towpath that led to Fridesley.

Kate's phone was ringing as she went through her front door: it was Gavin, sounding aggrieved.

'Look here, Kate,' he said. 'This Yvonne thing isn't going to stop us running the club race, is it? Not after the training we've done. You're still organizing it, aren't you?'

She had forgotten about it in the past forty-eight hours. The thought of ditching all the organization appealed to her.

'Well, perhaps as a mark of respect,' she said.

'Sod that,' said Gavin. 'The funeral will be long over by then. I expect the police will have arrested the vandal who killed her. I mean to say, how long are we supposed to let it affect our lives?'

A couple of weeks did seem on the short side to Kate, but perhaps she was being over-sensitive.

'No, Kate,' he was saying, 'you just go ahead with the arrangements, OK? Make sure you've got new batteries in the stopwatches, get the prizes bought and all that. Have you got permission to go through Wytham Woods?'

'Perhaps we should consult the others,' said Kate weakly.

'No need for that. And Kate,' a slightly different note caught her ear, 'why were you out with a clipboard, knocking on doors in Redbourne Road?'

'Just some research for the new book,' she fibbed.

'I thought you wrote historicals.'

She hadn't realized that Gavin had taken any notice of her writing. 'Well, we all get our ideas in different ways, don't we?'

'Yes,' said Gavin. 'I always wondered where writers got their ideas from. I didn't realize it was by going out asking people questions. What do you ask them?'

'Attitudes,' answered Kate. 'I find out people's attitudes. It helps me with the motivations of my characters.' She didn't tell him about the parrots: she wasn't sure what sort of attitude they indicated.

'I think you should be careful, Kate,' Gavin said. 'It looks a bit suspicious, walking round asking questions just when someone's been murdered. And suppose you asked the wrong ones, and someone thought you were getting too close to the truth? It's a bit iffy if you ask me.'

'Close to what truth?' Kate asked.

But Gavin said, 'If Penny asks you about it, you'll tell her what we've decided about the race, won't you?'

She would be in the wrong whether she answered yes or no,

she realized, so she just said 'Goodbye Gavin,' and hung up the phone. What truth was Gavin worried she might ferret out by her questions? And had he been threatening her?

Maybe he really had been concerned only about the club race. He thinks he's in with a chance of winning. He'd probably been out on his own, padding round the footpaths with a rechargeable lamp on his woolly hat, getting fitter and faster than the rest of them. Well, she'd see that they gave him a run for his money. She might even put on her trainers and creep out into the cold Fridesley dusk herself and run a few nine-minute miles before dinner. She looked out at the unpromising grey sky: on the other hand, perhaps she wouldn't.

The phone rang again. This time it was her editor from Fergusons. 'Just checking on progress on the new book, sweetie,' he said. 'Research going well, is it? Have you started the first draft yet?'

The truthful answers would be no and only just, but Kate flannelled. Elliot probably wasn't taken in by it, he heard too many excuses from too many authors not to recognize high-class flannel when he met it. 'Just so long as I have something to show people in June, sweetie,' he said. 'A synopsis, a chapter or two, would do. But real typewritten words on real paper.'

She promised. She rang off in relief. She would uncover her word processor that very evening and get down to some hard work. It was time she wrote an outline, a chapter-by-chapter breakdown, a list of things to find out. Other people did it and held down full-time jobs, so she should be able to fit in a little part-time sleuthing and get her book completed on time, surely?

Chapter Fifteen

Kate called Camilla first. 'My place, tomorrow morning, six-fifteen,' she said in a tone of voice that did not expect an argument.

'What's this about?' asked Camilla.

'I have some ideas and I want to ask some questions. And I want that rota of observers from Penny.'

'Wasn't Barbara in charge of it?'

'Whoever. I just want it. We ought to be able to work out who was where and when and who should have seen them. Any discrepancies should make us suspicious.'

'Why the "us" this evening, Kate?'

'It's a lonely job, being a sleuth, I've discovered.'

'I thought that was what it was all about: the mean streets, the solitary figure hunting the murderer through all the sleazy joints in town.'

'Just don't ever take up crime writing, Millie.'

'Camilla. Have you had any more thoughts about that Council agenda?'

'I think Yvonne may have been blackmailing Gavin over it, or at least contemplating doing so. That would have made life impossible for him, with pressure from both sides.'

'Have you thought who N.D. could be?'

'Not yet.'

'I've had a thought about it, but I'll keep it to myself for the moment, if you don't mind.'

'It occurs to me that Gavin had the best opportunity for bashing Yvonne over the head and making his getaway.'

'In which case, why didn't he remove the memo from the drawer?'

'Perhaps he was interrupted. Or perhaps he didn't know how methodical Yvonne was.'

'And there's something else: do you remember the scene in Rose's kitchen?'

'How can I forget it?'

'I'm sure that Gavin was one of the people who was dancing to Yvonne's tune. He was far too enthusiastic about the scheme to be natural.'

'You could be right. And there's someone else we've forgotten.'

'Who?'

'Rose. And I've even thought of a motive for her.'

'See you tomorrow,' said Camilla, sounding thoughtful in her turn.

There was a good response to Kate's phone calls and quite a crowd of runners arrived at the door of her house at six fifteen on Sunday morning.

'We're going ahead with the group race,' she told them. 'So we have to keep in training.' She had worked out that this was one way of getting them together to answer her questions. After all, it would seem natural to talk of the murder during their run.

'What could we have done to prevent it?' said Barbara, voicing the thought in everyone's mind. 'I feel so helpless and useless.'

'Have you heard any more news?' asked Penny. 'Has anyone been round to see Sophie? How's she coping, poor girl?'

'I'm seeing her later this morning,' said Kate. 'She didn't sound too good when I spoke to her on the phone.'

'Give her our love,' said Penny. 'And of course, anything that we can do to help . . .'

After a suitable pause, Gavin asked if they had seen the item on the local television news that said that a woman was helping the police with their enquiries.

'Isn't it dreadful,' said Camilla. 'Poor old Lynda. I wonder why on earth they've taken her in for questioning?'

'They're looking for someone to arrest. Once they've made their minds up that they've got someone likely, they're not going to go looking for alternatives, are they?' said Gavin. 'It isn't cost effective.'

'You're all out of date,' said Kate. 'Lynda was taken to the police station and questioned because she had been seen going into Yvonne's house just before the two of them went off to the Indian restaurant. But Theo called his solicitor, and the police let Lynda go after taking her statement. I think they can only keep you for two days without charging you, can't they?'

'I've always thought that anyone who calls for a solicitor must have a guilty conscience,' said Gavin.

'But why on earth would she have killed Yvonne?' asked Rose. 'It doesn't make sense. I don't like the woman, but that's no reason for accusing her of murder.'

'Look,' said Gavin. 'I don't know what all the fuss is about. The police will find someone to charge, and as long as it isn't one of us, it doesn't matter.'

'Of course it matters,' said Kate. 'How can you say that? Don't you have faith in justice? Don't you want to see the person who killed Yvonne arrested? I just can't believe I'm hearing this, Gavin.'

'Well, I suppose I would like to see them get the right person, but I don't see what I can do about it. What route are we running this morning?'

'Yes, shouldn't we start?' Penny said. 'I'm getting cold. And I've got the route worked out,' she said loudly, so that they broke off their conversation and listened to her. 'Across the Fridesley Road, down Rosamund Road, then round the recreation field and on to the footpath on the other side. We'll pick up the canal towpath at Osney Island and run down to Folly Bridge from there.'

'How many miles is this going to be?' asked Camilla.

'Chicken,' whispered Kate.

'Should be about eight miles by the time we get back,' said Penny. 'We'll have to get a few miles in if we're going to run the group race, remember.'

'Maybe we could slope off at Folly Bridge and cut back to Fridesley the quick way,' said Camilla.

'And what about the boxes?' said Gavin as they strung out along the road. 'What did the police say and do when Theo reported their disappearance? Why has no one been round to question us about them? We went through all that Jane Fonda routine just to give ourselves an alibi and it was never asked for. Why aren't they investigating the theft?'

'And what happened to my Oxford box?' asked Rose.

'I expect it's a different branch that deals with theft,' said

Kate, who didn't want to start speculating in front of Rose about Lynda and Carey, let alone Camilla. 'And can you imagine some big butch policeman coming round to find out about Yvonne's murder and to ask them where they both were, to be greeted by Theo rapping on about some missing boxes? They probably thought it was a diversionary technique and wrote it off.'

'Yeah, it means that all that effort of ours was for nothing,' said Gavin.

Kate was thinking that Gavin had been keen enough on the idea of recovering the boxes while Yvonne was alive. And she wasn't even sure he would have been noticed if he had made a detour into her house that evening. He had been distinguishable from the other members of the group when he had worn a beard, but now, if he covered his hair and wore a thick jacket, he could be mistaken for anyone. It wasn't as if he was any taller than the rest of them. There was one way of checking up on him.

'Do you think I could have the list you made?' she asked Penny.

'What list?'

'The rota of observers for the night of the burglary.'

'Sorry, I haven't got it. Try Barbara.'

'What doesn't make sense to me,' Barbara was saying, 'is why they ever picked on Lynda in the first place. She doesn't seem a very likely suspect, does she? Why did they start there?'

' "Was it you wearing the hat?" and she did go over the road and give her the box,' said Kate.

And, 'Perhaps she was being blackmailed by Yvonne,' said Camilla at the same time.

'What?' asked Gavin. 'What are you two on about?'

'Nothing,' said Kate.

And, 'Just thinking aloud,' said Camilla.

'Could you let me have the rota Penny made for the night of the theft?' Kate asked Barbara.

'I haven't got it,' she replied. 'Ask Penny for it.'

'She suggested you might have it.'

'I can't think why. But one of us must have thrown it away, I suppose. We didn't want it lying around when the police came to call, did we?'

'I suppose not.' Kate tried not to show her annoyance. Had Penny or Barbara thrown it away on purpose, or was it the simple tidying-up action of an innocent person? Gavin and Penny, she thought, I shall keep my eye on you two.

Ahead of her, Gavin's neat legs and feet in their resoled shoes moved in an economically efficient run. He was certainly strong enough to have killed Yvonne.

Kate was sitting in her kitchen, a hairdryer in one hand and a mug of coffee in the other, when the doorbell rang.

Penny thrust a plastic Sainsbury's bag at her. 'Your turn to look after the boxes,' she said, and left, quickly.

'Great,' said Kate. 'Just what I needed.' And she went down to her workroom and stuffed the bag behind a pile of old manuscripts in her filing cabinet.

Kate wasn't looking forward to her meeting with Sophie: asking impertinent questions of the recently bereaved was one of the aspects of sleuthing she hadn't considered when she took the task on.

When Sophie opened the door to Kate's ring at the bell,

she looked paler and thinner, and there were circles round her eyes. Her hair needed washing and she was wearing a shapeless grey jogging suit. Kate wondered whether she should embrace her in a condoling sort of way, but settled for making trite remarks and patting her, briefly, on the arm. Sophie thanked her, blew her nose, and led the way up to her room.

It was odd walking into a house as an ordinary visitor that she had previously entered only as a patient. At least this time, using the front door, she didn't have to pass the glass cases of plaster casts that reminded her of dead men's teeth, ready to bite if she didn't keep an eye on them. Had Yvonne intended to place the Oxford box in one of these cases, its lid open, the ivory death's head peering over the rim? *Die to live.*

'Everyone sends their best wishes,' said Kate, feeling inadequate. 'And if there's anything we can do . . .'

'You're all so kind,' said Sophie. 'And just knowing that the group is so supportive is a help.'

The door to Yvonne's studio was closed, and Sophie led the way past it, up the stairs. There was something odd about the house. She had never noticed before how different it was inside from its exterior. Outside, it was an ordinary suburban nineteen-thirties villa, enlarged by the addition of Yvonne's studio and the room above it, but still, exactly what one expected in a road like this. But inside, once you left the surgery and waiting room behind and moved through the double glass doors into the private section, it was as though you entered a different house, somewhere in the backwoods of Canada.

'It was the people before us,' said Sophie, as though she

read her thoughts. 'The husband had always wanted to live in a log cabin, so this is what he did.'

'It just seems odd to start with a 1930s house,' said Kate. 'Couldn't he have found something a bit closer in style? Or built from scratch?'

'That's difficult in Oxford,' said Sophie. 'And he wanted to do it all himself.' She spoke as if there was nothing unusual in this.

The walls were faced with split logs, the ceilings were low and timbered, the floors were of wood, with rustic rugs. With all this cedar-tinted wood about the place, the air was resinous, with undertones of creosote.

'I think it's what decided my mother to buy the place: she liked the idea of misleading people with an outer show while the inner identity was kept secret.'

Wow! thought Kate, you can say that again.

Sophie's room was the one above Yvonne's studio, and had originally been designed as a sitting room for her, where she could invite her friends in for food and conversation. But now it was dedicated, as was Sophie herself, to health, fitness, and the pursuit (so far unsuccessful) of the beautiful body. The wooden floor was covered in a pale vinyl, spotless and shining. Two of the log-cabin walls had huge mirrors hanging on them, like the ballet school that Kate and Millie had attended as children, presumably so that Sophie could check on her form as she exercised. There was a rack of hand weights and odd pieces of equipment with rings and heavy black elastic bands. There was an exercise bicycle and a rowing machine, and something that looked like a miniature trampoline. There was even a pair of roller skates in the corner.

'She did want me to look pretty,' said Sophie, her eyes bulging with unshed tears. 'But however hard I tried, I never quite managed it.'

'Yes, I can see you put a lot of effort into it.'

'Come and sit down,' said Sophie, leading the way to a chrome and plastic seat. 'I've made the coffee.'

There was a notice board at this end of the room, incongruous against the log cabin effect of the wall, and pinned to it were charts and schedules. The graph of weight against time showed a sharp fall for the previous week. Kate looked critically at Sophie: she was looking thinner, and something like Yvonne's sharp nose was starting to emerge from the pudding of her face.

'How's it going?' asked Kate. 'With the police, I mean.'

'I'm glad we decided not to tell them about getting back Rose's boxes. They were on at me for ages, but all I could say was that I was out for the evening and when I got home I found her.'

'How dreadful for you,' said Kate. 'Do you want to talk about it?'

Sophie took a tissue from a box on the table and wiped her eyes, then sat rolling it into a smaller and smaller wad as she talked.

'I keep going over it in my mind: walking through the front door and up the stairs. I stood on the landing and called out to see if my mother was in. I don't know what made me look into her room, but she should have been home by then. And then I found her, lying there. Every time I walk into the house now, I half expect . . .'

'It must be terrible for you. And I suppose that you'll go on feeling like that until they find the man who did it.'

'And yet another part of me refuses to accept that she is dead. I still expect her to walk in and tell me it was all a black joke. I know it isn't the same as when there was capital punishment, but they must catch the man who did it.'

'I'm sure they're doing their best,' said Kate.

'They kept suggesting such awful things,' said Sophie. 'They wanted to know about her friends, and kept hinting that there must have been all sorts of men in her life. How can they think such things?'

'Well,' started Kate, 'she was an attractive woman . . .' but she got such a reproachful look from Sophie's damp eyes that she stopped.

'It must have been an intruder or a madman.'

'How did he get in?' asked Kate. 'Was there a window broken or anything like that?'

'No. That's one of the odd things about it. Whoever it was must have used a key.'

Kate didn't like to say that that scotched the idea of the mad axeman or the casual intruder. It took planning to get hold of a key, as they well knew.

'Then there was the other thing they told me about her. I just didn't believe it at first.'

'Yes?'

'It gave me a terrible shock,' said Sophie. 'It's horrible. I won't believe it. And they keep asking me questions about that evening, going over and over it until I could scream.'

'That's to make sure you tell them every single thing that you remember: it's odd how the memory can throw up forgotten items that it has hoarded away.' Then she risked asking, 'Has anything like that happened to you?'

'No,' said Sophie. 'Why are you asking these questions?'

'Well,' said Kate slowly, 'since we're not being entirely open with the police about what we were doing on Wednesday night, I thought it would be a good idea if I just checked around to make sure that there was nothing important that was getting left out of the investigation.'

'I see,' said Sophie, and frowned.

'Do you want to tell me this shocking thing that the police revealed?' asked Kate, risking another reproach.

'They say that they've found evidence that my mother was blackmailing people, and they think that was the reason she was murdered. Can you understand how it felt? It's as though the person I'm mourning for isn't the same as the one who actually lived. I thought I knew her, but she's quite different. Can you believe it?'

'It must be difficult for you,' said Kate. 'Have you any idea what they found to make them say that?'

'They say they've found pictures and letters.'

'Do they know who the victims were?'

'They haven't said. They only tell me what they want me to know. So Kate,' the gooseberry eyes gazed at her, 'will you keep me up to date if you find out anything? It's awful being in the dark like this.'

'I'll try,' said Kate. 'And you must tell me of any little thing that occurs to you that might be useful. Is there anything else, anything in your mother's past, for example, that might have brought about this . . . this tragedy? Where did you live before you came to Oxford?'

'Nothing,' said Sophie, briefly. 'There couldn't be. We lived in a small town in Wiltshire. Denington had one of the lowest crime rates in the country: nothing ever happened there. And that was when my father . . .' She stopped, and even Kate hesitated to ask questions about the death of her other parent. Sophie was expelling spent breath in little snorts, as though the effort of talking was getting too much for her.

'Don't you think it could be dangerous, asking questions, I mean?' she said.

'I think we ought to continue stirring until the truth floats to the surface,' said Kate.

'Like scum on strawberry jam,' said Sophie. Kate shuddered as she made the childish association between strawberry jam and dead bodies.

'What are you going to do next?' asked Sophie, as she showed Kate to the door.

'I think it's time I went home and wrote another chapter of my book,' said Kate.

Chapter Sixteen

The skies were weeping down the steady, drenching rain that soaks through raincoat and shoes, that drips through hair and trickles down neck. Kate, as usual, had no umbrella with her. And so much, she thought to herself, for that beautiful red streaked dawn sky. She turned into Blackwell's, flying up the brass-edged steps and pushing through the narrow blue door into the fiction section. She might as well look at the latest in best-selling novels. It couldn't depress her any further about the slow progress of her own. She still had enough of her advance left to live on for another couple of months, but at her current rate of working she would need to look for a part-time job if she was going to be able to feed herself and pay her mortgage after that. She was feeling foolish, too, about what she was doing. Following a suspect seemed all very well when people did it in books, but it carried an unwelcome taste of melodrama when you tried it in real life.

The shop smelled of damp raincoats and was crowded with people with sodden shoulders and half-furled umbrellas. Kate pushed her way between a couple of browsing figures and picked up the nearest glossy-covered novel and started reading the blurb. If she stood by the window and looked over the top of her book, she would be able to see when her quarry went past. And if she didn't see him, she could tell herself it didn't matter, and go home.

'It's Kate, isn't it?'

She had to look up some way before she met dark brown eyes under black eyebrows. His hair was thick and well cut, and there were beads of rain caught in it. It was the man who had been eating in the Crypt when she had been lunching with Andrew. And she realized that he was also her fanciable runner. How did he know her name?

'You don't remember me, do you? But we met just a hundred yards from here, in Leicester Fellows' garden. It was raining, then, too.'

It was coming back to her: last June, at the Encaenia garden party. She had gone with Andrew, and in all that drought-ridden summer it had been one of the few days when the skies had opened and rain had fallen.

'You were wearing something pink and floating and a hat with roses.' Kate pulled a face at the thought of hats. 'And uncomfortable shoes. I remember you looked as though you wanted to take them off and walk around in bare feet.'

First the smell of strawberries, then the spattering of raindrops through the copper beech tree in the corner of the Fellows' garden. And a man who had volunteered his mortarboard as an improvised tray for her teacup and saucer. Andrew had introduced them briefly, 'Kate, this is Liam Ross. Liam, meet my writer friend, Kate,' then pulled at her sleeve and whispered in her ear, 'A musician from Leicester, no one special.' She had been aware only of someone tall, about her own age and vaguely pleasant looking. The three of them had run for cover together into the marquee, and ended up in the same group. She remembered drenched grass ruining her best shoes and there had been the same smell of wet clothing drying in a hot atmosphere. And then the drumroll of rain on the canvas roof of the marquee that had drowned out conversation and left them staring into each others' wet faces. Oh yes, she remembered his eyes now, and what a dark brown they were. Funny how it all came back after nearly eight months.

'We were eating strawberries and cream,' she said. 'And drinking tea from china cups with little pink rosebuds on, stuck in some time warp before the First World War.' She put the book back on the table and turned towards the door. Tall, dark, and skinny was her type, rather than red haired and middle sized like Andrew, she thought, so it must be time to leave.

'Have you got time for a cup of coffee?' he asked, turning with her. 'If we sprinted to the King's Arms we could hardly get any wetter than we are already.'

Of course she hadn't got time. She was following a suspect, if you could think of the witless Gavin like that. She was supposed to be writing a book. She was checking up on facts in a murder enquiry. She didn't need a man in her life. Particularly that.

'Fine,' she said, 'I'm sure I've got time for one cup of coffee.'

And then she got lucky. As they ran across the Bodleian roadway and dodged the cars on the corner of the Broad and Parks Road, she saw Gavin's green Goretex and Gavin's dark hair disappearing ahead of them into the

King's Arms. Even if he turned left into the no-smoking room, she still had splendid cover in the form of Liam. And she hoped that Gavin was going to drink at least one cup of coffee himself.

Inside, the coffee lounge was crowded, and there was a slow-moving queue stretching back from the counter, but no Gavin. Kate risked a quick look through into the bar, but couldn't see him. He must have moved into one of the rooms at the back, which was a bugger, she thought, because there was another exit into Holywell, and if he left that way, she wouldn't be able to see him.

And what had made her think that Gavin was witless and innocuous? Perhaps it was a careful mask that he had cultivated. The things that he had said to her on the phone the other afternoon, and again when she had rung him yesterday evening hadn't been at all harmless now that she thought about them. They had been threatening. How would he have behaved to someone who was trying to blackmail him? Sometimes, when she stopped and remembered that she wasn't in the middle of one of her own plots, she felt nervous about what she was getting into. After all, one person had been killed, and she was still a character in the story, with a killer on the loose out there. And the way she was behaving, sticking her neck out all over the place, asking questions, she was the obvious candidate for second victim. Pull yourself together, Kate, she told herself, this is going to be the one where the hero dodges bullets and speeding cars to arrive at the final confrontation. She tried to remember whether the hero always escaped unscathed, but wasn't too certain about it. And anyway, unlike art, life came with no guarantees. She should keep watching her back.

Meanwhile Liam was talking to her. He was probably used to a companion who listened to what he said, who gave him her full attention, not one who sat and stared out of the window and said vaguely, 'Sorry, what was that you said?' and spilled her coffee in her saucer.

'I read one of your books,' he was saying, 'after we met last June. I thought it was great fun: strong on plot, full of interesting characters, and very funny. Had you thought of trying a thriller? I'm sure you'd be good at it.'

'Actually,' said Kate, 'I do seem to be working on a crime novel at the moment. It was meant to be about a robbery, but it turned into a murder. And it was meant to be a historical, set in France during the Napoleonic Wars, but it turned out to be strictly contemporary.'

'And from the way you're staring out of that window, you get your ideas from close observation of the passing scene.'

'What was that?' said Kate, who had just seen a green rainproof jacket scurry through the rain and climb the steps to the Clarendon Building. No, it was all right, it wasn't Gavin. She drank some more of her coffee.

'Am I boring you?' asked Liam. 'Are you heavily involved with someone else? Do you particularly dislike tall thin men with dark hair? Would you like me to move on and leave you alone?' She looked at him then, meeting eyes that were both amused and concerned, and slightly uncertain. 'Or is it perhaps that you are deeply into that fascinating investigation that you were telling us all about at lunch the other day?' Kate felt herself blushing at this, but Liam continued, 'Only before I lost your attention, I was about to ask if you would like to come to a concert with me. Janáček, Tippett, Lutoslawski.'

'I'd really like that,' Kate said quickly, before she could

remind herself that she didn't want a new man in her life, making demands on the time she should be spending at her word processor. And that didn't sound much like her choice of music, either. Then she saw a flash of green Goretex and dark hair. Gavin was walking with a man in a grey suit and a Burberry, crossing the road at the lights, moving up towards Radcliffe Square. She had to go. Gavin's companion didn't look at all as though he was interested in saving the planet, more as though he had five new schemes for exploiting it.

'Give me a ring,' she said. 'I really have to go now.' She was standing up, pushing her way through the crowded room towards the door. 'And thanks for the coffee.' Liam was still sitting at the table, watching her.

'I know you're a runner,' he said, 'but really, this is ridiculous.'

She hadn't got time to worry about him at the moment. She would have to hurry if she was going to catch up with Gavin and his companion and not lose them in the crowds in the High Street. She padded across the cobblestones of Radcliffe Square. On her left, the Camera sat like a fortress behind its defensive circle of chestnut stakes. This was the low season for tourists, but the Curators were determined that the summer invasion would not destroy their smooth green turf this year. Then she was dodging a couple of cyclists in the narrow lane beside the church of St Mary the Virgin and coming out into the High Street. She was glad she was wearing trousers and flat shoes: what they lacked in elegance they certainly made up in practicality, and she could move in and out of the meandering shoppers in the High Street always keeping Gavin and his companion in sight. They crossed on the pelican crossing. Luckily there were other people crossing at the same time and she lowered her head and hid behind them. Gavin and his companion were talking hard, but she didn't dare get any nearer so that she could overhear. She was getting scared of Gavin, she realized. She wanted to find something concrete to tie him in with the developers, and to Yvonne's blackmail.

Gavin and his companion were walking down King Edward Street towards Oriel Square. Kate gave a quick, covetous look at Liberty's window before hiding her face in the special offers in Oddbins.

Without looking behind them, the two men turned into a dark brick office block, built at a time when the Victorians went in for white decoration on their red buildings. A sad gargoyle dripped rain on to their shoulders as Gavin's companion let them in with his key. Kate stood wondering whether to go into the shop and get a bottle of the special-offer Bulgarian red, until the door closed behind them. Then she cautiously made her way over to the black-painted door with the shiny knobs and brass letterbox. If she were Gavin, she thought, she would at this moment be looking down from a first-floor front window, to see whether anyone had been following him and was lurking in the neighbourhood. But then, Gavin perhaps didn't read the same fiction as she did, and maybe Gavin wasn't guilty of anything or feeling trapped and followed. Maybe.

There were brass plates set into the wall on one side of the porch. She pulled out her notebook and found a page with 'yellow shirts? starched?' written on it, and copied down the names of the companies that were listed on the brass plates. They looked like dentists. White and Darke, she wrote. Planning Consultants. Not dentists after all, but an unlikely name. Grant Investments. Grant Holdings. Oxbridge City Leisure. And what on earth did that one mean?

When she had finished she moved a little way up the street and stared into the window of the health-food shop. The food looked good in a wholesome and handknitted sort of way, but she wondered why people stuffed themselves with some of the other things in the window.

After five minutes, Gavin had not emerged from the building and Kate was bored. It was time to move on. She walked back across the High Street and through Radcliffe Square into the Schools Quadrangle of the Bodleian. The porter in the Proscholium, through the big glass doors, would let her use his phone to call Andrew.

'How about tea?' he said. 'In the Convocation House. I rather fancy a large slice of their frosted carrot cake. And it must be doing me so much good, don't you think?'

Well, thought Kate, as much good as the red kooga and garlic capsules in the shop window. But it was kind of Andrew to meet her and offer his help. She mustn't think of his incipient paunch or remember the lean figure of her running don, Liam. Not *your* running don, Kate, she reminded herself, while wondering if he would be clever enough to find her ex-directory phone number.

The Convocation House coffee shop was noisy and echoing, but thankfully smoke-free, and she and Andrew chose themselves large slices of cake and a pot of Earl Grey tea. Kate paid for both of them.

'Now,' said Andrew, when they had sat down at an empty table in one corner, 'let's look at this list of yours.' He read it through. 'Hmm. Well, these names don't mean much to me, but I'll see what I can find in the reference section, though they might just be too recent to be listed in the current editions.'

'They looked venerable to me,' said Kate. 'Old. Well established.'

'Brass does that,' said Andrew, pushing back a lock of red hair with sour-creamed fingers. 'And if you were planning something dodgy, that's just the image you'd go for, isn't it?'

'So you don't think it's all in my imagination?'

'Yes,' said Andrew. 'I do. But I'm a sweet and lovely man and I'll look them up for you anyway.'

Kate wondered whether she should tell him about the lemon-flavoured frosting in his hair, or whether she should ignore it, like the lady she wasn't. She opted for restraint.

When she got back to Fridesley, on an impulse she turned down Rosamund Road and stopped outside 23: Gavin and Penny's house. Gavin was surely still inside the planning consultants' office in King Edward Street. Penny would be at work for another hour, and she would collect the children from the minder on her way home. It was odd how you could tell from outside that a house was empty, but even so, it would be reckless to try and get into it. But why not? If she could look around while Gavin and Penny were out, she might find evidence that Gavin was being blackmailed by Yvonne, or that he had been feeding information from the Council to the Planning Consultants. The thing to do was to get on and do it before she thought about it and changed her mind.

She walked up the path and rang the bell. No reply. She stepped across a flowerbed to the side gate: it wasn't bolted, it opened easily. She closed it behind her. Now she was hidden from curious eyes. She looked around. If you had young children, you would leave a key hidden somewhere, just in case. Under that brick, for example. Oh yes.

Inside, there was a smell of cooked mince and damp laundry. Kate moved swiftly through the kitchen. Behind the large front room, scattered with construction kits, was a small room, dominated by a large photograph of a whale, that appeared to be dedicated to Gavin. Kate went to the desk and started leafing through the papers piled on it.

She recognized Yvonne's handwriting on a postcard: 'Thank you, Gavin. How sensible of you, and how kind!'

She thought about slipping it into her pocket, but what sort of evidence was it? She could put the interpretation she wanted on the message, but it would be difficult to convince anyone else that it referred to blackmail. Perhaps Gavin had lent Yvonne a running schedule, or Xeroxed some posters for the Friends of Fridesley Fields. She looked quickly through the rest of the letters and notes, but there was nothing that looked like hard evidence. And she could scarcely expect Gavin to leave traces of his dishonesty over planning applications lying around for people to find.

She looked round the room again: pinboard with details of meetings, shelves full of paperbacks, a dusty Amstrad PCW.

Like most writers, Kate's first word processor had been an Amstrad and she knew how to boot it up and search through the floppies that Gavin had labelled and stored in a clear plastic box. She found the Locoscript disk, switched the machine on, and pushed the disk into the drive.

The telephone rang.

The sound was so loud in the empty house that Kate's heart started thudding in her chest. She ejected the disk, threw it back in the box, switched off the Amstrad and ran from the room, banging into the lump of metal that Gavin used to prop open the door. As she rubbed her shin, she saw that it looked like an oversized version of the key that she had used to put her quick-assembly bookcase together, the one that had always leant drunkenly to one side. Whatever it was, it was solid and heavy, and it hurt.

She let herself out of the back door again, locked the back door, hid the key under the brick, and slipped out through the side gate, as the phone at last stopped ringing. By the time she got home, she felt as though she had been for a long, hard run.

Half an hour after she got back to her house, there was a ring at her doorbell.

'May I come in?'

Detective Sergeant Taylor. Clean, neat, conservative, alien.

'What is it this time?' she asked, when they were both sitting down. 'More dirty pictures for me to look at?'

'We're investigating another crime, that may or may not be connected with the death of Mrs Baight,' he said in his careful, neutral voice. Kate was tempted to needle him again, but resisted. Had she been spotted coming out of Gavin's house?

'The disappearance of a collection of enamel boxes,' he said, and Kate was glad she had kept her mouth shut. 'Any idea what I'm talking about, Miss Ivory?'

They both looked over towards Kate's mantelpiece with

its assortment of figures and small objects. 'Nothing in enamel, I'm afraid,' she said. 'One flower-decorated porcelain box, a present from a friend, but enamel is a bit pricey for me.'

Paul Taylor got up and wandered across to the fireplace, the way he had the previous time.

'And if you want to tidy something up, there's a really challenging cupboard under the stairs,' said Kate, before he could touch anything.

He turned and grinned at her. 'I like straight lines.'

'I noticed.'

'I'm talking about a collection of early nineteenth-century enamels, the property of a Mr Keith Smith.' The voice was impersonal again.

Kate looked puzzled.

'You may know him as Theo.'

'Oh, Rose's husband.'

'He is at present living in Redbourne Road with a friend, and the collection of boxes disappeared on the night of Mrs Baight's death. We don't like coincidences.'

'Neither do I,' said Kate, without thinking. 'They must be connected.'

'Yes.' And he waited for her to speak.

'Sorry,' she said. 'Like I said before, I'm a simple, hardworking writer, and I have no information for you.' She thought of the Sainsbury's bag in her workroom and hoped he wouldn't ask for a tour of her house.

He looked as if he wanted to shake her, but he stared at her for a few moments instead and then walked towards the door. As she let him out, she thought she heard him mutter, 'Stupid cow.'

Kate closed the door and went to phone Rose.

'Come and get the bloody boxes back,' she said. 'They're not safe here.'

Chapter Seventeen

'Hallo, Kate? Liam Ross here.'

Kate's spirits lifted out of their despond.

'How did you find my number?'

'That bit was easy: I popped into Bodley and tracked down your foodie friend.'

'And he gave it to you, just like that?'

'He did after I'd told him a tiny fib, or a slight exaggeration, maybe, about how well we knew one another and how I had promised to let you know about a Janáček concert.'

'But I hate Janáček.'

There was a short silence while Kate realized that she had said the wrong thing.

'The tricky bit,' said Liam, eventually, 'was ringing your number and finding you at home.'

'I've been out on my researches,' said Kate. 'For the new novel.'

'What happened to the murder investigation?'

'Does *everyone* know about that?'

'Well, everyone who was in the Crypt and within hearing distance of your clear and carrying voice.'

'And who were listening to other people's conversations.'

'Doesn't everyone? I thought it was why people ate alone in restaurants. But I had to track you down after that and find out what it was about. It was like finding an exciting book, getting as far as chapter five, and then leaving it on the train.'

'So what about this Janáček concert?'

'But you hate Janáček.'

It was Kate's turn to fall silent.

'What about going for a walk, instead,' said Liam. 'We could take a look at Fridesley Fields and see what's happening there.'

Fridesley Fields were not an attractive sight in March.

'I don't know how you can be so lukewarm about it, Kate,' said Liam the next afternoon, as they walked along the footpath.

'Not so much lukewarm, just uninvolved,' Kate replied, feeling that she was being got at, and resenting it. 'There's only time for so much involvement in my life. You have to choose your priorities, don't you? And protecting every square yard of Oxford from development isn't mine.'

'But this is where you live. You have to protect it. This development that everyone's talking about is just behind your house. Well, a quarter of a mile away, anyway.'

'But you can't conserve every little patch of green; there's too much of that going on, with Oxford's privileged defending everything they own, and keeping out the rest of us. And I have got involved now, you know. I've looked at the Structure Plan and seen where the Green Belt goes. I shall turn up at the public inquiry and make my voice heard, too.

But this piece of land is quite uninteresting as it stands, so why not build a wonderful great leisure complex all over it?'

This wasn't the way she had planned it. They were supposed to go for a gentle walk through the Fields and along the Meadow, while they talked about their lives, their dreams, their interests. But somehow she found herself telling him about Rose, Theo, and the boxes. She hadn't meant to, but she found that whatever problem was absorbing her at a given time, that was what she talked about.

Obviously, Liam hadn't understood why she was doing the investigating: any sensible person left that sort of thing to the police. So she told him about Yvonne and the blackmail, while managing to hide the details of Camilla's involvement. The explanations had taken them across Port Meadow to Wolvercote and back. They were not supposed to have a loud argument about the merits or otherwise of the development scheme, either, but as they looked out over Fridesley Fields, the subject came up.

'You can't take this place for granted: it won't be here for anyone, however privileged they are, in a few years' time if you do that. Haven't you walked along here in the early morning, watched the mist clear, seen the horses and the cows grazing there, maybe even a heron fishing by the riverbank? And all that almost in the shadow of the colleges. You look across to Oxford and all you can see are green trees with the yellow brick tower of St Barnabas' with its triangular green hat and the spire of St Andrew's sticking up out of them. It's not just the University, is it, Kate? It's a city that belongs to all of us. You think how beautiful it is from a distance when the sun catches its spires, and then close to, when you see the detail of those golden buildings, it's even better.'

'They're not taking away the whole of Port Meadow, just a swampy bit of the Fields. I didn't know you felt so passionately about it.'

'You think of me as living in my college world, cut off from the rest of the life of the city, don't you? You think I go in through that small black door in Broad Street, chain my bike up in the shed, and go off into my medieval maze of buildings, my village in the middle of a city, and forget about everyone else. And yes, that is part of the truth about me, I admit it. It's very important to me, what happens at Leicester: it's like my family. For a lot of my day I live behind the grey stone wall that stretches down Parks Road, and I look out across green velvet lawns to the grey stone-work of the New Bodleian, and I invite my students to my rooms for their tutorials. But I get outside too, you know. I put on my tracksuit and my running shoes and I watch the sun rise as I come out of the darkness of Wytham Woods. I see the sky streaked grey and gold, and I love the way I can live in a city that is surrounded by wild open spaces, where I can breathe without taking in car exhaust fumes, and run for miles over footpaths without seeing anyone but a fellow runner or a crew out practising on the river.'

'And so? I run through Port Meadow and up through Wytham Woods. I go along the bridle path to Chilswell Farm and up through Boar's Hill. I can stand up on the hill and see the view that inspired Matthew Arnold, and I can look across to the Chilterns and watch a dozen gliders floating on the golden air of a summer's afternoon. And my spirits lift and I think how lucky I am to live in such a beautiful place. But what difference is one small development going to make to any of that? He's going to build a new road, he's going to provide minibuses into town, he'll even build a new swimming pool. Oxford isn't just for people like you and me, it's for ordinary people who need jobs and whose children need schools and entertainment and hope if they're not going to go hotting in Blackbird Leys. He's going to tidy the place up, isn't he? The Postle may be a naturalist's delight, but it's an eyesore at the moment. It's full of New Age travellers with their empty beer cans and their mess and noise, and squatters and their pack of flea-ridden dogs. They break into houses and warehouses and help themselves to what they want. They demand money for food for their dogs when they meet you in the street, and they swear at you when you refuse. Is that what you're trying to protect?'

'You don't realize what he's going to do, do you? You've been taken in by the public relations exercise the man's been mounting.'

'I've looked at the plans,' said Kate, indignantly.

'And would you trust a man who got rid of the original people who lived on the Postle in the way he did? Do you realize how they were terrorized for the year before they went? Yes, the squatters are there now, because they'll move into any empty house and they like to defy authority. But there were six ordinary, not very well off, families living there before Tom Grant made sure their electricity was switched off and their phones were vandalized. Their post wasn't delivered, because the postman was attacked in the dark mornings and they had to collect their mail from the sorting office. Their small shop, where they could buy bread and milk and a tin of baked beans, was closed. Didn't your information from the Friends tell you all this?'

'The odd thing is,' said Kate slowly, 'that it didn't mention any of it, and I'm beginning to wonder why. It's just possible that the Friends were dominated by someone who was secretly in favour of the scheme.' Penny, she thought. Gavin? Yvonne? No, not Yvonne. Barbara, perhaps. Gavin was favourite.

Their footsteps thundered over the wooden bridge at the Peter's stream, the sound magnified as it bounced off the water racing and foaming below them, and seeming to echo Liam's anger at Grant. They stopped and leaned over the bridge, staring into the water below them. The canal above was dark green, still and secretive. Kate stared into the water, wishing that she could love Janáček, wishing she could care as much as Liam did about Fridesley Fields instead of being obsessed with finding the murderer of Yvonne Baight.

A figure was approaching, joining them on the bridge. Kate heard his footsteps, not as firm, not as angry as hers and Liam's. She turned round. The man was in his sixties, hardly her own height, but broad and wind tanned, with the ruddy complexion and coarsened features of the heavy drinker. He held a long T-shaped metal rod in his hand. Now where have I seen one of those before, wondered Kate, as she pressed her back against the bridge and hoped that Liam was as strong as he looked.

'I'm just closing the sluice,' said the man. He must have noticed how nervous Kate was, because he smiled at her, and breathed beer fumes all over her while he climbed laboriously up a couple of steps and fitted his windlass into a socket. 'Floods are subsiding now,' he told them, as though they hadn't noticed for themselves. 'No more rain forecast for the next few days. If you can believe the silly buggers,' he added.

'You do that, do you?' asked Liam. 'Open and close the sluice gates when there's danger of flooding? I'd have thought it was done by a computer these days.'

'Stand us a drink at the Cobblers and I'll tell you all about it,' said the man, slyly.

'I don't think the Cobblers is open yet,' said Liam, digging in a pocket and finding a couple of pound coins. 'But have one on us later.'

'I look after the next lock along,' said the man. 'Fridesley Lock, that is. I come down here and open and close this sluice gate, according to the weather. Maybe it is only three or four times a year there's danger of flooding, but it's on the wild nights they want me out here in the dark and the rain, frigging around with a bloody windlass.'

'Pity they don't have to do it themselves a few times,' said Liam sympathetically. 'Still, I expect you've got a mate helps you out, haven't you?'

'What you trying to say?' he said, belligerently. 'You can't tell me I've neglected my job.'

'We wouldn't dream of it,' said Liam, smoothly, and he took Kate's arm and led her away from the bridge and towards Binsey and Port Meadow.

'You think that's what happened?' asked Kate when they were out of earshot. 'Someone opened and closed the sluice at the wrong time. They flooded those houses on purpose to persuade the people in them they should move on or sell out to Grant and his partners?'

185

'Yes,' said Liam. 'I do. They were two feet under water. Their cellars were flooded, their carpets and furniture ruined.'

'I wish we could have found out who did it.'

'You'd have thought that a man walking round with a windlass in his hand would have been pretty noticeable.'

'Not if it was in the boot of his car. He could have driven up to the end of Peter's Lane and parked behind those trees over there,' said Kate. 'Even the people on the Postle wouldn't have seen him if it was a dark night, and I've seen one of those key things before somewhere, but I can't think where at the moment. It'll come to me, I suppose,' said Kate.

Above them came the stirring of wings and the syncopated honking of a skein of geese as they flew in their wedge-shaped formation back to their grazing on the Meadow for the night. The sky on their right was turning from blue to a pale green colour, and ahead of them crouched the darkly wooded hill of Wytham. They couldn't see the foxes, the badgers, the deer, but they knew they were there and would stay as long as there was a habitat where they could live and breed.

Liam turned back to look across the Fields. To Kate, they looked like any other stretch of rough ground, with waving, yellowing grass and a few dull leafless bushes. 'Does it really matter what they build on it?' she asked.

'It's not going to be some People's Temple, you know,' Liam said, waving his long arms at the green water of the canal, the unattractive hump of the Postle. 'It's going to be one expensive development, catering for the rich. They'll be able to stay at his clubhouse, have an office or a flat in his expensive block, park their BMWs and their Mercedes in his underground garage. And how many jobs will that keep going at Cowley? You think the Maestro drivers will be able to afford his prices? And when the customers have overeaten in his restaurant and indulged in his bars, they can go and work it off in his gymnasium, with all his shiny equipment. They can swim in his azure-blue fifty-metre pool, play squash on his glass-backed courts, and sweat in his sauna.'

'But we need a swimming pool on this side of town, and more sports facilities. What's wrong with that?'

'They're not going to be open to people like you and me, Kate. There's going to be a club with a four-figure entry fee and a long waiting list. "Exclusive" is the word he'll use in his brochures. And that means that ordinary people, people who need those facilities, people who today can walk over those fields for free, will be shut out.'

'You're exaggerating. You must be. How do you know it was Grant who did all that on the Postle? Have you got any evidence?'

'Ask yourself who benefited and the answer is Grant and his associates. But no, there's no evidence. It looks as though a man that rich is above the law. Oh, I think they caught one thick lad from Berinsfield with a shaved head and tattoos on the back of his hands, who had a crowbar in his hand and was smashing windows. They gave him thirty days. I expect Grant compensated him for his time when he got out, don't you? Just one more thing, though. I suppose you know that the original application was turned down?'

'I read about it. And then he put in a second application with modifications.'

'The plan was almost identical, but this time he used a different planning consultant. It's an odd thing, but there's one agent in Oxford who always seems to get plans through for people, even when they've been turned down before.'

'Gavin,' said Kate, thoughtfully. 'Have you heard of a firm called White and Darke?'

'Yes. That's the one I'm talking about.'

'This is starting to fit together,' said Kate.

The light was leaving the sky as they turned down Binsey Lane and then took the left turning to Fridesley.

'Are you coming back to my place?' asked Kate. The question, with its reverberations, hung in the air. It should have been a simple query, but somehow this evening it wasn't.

'My bike is chained to your lamppost.'

'And I still don't see what any of this had to do with Yvonne,' said Kate. 'OK, so she was an enthusiastic member of the Friends of Fridesley Fields, but so were plenty of other people. And from what you were saying, a little preservation society like ours wasn't going to worry Tom Grant much, was it?'

'She was a powerful ally to have,' said Liam. 'She had some standing in the community, after all.'

'Oh, come on,' said Kate, 'who takes a dentist that seriously? Doctors, yes. But dentists, unless you've got an abscess or a filling has just fallen out, you don't take them seriously. They're a bit of a joke. I mean, can you imagine a dentist as the hero of a romantic novel?'

'That's the criterion we're applying, is it?' said Liam.

'You know what I mean,' said Kate, hating the way he was being pedantic and donnish at her woolly thinking.

'What was she going to do to stop Grant? Attack him with her high-speed drill? Threaten to floss his teeth for him?'

Now that the wind had dropped, it was warm for March, and the sky had a clear, rainwashed look, with flecks and streaks of cloud like the feathers of Miss Price's grey parrot. She wished that she could get out of this argument with Liam. This wasn't how she had imagined their time together. She wished he would shut up about Fridesley Fields and Grant and the Postle, and just take hold of her hand, so they could walk – like what? old friends, lovers maybe? – back to her snug little dolls' house. They could share a bottle of wine, she would cook them a simple but sophisticated meal, they would sit side by side on her pink velvet sofa and lean against her hand-embroidered cushions. She had even washed up her breakfast dishes. She had food in her fridge. She could put the sort of music that even he would approve of on her compact disc player. She would have to invest in a whole collection of new CDs, because she couldn't play him anything as naff as Tchaikovsky, or as overplayed as Mozart. Why couldn't he be a historian instead of a musician? She could have left out all the books she used for background information and only hidden her Dorothy Dunnetts, and played the sort of music she enjoyed herself without worrying that he would disapprove of it. It was as bad as cooking a casual meal for a renowned chef.

'Ignoring your flippancy for the moment,' said Liam, still waving his arms around and scowling at the beauties of the evening sky, 'there might have been something that Grant was afraid of. There might have been something that she had found out and was going to use against him. After all, we do know that she was a ruthless woman in that way: using information that came into her hands for her own ends.'

They turned the corner into Josephine Street. Just a few yards away was Agatha Street and the lights of her house, that she had left on as always so that there would be something to welcome her home. Perhaps the evening would end up the way she had planned, after all. Mind you, she wasn't sure about this man. She certainly couldn't read him the way she could Andrew.

'Would you like to come in for tea?' she asked. 'I could make us a simple meal later, if you like.' But Liam was looking at his watch.

'Sorry, Kate,' he said. 'I'd love to, some other time. But now I have to get back to a rehearsal. There are a dozen people turning up at Leicester for me in fifteen minutes' time, and I'd better be there.'

He had left his bike chained to the lamppost by her house, and it took him only seconds to unchain it. 'I'll be in touch,' he said as he mounted. He stared at her as she stood in the dusk, getting cold, wishing he would stay. 'Why couldn't you have got involved with the Friends of Fridesley Fields earlier?' he said, as though he was angry with her. 'We could have met a year ago, instead of . . .' But he was mounting his bike, and she wasn't even sure that he intended to finish his sentence. Then he was riding down Agatha Street, disappearing round the corner into the Fridesley Road.

Kate let herself into her house, thought about the wine in the fridge and the chicken in its marinade. She rang Andrew, who could always be relied on to be hungry, then went back into the kitchen to peel a lot more potatoes. Perhaps he would have news for her about the names she had copied down from the door of the offices in King Edward Street. At least he would fill up the empty space left by Liam's departure.

The phone rang.

'Kate, it's important. I have to talk to you. Now. I've been trying your number for hours. Where have you been? I'm coming round right away.'

'Calm down, Millie.'

'You wouldn't feel calm if you'd just learned what I've learned.'

'Give me a chance to speak, will you? I've got Andrew turning up in the next half-hour.' She licked whipped cream and melted dark chocolate off her fingers. It needed the addition of alcohol. 'Do you want to unburden yourself to him, too?'

'No.'

'I thought not. Now, why don't you tell me all about it on the phone? Or in the morning: that would be even better.'

'It's not a phone sort of thing. Can't you get rid of Andrew?'

'No, he's bringing me some information, and he's hungry.'

'Sod Andrew, he's always hungry. Well, I suppose it will have to wait until tomorrow. I'm tied up most of the day; can you make it sixish?'

Camilla sounded calmer, but not a lot.

'Come round here at six, and I'll pour you a large drink.'

She remembered after she had put the phone down that

sixish was the time she had promised herself she would sit down at her word processor and start drafting chapter two of her book. She went back into the kitchen, poured a glass of rum into the chocolate mixture, and started gently whisking.

Chapter Eighteen

Andrew wiped sauce from his face with Kate's best table napkin and said, 'That was delicious. Have you made one of your marvellous puds for us, too?'

In spite of Camilla's phone call, she had made two. There was homemade lemon-flavoured ice-cream with chunks of preserved ginger folded into it and a sprinkling of toasted almond flakes, which she served with *langues de chat*. And then, when she realized that it was going to be Andrew rather than Liam, she had put together something in a crisp shell, rich with chocolate, rum, and too much double cream. She poured out the rest of the wine for him before she brought in the puds. His face was already glowing pink, and she thought it would not be long before the small blood vessels gave his face the permanently healthy glow of the heavy drinker, and his figure the paunch of the greedy man that he was becoming. Oh well, at least he was more interested in food than in sex, and needed only the slightest of refusals to give up his attempts to get her into bed. He was a good friend, but really she didn't fancy him very much these days, and their occasional trips to bed, which she thought they both accepted out of politeness rather than lust, were friendly but unexciting. It was a pity that he wouldn't come out running with them: a bit of exercise would do wonders both for his libido and for his attractiveness. But she knew, really, that Andrew was happy the way he was. He didn't want a woman to tidy up his untidy house and invade his life.

She let him spoon in the last of the rum and chocolate, then carried in strong coffee for him, a glass of mint tea for herself.

'I don't know how you can drink that muck. What is it tonight?'

'Infusion of spinach,' she said, just to confirm his prejudices. 'Now, I've been wonderfully patient, don't you think?'

'You want to know what I've found out for you?' He pretended surprise, though he must have known that she had been waiting all evening to hear what he had brought. As he spoke they moved from the table to settle themselves in comfortable velvet-covered chairs in front of the gas fire. Andrew sank back into his chair, stretched out his legs and undid a button at his waistband. 'Well, your detecting led me to three people who are relevant for our enquiry. One of them we might have guessed, the other two are more surprising.'

Andrew was going to be pompous again, she thought, and if she tried to hurry him into giving her his findings he would get increasingly pedantic. He would even move into the passive voice, which drove her wild. He does it to annoy, she reminded herself, so that he can laugh at my over-reaction, and she kept quiet with an effort.

'The first person, the one we already knew about, was Mr Grant,' said Andrew. 'Thomas Grant. He appeared from nowhere in the sixties and started making money. Big money, Kate. He had a nose for what would be successful and he got in on things before other people, and while there was still a lot of money to be made. He also got out of areas that were going down. He took risks, he borrowed money, and made more. He made his base in Oxford back in the mid-seventies. All in all, the man is worth hundreds of millions. And as you have probably guessed, that money gives him power. He can buy people and permissions. He has a stake in television companies, newspapers, and magazines, as well as in book publishing. He owns a shipping line and a finance house. With that money and power he can defy the law. He will happily pay a fine for demolishing a building he should not have demolished, because the profit he receives makes the fine derisory. Too many people are in his pocket, and you and I would like to see him fall, but we are not likely to succeed, I am afraid. Perhaps already you are hoping that we can pin the murder of Yvonne Baight on to him, but I have to disappoint you. Mr Grant has been in North America for the past three weeks, and is even now boarding a plane from New York to Toronto. So cross him off your list, Kate. His influence and his money are involved in this story, I'm sure, but Mr Grant himself is not.'

'And what are your other finds?' asked Kate, knowing that Andrew wanted to be coaxed and appreciated. 'This is awfully clever of you, Andrew. I hope it didn't take you away from your real work for too long.' Was she overdoing it? No, Andrew was smiling at her.

'It's a question of knowing where to look, whom to call, isn't it, Kate?'

'Yes, Andrew,' she said dutifully, 'what would I do without you?'

'Well, we can write off Mr White, too. I think he was only taken on for his inoffensive name and his impeccably upright reputation. He's lost most of his marbles now, though, poor old boy, and his share of the loot from the company which has his name is keeping him in an expensive nursing home in Buckinghamshire.'

Kate refused to ask about the last name. She had done enough, feeding Andrew's ego and stomach, for one evening. He wouldn't be able to resist telling her in a minute, anyway. She thought about pouring him a brandy to help his recall, but she didn't want him to tell her later that he had had too much to drive home, so could he stay here with her?

'Darke,' said Andrew. 'Again, just a planning consultant with no apparent connection with anyone else in your story, until I looked up his family.'

'I didn't realize you had friends at St Catherine's House, Andrew.'

'Nice girl, Julia. We met at Library School. Didn't I ever tell you about her?'

'No, and I don't want to hear now, either.'

'Well, Mr Darke has a daughter, and her name is Barbara.'

'Barbara Darke? I don't think I know her.'

'You might do. She married a man called Davies.'

'Barbara Davies. But it's still quite a common name; it doesn't have to be our Barbara.'

'Do you know her husband's first name?'

'No. If she's ever mentioned it, I've forgotten.'

'Barbara Darke married a Nicholas Davies.'

'Nicholas Davies? N.D.? It would fit in rather neatly.'

'You've got me hoping for one of your coincidences.'

'I'll check; it should be easy enough to find out Barbara's husband's name. He's a councillor, too, apparently on the opposing side to Green Gavin, but maybe that's just for public consumption.'

'So I think I've given you plenty to work on here.'

'You have, Andrew.' She checked off on her fingers. 'A firm of planning consultants sharing a building with the company who are seeking to develop Fridesley Fields, and a lot of familiar characters walking on and off the set. You've given me a possible second bent councillor who is in the pay of Tom Grant and who may or may not have been blackmailed by Yvonne Baight. And I've just remembered something else: Barbara is the most likely one to have destroyed the rota for Wednesday evening.'

'So all you have to do now is establish links between all these and Yvonne, find motive and opportunity for her murder, and present the lot to the police. With a flourish.'

'Thanks, Andrew. I'll start tomorrow, rather than tonight, I think. There's something else I want to check with Sophie, too. And if I'm to sort out all that, I'm going to need an early night. Would you like to give me a hand with the washing-up?'

'Umm,' said Andrew. She knew that the mention of a household chore would shift him. 'I think it's time I got moving, too, Kate. But let me know how you get on, won't you?'

At least the weather had improved. The gales that had

blown for weeks had dropped. The morning's mist had receded and a warm and balmy air had come in from the west. It even felt as though spring flowers might burst into bloom in the next couple of weeks instead of being flattened and pulped by the storms. Kate crossed the Fridesley Road to the church of King Charles the Martyr. A few elderly people were going in for the Sunday morning service. Kate turned right along the Fridesley Road, over the bridge, and left into Christie Road.

There was activity at the Davies's house. Someone was unhooking the curtains in the front room and Kate could hear Barbara giving instructions to someone else. When she opened the door, she was obviously not in a mood to be sociable.

'Yes?' she asked briskly.

Kate looked at her objectively. She was tall and thin, with dark brown hair pulled back off her face. Lines of discontent pulled her mouth down and her once fine skin was March-pale and dry. No one would ever mistake her for Rose, or even for Lynda, and that bossy voice had been urging them to lift and kick and circle for most of the evening.

'I was wondering if I could speak to your husband?' said Kate.

'Nick? Whatever for?'

Bull's eye! 'It was to do with the Friends.'

'Well, you're out of luck. He's in France at the moment and not expected back until tomorrow evening.'

'Has he been away long?' Kate chanced. Nick Davies was in there with a motive if Yvonne had been blackmailing him about accepting bribes to push through a planning application. And Barbara could have told him about the plan to steal Rose's boxes. It was a comforting idea that someone she had never met might have killed Yvonne, instead of one of her friends.

Two vertical lines had appeared between Barbara's eyes and she shouted over her shoulder, 'Be careful with that stereo!' Kate continued to look persistent and Barbara finally answered, 'Since last Tuesday morning, but I don't see it's any of your business if we're buying ourselves a holiday cottage.'

'Thanks so much,' said Kate, and left. Reluctantly, she crossed Nick off her mental list of suspects. If Barbara was telling the truth, Nick Davies couldn't have done it. It still left Barbara as a possible, though. She walked back towards Redbourne Road and the Baight house.

'You know I'll help in any way I can,' said Sophie, after she had shown Kate up to her studio room. 'Have your questions led anywhere yet? What is it you need to know?'

'Not yet. You said that no one broke into the house,' began Kate. 'So I was wondering how many keys there were, and who had them.'

Sophie thought for a moment before answering. 'Well, I had one, of course, and so did Yvonne. Then Jean, who runs the cleaning service, had one that she gave out to the team that came in to do the housework.'

'I suppose I ought to check that one out,' Kate said, without enthusiasm. How could she, without the resources of the police, follow up all the cleaners employed by an agency?

'I think that the police already enquired into that and found that it didn't lead anywhere,' said Sophie. 'They thought it was more likely that someone knew that we kept a spare key in the garden shed and used that. But I don't see how anyone could know, do you?'

'I wouldn't be too sure in this road,' said Kate. 'People seem to know an awful lot about their neighbours.'

'But what I did forget to tell them,' said Sophie, 'was about the key that Yvonne gave to Carey.'

'Carey! Carey Stanton?'

'They were very good friends,' said Sophie. 'They shared an interest in photography. I think Carey even knew something about those things that people perch on their shoulders and walk around with.'

'Parrots? Or video cameras?' guessed Kate.

'I think Yvonne liked the idea of movement, and sound, of course.'

And when Kate thought about the sort of photographs that Yvonne had been in the habit of taking, that made sense.

'Thanks very much for your help,' said Kate, standing up. 'I'll have to be going: I've got some more questions to ask people about the night of the . . . Wednesday night.'

'I'll come with you,' said Sophie, unexpectedly.

'I don't think—' started Kate.

'I know most people round here: they came to get their teeth fixed by Yvonne, you see. She had a very good reputation as a dentist.'

Kate's teeth ached at the thought of Yvonne prodding at sensitive nerves, but she stopped arguing, smiled and nodded and followed Sophie out of the room.

'Would you like to see where it happened?' Sophie asked, as they went down the stairs.

It should have been easy to say no. 'Yes,' said Kate, who didn't want to see it at all.

Yvonne's studio was different again from Sophie's room above it. The walls were the rough-cut wood of the rest of the house, the curtains were the thick dark blue velvet that Camilla had described, the floor covered with a blue and green patterned fitted carpet. In one corner stood the standard grey filing cabinet, all the drawers closed now. The large table was furnished with an efficient-looking light and there were machines that Kate didn't recognize, presumably to do with Yvonne's photography and video making. Kate, who couldn't even use an Instamatic with any competence, knew nothing about any of them.

Also in the room was a velvet-covered *chaise-longue*, draped with an old sixties shawl, and a series of Georgia O'Keefe posters: huge, brilliantly coloured, erotic flowers. A pansy, a canna lily, a camellia.

Kate started to make a connection with something she had seen recently, but Sophie said:

'She was lying over there,' pointing to a patch on the carpet that looked like every other patch.

'Have you any idea at all who might have wanted to kill her?' Kate asked.

'No. I can't imagine. What about you? Have you come across anything that might give someone a motive?'

'Not yet,' said Kate, conveniently forgetting all she had learned in the past twenty-four hours. 'Have you heard any more about her blackmailing . . . *if* she was a blackmailer, of course?'

'No. And I still refuse to believe it.'

'I have an idea her death might have something to do

with the development scheme for the Fields,' said Kate, hoping that Sophie would add something to what she already knew. 'Yvonne was a very effective campaigner, and I think that the people she was opposing may have been pretty ruthless. There's a man called Grant, who seems to have been behind it all.' She wished now that she hadn't said so much: it was all supposition; she shouldn't be spreading gossip like this.

But Sophie said, 'Tom Grant? But I like him.'

'Have you met him?'

'Once or twice. And I know about his plans for the Fields. Yvonne had her own reasons for opposing him, but that was because she didn't understand properly what the development would mean. And anyway, it was more of a vendetta with her.'

She and Sophie left the room and carried on downstairs, where Sophie picked a navy jacket from a row of coats by the back door. It looked as though Yvonne's had not been moved yet. Had the police asked her to leave everything as it was, or hadn't Sophie come to terms yet with Yvonne's death? Perhaps she was unable to do so until her mother's murderer was found.

They walked down the tarmacked path that ran along the northern edge of the playing field. The floods had subsided at last, the seagulls flown. The ditches at the far end were still full of water and in the pearly light the grass was a brilliant poisonous green. But although it still looked very muddy, the local children could once more play football on it, the local dogs deposit their faeces.

A few yards down the path and there was another small street leading up to Fridesley Road: Wheatfield Road.

Kate, and presumably the rest of the group, had run down this way on Wednesday evening when they had been out on their lap of the lookout run. It all looked quite different today, in daylight, with twigs and roof slates all cleared up. But the same man was encased in black leather, bum cleavage in evidence, revving the engine of his powerful motorbike, threatening to leave another layer of rubber on the tarmac as he accelerated away.

'Clarke!' came a voice from the corner house, and a small, thin grey-haired woman in a blue pinafore and felt slippers came out of the house. 'Just you come back here, my lad. Don't you go off like that without a word to me.'

The young man removed his helmet and turned from alien being to a balding, plump-faced middle-aged man with the expression of a guilty twelve-year-old. 'Sorry, Mum,' he said. 'What did I forget?'

'You didn't tell me where you was going and when you'd be back,' she said, and her son dutifully replied, 'Down the Club,' and 'back for me dinner,' before putting his helmet on again and disappearing in blue exhaust fumes up the road.

'Hallo, Mrs Graybel,' said Sophie. 'How are you this morning?'

'Can't complain,' said Mrs Graybel, looking as though she was about to.

'I was just wondering whether you saw anything on the night of the murder,' said Sophie.

'Wednesday? Well, Clarke was off on his bike again, and I was asking him where he was going, and we saw the girl with the fat bum in the baggy trousers and the funny hat go running by. I dunno why she was out in all that storm, it doesn't seem right to me, a big girl like that, but then, it takes all sorts, I suppose, dunnit?'

'Too right,' said Kate, wondering which of them qualified for the description of the one with the fat bum. She looked at Mrs Graybel: she weighed all of six and a half stone, and any of them would look enormous next to her. And so much, she thought, for their wonderful alibi. Half of Fridesley seemed to have noticed them out and running that night, though no one seemed able to tell them apart. And what sort of hat would Mrs Graybel describe as 'funny'?

'Course,' Mrs Graybel was saying, 'you both go out, doing that jogging, don't you. You wouldn't catch me at it, I can tell you.'

'Quite right,' said Kate, who was used to insults about joggers. 'They say it's bad for you, don't they?'

Mrs Graybel looked put out at having her line pinched, and Kate and Sophie said goodbye and moved on up the road. But although she had Sophie to tell her who people were and what they did, and to introduce her to those who were available to be questioned, Kate didn't meet anyone who had seen anything or heard anything at all useful, though she did pick up on the local gossip.

Sophie looked at her watch. 'I've got another policeman coming to see me in half an hour. I'd better get back and get the place tidy for him. I hate people to come in and find the place in a muddle.'

'Thanks for your help,' said Kate.

'We don't seem to have learned much, do we?' said Sophie. 'Isn't it awful the way no one sees and hears anything? Are you going to try any more doors?'

'I think I may knock off for the morning.' It must be

getting on for lunchtime after all these house calls, surely.
She tried to remember whether Gavin was one of the
people wearing a funny hat – one of Rose's hats, that was
– on the night of the murder, but it was no good, she
just couldn't.

'Can you remember who was wearing Rose's hat on
Wednesday?' she asked. She still couldn't describe it as 'the
night of the murder' when she spoke to Sophie, though she
noticed that Sophie herself used the word.

Sophie thought for a moment. 'I think Barbara wore it,
and didn't she pass it on to Gavin? But I'm afraid that my
memory of that evening is a bit hazy. Everything got pushed
out of my mind by what happened later.'

'You've been a great help,' said Kate.

'No, you're the one who's helping,' said Sophie, looking
earnestly into Kate's face. It really was a pity about the
moustache, thought Kate. But the woman could make
something of herself if she had a bit more style. 'You're
really going to find out who killed Yvonne, aren't you?'

'I've got a good idea already,' said Kate. 'But proving it's
the tricky bit. And I'm not looking forward to trying to
convince the police about it. But I can't let him get away
with it, can I?'

'Let me know how you get on,' said Sophie. 'The police
don't tell me much at all, and I want to know what's happening.' She put her hand on Kate's arm for a moment. 'We've
got time for one last call, haven't we? Why don't we go and
talk to this man who's your prime suspect? It would be less
dangerous with two of us there.'

It would, though Kate hadn't wanted to confide her
suspicions about Gavin to anyone else at the moment. She

could so easily be mistaken, and it would be wrong to leave people with the vague feeling that there was something sinister about him if in fact he was innocent. But then, this was Sophie, and if anyone had a right to know it was she.

'Don't you want to tidy up for your policemen?'

Sophie shook her head. 'There'll be enough time afterwards.'

'Come on, then,' said Kate.

'Where are we going?'

Kate led the way to Gavin's house.

It was one of those that had been recently tarted up, with a new front door, and none of your softwood from MFI, either, but something heavy in hardwood, with brass door furniture. There were indeed Austrian blinds at the windows, and Kate recognized a Liberty print that she had rather fancied for her own sitting room before settling for something cheaper at Debenham's. She concentrated on all these details so that she shouldn't feel embarrassed to remember her last visit to the house and the way she had let herself in through Gavin's back door.

'Do you want to ask us some questions, or will staring through our windows do you?'

Gavin. She hadn't noticed him coming out through the gate that led to the back of the house, wheeling a bicycle. It was a plain but expensive-looking bike and it looked as though Gavin had been spending his Sunday morning looking after it.

'I thought he usually rode a tricycle,' whispered Sophie. 'With a trailer on the back for collecting recyclable material.'

She wasn't sure that she had the nerve to ask Gavin any

questions, although she wanted to know exactly where and when he was doing what on Wednesday evening, and how he had come by all the money that had paid for the expensive extras that she could see lying around. And what was it he did for a living? But Sophie was whispering again in her ear, urging her to go on, ask Gavin some questions.

'We're just out for a walk,' she said to Gavin, after far too long a pause. 'And I thought I'd let you know: the group race is on, after all. I've got permission from the Estates Office to go through the woods, and I'll be printing out the application forms on the word processor this afternoon.' She smiled brightly at him, pleased with this piece of creative dialogue. 'Could you ask Penny to get the maps done as usual: she's so good at routes.'

'Right, well then. Yes.' Gavin had lost the initiative, she was glad to see. It's difficult to be angry with someone openly when they've just given you the thing you said you wanted. 'May the best man win and all that,' he added.

She looked at him as though for the first time: that wasn't a soft face at all, but a weak one with a strong trace of self-interest. He could be dangerous. She smiled brightly at him and pulled Sophie's arm. 'Come on,' she hissed. Sophie was staring openly at Gavin, at Gavin's house with its expensive additions, at Gavin's bicycle. Gavin stared back at them as they walked on down the road.

'But he's something quite junior in a big firm of accountants; does he really earn enough for all that?' said Sophie.

'Maybe someone left them something in their will. And Penny goes out to work as well, which must help with the money.'

'Yes, but she works so that they can afford to eat. There

are the two children and Penny's mother's always staying.'

Kate couldn't tell Sophie she thought Gavin was on the take from Thomas Grant, since she didn't want to admit to how she had broken into his house and gone through his desk. She didn't like to say, either, that he was probably being blackmailed by Yvonne for it. Even if she didn't want his money, Yvonne knew how to inflict pain all right. And she thought, too, that if he was on the Planning Committee, Gavin could well be part of the reason for the success of Messrs White and Darke, Planning Consultants.

'Isn't it time you got back to your policemen?' she asked Sophie. She wanted time on her own to think about what she had seen and heard.

Sophie seemed unwilling to leave, but when she checked the time, she said that yes, she was cutting it a bit fine, and she thanked Kate effusively again and finally left.

Now that had been a useful bit of sleuthing, Kate thought. She was getting close to the truth there. But she'd have to take a good look at Penny's route for the group's race through Wytham Woods and down through the Meadow and Fridesley Fields. There were too many dark, lonely places, and too many simple blunt instruments around for her safety, and now she came to think of it, she couldn't be sure that Penny was ignorant of what Gavin was doing. She must be very careful of them both until she got him nailed for the murder of Yvonne Baight.

Hold on, she told herself. How are you going to nail him? Should she go to the police at this stage? She would prefer to talk to Andrew, or Liam – though what good an expert on bloody Janáček would be in this situation she wasn't at all sure. She just had this sudden feeling that she would like to lean against the shoulder of a tall, dark man and let him take care of all her problems. It was just as well that there wasn't one available at the moment, or she could make a fool of herself.

Kate stood on the corner of Wheatfield Road, looking up towards the Fridesley Road. She watched as a Morris Minor with large patches of rust remover on its wings drew up at the house a few doors away from her. Two small girls with fair hair escaping from blue scrunches, globular in their duvet coats, got out of the back. One held a violin case, the other a cello. Their mother, who was simply a larger version of the two girls, fixed a Krooklok to the steering-wheel of the car, locked the doors carefully, and shepherded them to the front door.

'Hallo, Valerie,' Kate called. 'Hallo, Amelia and Dorrit.' The children stared at her with veiled blue eyes. *Got it*, thought Kate. Valerie Binns and her two daughters. The delightful Miss Binns. Carey must have been talking about one of the children. And weren't children reckoned to be good and truthful witnesses? She would make one more call before going home. She waved her clipboard at them. 'Just asking a few questions,' she said, as though it was the most natural thing in the world.

'Research for the new book?' asked Valerie. 'But I thought it was a historical thriller.'

'Sort of,' replied Kate. 'But it has modern repercussions.'

'I always wondered where you writers got your ideas from,' said Valerie. Then she opened the front door of number 25. 'Come in, Kate. And in you go, girls. You'll get cold standing about outside.'

The girls dutifully went indoors and disappeared, presumably to put their musical instruments away.

'Aren't they wonderful at that age,' said Valerie. 'So innocent and untouched by the materialism of the modern world. I'd like to keep them like that for as long as possible.'

Perhaps, thought Kate. But that had been a pretty cool and assessing look that young Amelia had shot in her direction before she disappeared. She thought that any information she gained from young Miss Binns would cost her as much as the snippets she extracted from the lock-keeper. She started feeling in her handbag to see what she could find.

'What I mean,' said Valerie, 'is that I know that you've been going round asking everyone questions about Yvonne's murder, and I can see that you want to ask me and the girls something, but I don't want them touched by the sordidness of it, Kate. I want to help you in any way I can, of course I do. I think it's terrible the way that wicked man is still stalking the streets so that none of us is safe, but I want my girls to keep their innocence and their trust in people. You'll have to think of a way of talking to them that doesn't involve murder or anything at all nasty.'

'Trust me,' said Kate. 'I'm the creative one, remember?'

Chapter Nineteen

The three female Binnses all had fair hair escaping from scrunches and falling over their foreheads; they had round blue eyes and submissive mouths and they were dressed in corduroy dungarees and white Reeboks. They sat in a row on Valerie Binns's pretty flowered sofa and looked at Kate with identical expressions and waited for her to begin. Kate smiled her new, dishonest, smile.

'You're so good at noticing things, I've been told,' she said to the two children, 'I'm hoping you can tell me what you saw on Wednesday evening.'

'Why?' said Amelia Binns.

Her younger sister made a long, burbling noise.

'Dorrit sees everything, don't you darling?' said Valerie Binns. 'She takes everything into that little head of hers. But I'm afraid she hasn't quite made the breakthrough into talking. Her sister can understand her, but the rest of us have problems with interpretation. You'll try hard for us, Dorrit darling, won't you?'

How old was she? wondered Kate. Coming up for four, surely? Not backward, just obstinate.

Dorrit made a different burble and her mouth looked less submissive.

'Wednesday evening,' prompted Kate. 'There was an awful storm: the wind was howling, the rain was falling and the dustbin lids were clattering along the road. I expect you had to make sure your bicycles were put away properly.'

Dorrit burbled.

'I had to talk to Elfred,' said Amelia, 'because he was frightened.' She took a small teddy bear from the pocket on the front of her dungarees. 'Elfred,' she said, holding him up to Kate.

'Aren't their imaginations wonderful at that age,' said Valerie, looking fondly at her two daughters. Kate wished that they would answer her questions and let her go home. She wondered if she would get on better with the children if their mother weren't present.

'Do you think I could have a glass of water?' she asked, since nothing more original came into her mind.

'Would you rather have rosehip tea?' asked Valerie.

'Even better,' said Kate, calculating that it would take longer to prepare.

'Now,' she said, when Valerie had left the room, 'tell me what you saw on Wednesday.' She had found a packet of chocolate in her bag and she held it in her hand, but without offering it to the children. She was pretty sure that Valerie wouldn't let them have it to eat if she knew, but Amelia's greedy eyes had taken in the situation.

'There was something,' said Amelia. 'I didn't see it, but Dorrit did.'

Dorrit made an affirmative sound.

'In our shed, where we keep our bikes and some of our

big toys,' said Amelia. Kate handed over two squares of chocolate. There were eight more.

'Rosehip tea,' said Valerie Binns, coming back into the room and putting a cup and saucer on the table next to Kate.

'Have you a little honey to go in it?' asked Kate, who hated sweet drinks. Valerie disappeared.

'She was supposed to be in bed,' said Amelia. 'But she was worried about her dolls' pram, so she went out to the shed.'

'Acacia or orange blossom?' called Valerie from the kitchen.

'Have you got Scottish heather?' called back Kate, handing over two more squares of chocolate and thinking that she would have to supply a damp handkerchief in a moment to remove the evidence from Dorrit's face.

'She found something inside the pram,' said Amelia, eating her chocolate neatly.

Dorrit made a wailing noise, and Amelia produced a tissue, to Kate's relief, and wiped the mess from her sister's face.

'What was it she found?' asked Kate desperately, but Valerie came back into the room with a jar of honey and a long-handled spoon. As she sipped the sweet rosehip tea, Kate thought that it served her right for corrupting the young Binnses like that. Through the french windows at the end of the room she could see into the Binns's garden, with its swing and its climbing frame. On the right-hand side, towards the end of the garden, she saw the shed that Amelia had spoken about. A few feet beyond it was the back wall of the garden, and then the back gardens of the houses in the next road. That must be Redbourne Road, thought Kate, and Theo and Lynda's back garden.

She could see that she was going to get no more information out of the child while her mother was there, so when she had finished her tea she got up to leave.

'I hope you find out who killed Yvonne,' said Valerie as she showed Kate to the door. 'She was our most committed member, you know. Quite frightening in her intensity sometimes, but she really knew how to fight for the Fields, like a crusader, you might say. It really mattered to her, what the outcome was.'

And that, thought Kate, though she didn't say anything, was probably why she was killed. She was just too successful at stopping the scheme from going through.

'What's that on your hand,' Valerie asked Dorrit suddenly. 'It looks like . . .'

Dorrit wailed.

Amelia took the offending hand and looked straight into her mother's pale blue eyes. 'Dorrit says she needs her potty,' she said. 'I'll take her upstairs.'

Dorrit let out a long and protesting burble, but Amelia refused to recant. Kate managed to slip her another two squares of chocolate as she left the room. She thought she might get back to young Miss Binns, and she should keep on the right side of her.

'What lovely children,' she said insincerely to Valerie as she left.

'Aren't they?' said Valerie. 'We do do our best to keep them unspoiled by modern life.'

Actually, Kate thought, Amelia's smile was as dishonest as her own. And as for young Dorrit, she thought she would start talking in a comprehensible way just as soon as she thought it was in her own interest to do so.

She walked back towards the recreation field at the end

of Wheatfield Road and turned right. Ahead of her, leaning out over the field itself, was the Baights' house.

She turned into Redbourne Road. Lynda and Theo's house showed no signs of life at all, but there was a certain amount of geriatric noise coming from the house opposite.

The Gatlocks, thought Kate. And Elma and Betty. She knew she should take the chance to call in and ask them what they had seen, if anything. It was true that Mr Gatlock kept a permanent watch on the street and its happenings, but he was also as deaf as a post, and conversation with him had to be conducted through Elma and Betty, his sisters. Kate wanted her lunch, and she wanted to get on with her book. Boulogne, 1803. She wanted to walk away from Fridesley and into France under Napoleon. And now she remembered that Millie was coming round at sixish, so she would have to stop work again then. Why did detectives in stories never have these problems? They never seemed to get hungry the way she did and yearn for plain chocolate digestives, either.

The old man, with his white hair and deeply tanned, thin, lined face was at his post at his front window, which was, as usual, open so that he could conduct his exhausting conversations with the passers-by. In front of him his tiny front garden was about to burst into bloom with its spring bulbs. His shrubs had been pruned, his leaves picked up, his path swept, and Kate was sure that his back garden was in equally beautiful nick.

'Good morning, Mr Gatlock,' she bellowed. 'Weather looking up a bit today, isn't it?'

'Did you hear what the lady said, Arnold?' shouted Betty.

'What was that? Who's this one?' grumbled Mr Gatlock.

'These females in their trousers and their funny hats, they all look the same to me.'

Oh dear, thought Kate. This is going to be a long session. She took another deep breath and inhaled the smell of Mr Gatlock's well-disguised compost heap.

Betty was leaning close to Mr Gatlock and shouting in his ear. 'This is the one who writes the books, Arnold, and I expect she wants to ask you some questions: she's been around asking everyone else.'

'You can tell her it's no good asking me,' said Mr Gatlock, 'I never read books. Haven't got the time.' When he wasn't in his garden, Mr Gatlock spent his time making dresses for his sisters. It had started as an economy to help his widowed mother when he was a young man and the girls were still children, and had continued as an obsession after the death of his wife. Unfortunately, he had never progressed past the gathered skirt, the Peter Pan collar, the short sleeve, and the sash, of their childhood. Not that Betty and Elma seemed to mind about this, and his sewing was excellent. His brown-spotted hands were working at this moment, on something in pale blue with a pattern of pink rosebuds.

'It's about the night of the storm,' said Kate, loudly, 'the night of Mrs Baight's murder. Did you see anyone, Mr Gatlock?'

'Night of that old dentist's murder, Arnold,' shrieked Elma. 'What was it you saw?'

'She come from over there,' said Mr Gatlock, pointing his tacking thread towards Lynda's house. 'Some female in a hat with dahlias and daffodils on. Don't get them flowering at the same time of year, do you? It don't make sense.'

'And then?' asked Kate. 'Where did she go then?'

'Stop going on about bloody flowers, Arnold,' shouted Betty. 'Where'd the woman go?'

'Over the road to the dentist's,' said Arnold. 'I didn't see no more, I was too busy tying down the lid of the dustbin.'

'That wasn't you, that was us,' said Betty. 'You was just telling us what to do, we was doing all the work.'

'Stupid women,' said Mr Gatlock. 'Wouldn't know what to do if I didn't tell them. But it was a bugger of a night, all right.'

'Didn't you see who it was?' shouted Kate, who was starting to get Mr Gatlock's range. 'It's important.'

'You young females all look the same to me,' said Mr Gatlock. 'And I wasn't going to let my dustbin go flying off over the Fields to go peering up into people's faces, was I?'

'Did you see what she was wearing?' asked Kate. 'Apart from the hat.'

'Some sort of jacket thing,' said Mr Gatlock. 'Darkish. Brownish, maybe. I dunno. Couldn't tell what colour it was in that light. Don't wear proper clothes no more, the females round here. Except for my Elma and Betty.'

Betty and Elma beamed at Kate from over their white Peter Pan collars.

'What's she asking all these questions for?' Mr Gatlock asked them. 'What's she on about, then?'

'She's going to put us in a book, Arnold,' shouted Betty.

'She's writing us all down,' shouted Elma.

'Stupid female,' said Mr Gatlock.

Kate bellowed her thanks and left.

She had reached the corner of Redbourne and Fridesley Roads when she met Rose Smith.

'I've got a confession to make,' said Rose, and paused.

'Yes?' Kate queried, her heart at boot level.

'I know you've spent so much time and trouble over getting my boxes back, Kate.'

'It wasn't just me,' said Kate, awkwardly. 'Everyone was involved.'

'Yes, but you've done more than the others. And I'm grateful, really I am. But now you're trying to find out what happened to the Oxford mourning box, aren't you?'

'Yes,' said Kate, guardedly.

'But you see,' said Rose, 'really, I don't want it back.'

'Isn't it the most valuable box in the collection? Didn't we hear all that stuff about the John Parrish works at Wolvercote and special enamels?'

'All that's true, but it was Granny, and then Theo, who liked it so much. I always found it morbid and horrible, and now it's gone, I'm glad. If Granny asks where it is, I shall have to tell her a fib. I'll think of something. I suppose I could even tell her that it was stolen. I don't care who's got it, Kate. They're welcome to it. I hope I never get it back again.'

'Any special reason?' asked Kate.

'It seems that Yvonne rang up and asked Lynda to bring it to her on the night she was killed, and maybe the box has something to do with her murder. It's all mixed up with killing and death and it gives me the horrors just to think about it. I couldn't touch it; I don't want it in my house again: it's unlucky.' As Rose spoke, her voice was rising towards hysteria. 'I hate the thing. Don't get it back for me: I don't want it, Kate. The money for it would be great, but I never want to see the box again.'

Kate stood watching as Rose walked down the Fridesley Road and disappeared into Flack's newsagents. Why had Yvonne rung Lynda that night? She pictured her sitting in her warm house as Lynda and Theo got ready to go out into the storm and the rest of them prepared to steal back the boxes. No, Yvonne wouldn't be able to resist the temptation to pull on the puppet-string attached to Lynda and remove the most valuable, the most desirable box from the collection before Rose got to them. The woman really was a bitch. And Rose was probably right that the blue enamel mourning box was involved in some way in her death, though at the moment she couldn't see quite how.

But that was the end of Rose's motive. If she didn't want the Oxford box back – and Kate believed that the vehemence of her speech was genuine – then she was hardly likely to have gone rushing over the road to beat Yvonne over the head and grab it back. Unless she had some entirely different motive, there was one person Kate needn't be nervous of on the woodland paths during the group's race.

Kate spent an afternoon on the chocolate biscuits and the word processor, creating an outline of the new book. Her workroom was in the basement of her house and had only a narrow view of uneven green grass and some tired-looking leaves. She had tried to keep it as functional as possible, with no distractions from her work, but had gradually added pinboards with postcards and cuttings and cryptic messages to herself. The room was dominated by her desk with its computer and printer, but there were cushions on the seat of her chair, and the four-drawer filing cabinet and the stationery cupboard were a burgundy colour rather than functional grey.

Her manuscript looked very neat and impressive when she printed it out, but she had to admit that there was still a lot of work to do before she could type 'The End' on page 380. She spent another hour scribbling a few lines of text under the chapter headings. Even if it bore no relation to the finished book, it might keep Elliot happy for a few weeks. Then another idea for the opening chapter came to her and she returned to the keyboard and started writing in earnest.

The doorbell rang. Kate looked at the clock: two hours had passed and it was sixish. This would be Camilla. She opened the door. Camilla stood there, sure enough, but there, too, was Carey, his wrist held in a firm grip and looking like Camilla's prisoner.

'I thought it would be best if Carey told you about it, himself,' Camilla said. Kate had never seen her so angry, the anger battened down, but trying to escape through her eyes and mouth.

'Come in, both of you,' said Kate, taking coats and hanging them up. She had to prise Camilla's hand away from Carey, and that was no lover's clasp, she thought.

The phone rang. 'Go into the sitting room and pour us all a drink,' she said to Camilla. If there was enough gin in the bottle she kept for Andrew, it might take the emotional temperature down a bit. She picked up the phone and snarled her name into it.

'Couldn't you get a machine to answer your phone?' Liam asked. 'It might sound more welcoming and it might be at home more often.'

'But I've been in all afternoon. Working,' she added virtuously.

'I've been working too, which is why I couldn't phone you earlier. Are you free next Saturday?'

He sounded as though he wanted to rush off somewhere else right at this moment. Next Saturday? No, she should be working at her book, she should be pinning Gavin down, and finding out who murdered Yvonne, and how and why. Perhaps it would all be solved by then. And if she posted off her outline and first chapter, Elliot would be off her back, too.

'Yes,' she said.

'I wondered if you'd like to come down to Bath with me. I have to check some eighteenth-century sources in the public library there, but afterwards I thought we could have lunch, go for a walk, whatever it is you like to do on Saturdays.'

'Do you want to drive down?'

'Have you got a car?'

'Yes.' Was this why he had rung her? 'I'll pick you up at Leicester. What time?'

'Would eight-thirty be OK?'

'Fine.' That would give him the whole morning to find out what a lousy driver she was. And on the way back she could check out another idea.

Camilla was looking agitated in the sitting room doorway, miming winding-up. She wished she could stand and talk to Liam, but he was sounding pressured, too.

'I'll see you on Saturday then. Come to the Parks Road entrance, you can stop the car in the bay outside the college for twenty minutes without getting clamped or towed away.'

'Opposite Wadham?'

'Yes.'

She put the phone down. Now she had to go and face Camilla and Carey and the emotional scene that they were determined to have all over her sitting room. She hadn't forgotten the flash of blue that she had seen while Carey was juggling, and she mustn't be taken in by his charm this time so that she dropped her suspicion of him. Or of Camilla.

'Thank goodness you're off the phone at last,' Camilla was saying. 'I thought you were going to stand there chatting with that silly expression on your face all evening.'

'Haven't you poured the drinks yet? Why don't we sit down, and you can tell me what this is about.' She didn't want Camilla commenting about Liam before she had some idea what he meant in her life, if anything. And let me guess, she thought, when you're this agitated, it must be something Carey's done.

'It's Carey,' said Camilla.

'Trouble?' asked Kate, looking at Carey.

'If you're going to talk like that I shall go home straight away and not tell you the news.'

'I will keep my opinions strictly to myself,' said Kate. 'So get on with the story.'

'You know I always wondered how Yvonne found out about me and Carey. And how she got the photographs of . . . well, of me, and me and Carey. Tell her,' Camilla said to Carey, pink in the face, drinking her gin too fast.

'She's trying to say that I told Yvonne about the two of us. It amused Yvonne when I told her about me and Camilla. She wanted to know more about it, so she lent me the equipment. I took the photos and the video films, and gave them to Yvonne.'

Kate tried to work out the logistics of this, but failed.

'That's sick,' she said. 'How did you do it?'

'A wall-mounted video camera,' said Carey. 'Of course, I wasn't to know what use she was going to make of them, was I?'

'You thought you and she would spend cosy evenings in her studio watching her blue videos, and that would be an end to it?' She didn't believe that, and he knew it. 'Why don't you throw him out of your life?' she asked Camilla.

'She's still hoping that public confession will cleanse my soul, show me the error of my ways and persuade me to change,' said Carey. 'And anyway, she knows how much I love her.'

The phone rang again. Kate picked up the extension and shouted, 'Yes?' then regretted it as she thought it might be Liam back.

'Kate dear? Are you having a bad evening?' It was Andrew and she tried not to feel disappointed. It wasn't his fault that he wasn't someone else.

'Tell him to hurry up,' shouted Camilla, loudly and rudely.

'I was ringing to ask you whether you wouldn't like to get away from everything this weekend.' Andrew sounded huffy, as well he might, thought Kate. 'I though we could go over to Suffolk, to this little hotel I know where the food is absolutely wonderful, relax completely, just enjoy ourselves.'

'It's a marvellous idea,' said Kate. 'But I'm afraid I'm rather busy this weekend.'

'You need a break,' said Andrew. 'Why don't you drop everything and come away. It's a long time since we really had time to ourselves.'

'I'm sorry, Andrew, I just can't make it, I'm afraid. But some other time, maybe.'

There was an audible silence at the other end of the phone, full of accusations of disloyalty.

'Well, if you can't, I suppose that's it,' he said.

'But come to supper next Tuesday,' she said impulsively.

'I'm not sure I'm free,' said Andrew. 'I'll give you another ring.' And he hung up. Kate felt guilty for a moment, but she was too interested in the scene that was emoting all over her sitting room to worry about it for long. Carey was smiling and Camilla was pink faced and still angry when she got back.

'He's enjoying this,' said Kate to Camilla.

And suppose he had done something similar to Yvonne, wondered Kate. She was a lot more dangerous than Camilla. Though, watching her friend pour the last of the gin into their glasses and top it up with a very little tonic, she wondered if she had been underestimating Camilla, as well. She looked as though she could commit murder at this moment, and Kate was afraid that it wouldn't be Carey, who deserved it, that she would take the axe to.

'Didn't you wonder why the police picked up Lynda and accused her of killing Yvonne?' Carey asked. 'She was hardly the most likely candidate, was she?'

'Are you going to explain?' said Kate. 'Or am I going to go back downstairs and get on with some real work?' She drank some of her gin to catch up with Camilla and Carey. 'Lynda,' she prompted, trying not to cast Carey as the fanciable hero of her book.

'You were screwing her, too,' said Camilla to Carey, seeing it at last.

'We used to enjoy pleasant afternoons on her lilac-coloured sheets, yes,' said Carey. 'But then we were both young and free, so why shouldn't we?'

'What about Theo?' asked Kate. 'Did he know about this?'

'Now, there's Lynda's problem,' said Carey. 'I'm afraid she didn't quite give up her afternoons with me before landing Theo. Funny how a wedding ring can mean so much to some girls, don't you think? Lynda wants to be respectable. She wants to marry Theo, and she thought it would reduce her chances if he discovered she was spending such amusing afternoons with me at the same time.'

'At the same time?'

'You had the video set up again?'

'It would have been a bit tricky in her house, don't you think? No, she liked the idea of being photographed by me. She was quite imaginative in her poses, too, which is surprising when you think what a rather boring little girl she is in other respects.'

'And you gave the photos to Yvonne?'

'Lent, sweetie, just to amuse her for the evening.'

A picture of a red canna lily came into Kate's mind: hanging on the wall of Yvonne's studio; out of focus in the background of Detective Sergeant Taylor's photograph. Threes, Carey liked them in threes, he had said, as he juggled with folded socks.

'You were Yvonne's lover, too,' she said to Carey.

And had it dawned on Camilla that Carey had been Yvonne's lover as well as her own? What did it do to her if Carey told her about it? Or perhaps Camilla had guessed, after all, and had picked up the blue enamel box and given it to Carey, who hadn't realized its significance and had juggled with it in front of Kate in all innocence?

'The only thing I like about this,' said Kate, 'is the fact that if you were in on the blackmailing with Yvonne, then you're heavily at risk from whoever killed her, aren't you, Carey?'

'I would be, if I were. Which I'm not.'

'And the police found the photos? At Yvonne's?'

'They were the ones that were on the floor, underneath the body. They can hardly have missed them.'

'And what about you? Doesn't it make you a suspect, too? Why haven't the police questioned you, as well as Lynda?'

'She was the one with something to lose, not me. And then again, I believe she was seen tripping across the road from her house to Yvonne's at just the inconvenient time. And I opened my eyes wide for them and did my butter wouldn't melt act, and told them who my father was.'

Kate wondered fleetingly whose son Carey might be, but knew it would give him pleasure if she asked. Carey would do anything for kicks. If it amused him to kill Yvonne and leave compromising photos of Lynda all over the body, then that is just what he would do.

Chapter Twenty

The sun was shining through a web of chestnut branches when Kate drew up in the bay in Parks Road on Saturday morning. Notices warned her that her car would be clamped or towed away if she was parking without authority, and other notices warned her that her car was likely to be broken into or stolen. They fitted in with her mood. Her day had started with an electricity bill that was higher than she had expected, and a polite but insistent letter from her editor, and carried on through an empty bottle of *Ivoire* and a jammed zip on her jeans. Her mood wasn't helped by the knowledge that she always felt inadequate and under-educated when she visited an Oxford college, as though the words 'not a graduate' were branded on her forehead.

She went through the archway and asked the porter in the lodge to ring Liam and let him know that she was there. To her left lay a smooth quadrangle of green lawn and an eighteenth-century façade. There were sounds of a piano playing coming from a room above, and a couple of under-graduates moved from left to right towards an archway and disappeared. Then, from the opposite corner, she saw Liam, moving in his co-ordinated runner's way. He paused to greet a slim blonde woman who looked sharply at Kate before turning away, and then he was standing beside her. Her shyness came out as a brusque greeting, and they walked in silence back to her car.

'I hope you're good at map-reading,' she said, 'because I'm not sure where it is we're going, and I have to concentrate on the road.' She sounded cross and she wasn't looking at him as she switched on the ignition, but she could feel him looking at her, and his voice, when he spoke, was amused.

'Leave it all to me,' he said. 'Turn right into South Parks Road and right again into Mansfield Road. But before you do . . .'

'Yes?' He was going to complain about her bad temper.

'You'd better do up your seatbelt.'

After that the day improved. The sun behind her warmed the nearly-spring landscape, and reminded them that daffodils would soon be joining the snowdrops and crocuses in front gardens. They took the A420 west and stopped off for coffee in a small town and Kate could relax and talk, away from the wheel of her car. Liam hadn't said anything about her driving, but she had felt him tensing, and his right foot pressing vainly into the floorboard as she had approached that last red light a little too fast. Well, she had stopped in time, hadn't she? After that she had got them into Bath safely, and parked in a multi-storey car park, even if she had left a few irate drivers behind her. She had to admit that Liam was an excellent map-reader, telling her in plenty of time to move into the left- or right-hand lane before a turning.

Then Liam disappeared off to the library, leaving her to

spend time staring into shop windows at clothes she couldn't afford and didn't want to wear, and wonder why she couldn't behave in a natural and friendly way to him. Maybe if her father hadn't died when she was ten? But whatever the reason, and perhaps after all it lay in her own spiky personality as much as in childhood trauma, she would have to make more effort to relax and not be on edge when she was with Liam. She had managed it with Andrew, hadn't she? But then, Andrew was twelve years older than she was . . . At least she managed not to scowl at Liam when they met up again.

'I've looked up a place for lunch in the Good Pub Guide,' she said, as they walked back to the car. 'It has a river to stroll by afterwards, too. It will take us home by a longer route, though. Do you mind?'

'No, I'd like that,' said Liam bravely. 'What's the place called?'

'Denington. It's in Wiltshire.'

After lunch, which was as good as the guide had promised, they walked down through the wide and only street towards the bridge over the river. They wandered past the old-fashioned windows of the shops and Kate found herself as usual making mental notes of the goods displayed, in case they came in useful for detail for a character – if she ever managed to fight her way back to the twentieth century. First came a dress shop whose clothes she couldn't imagine having the social life to wear. And how on earth could you possibly fit all your needs for a day out into that neat little handbag? She hitched her large, scuffed leather one over her shoulder and they moved on. Next came a shop selling fishing bags and body warmers, green Wellingtons and waxed jackets. Then she stared into the biggest shop so far: double-fronted this one, with a faint expensive smell drifting out through its front door. It was an old-fashioned chemist's shop, with a window full of packaged scents and boxed soaps and hints of even lovelier things inside.

'*Ivoire*,' she said into the companionable silence that had wrapped round them since the end of lunch. 'You can't get it in Oxford, and I'm running out. It's the scent I usually wear,' she explained, seeing his blank face.

'Well, I suppose you'd have to,' he answered, straight-faced.

And then she noticed the name of the pharmacist painted over the door.

'Look,' she said, staring at it. 'We have to go in.' It was the reason she had suggested lunching here, but she hadn't really expected to fall over the name so quickly.

A man of about sixty, rather broad shouldered, with dark hair that had gone a pewter colour and a dark complexion, came out from a back room. His face, with its greenish-hazel eyes was familiar. No, it couldn't be a coincidence, he had to be related.

She tried her most captivating smile and hoped that he was more susceptible than the Oxford members of his family to her charm. 'Mr Baight?' she asked.

'Yes.'

'I was looking for Balmain's *Ivoire*,' she said. 'It's so hard to come by, I'm afraid. The eau de toilette or the perfume would do.'

'Yes, I have them, but I'm waiting for a delivery of the smaller sizes.'

Kate knew the prices and realized that this purchase of goodwill and information was going to cost her a lot more than the exchange with the lockkeeper at the Postle. She had been to the bank on Friday afternoon and taken out enough to get her through the coming three weeks. It should be enough to get her on the right side of the pharmacist. 'I'll take the perfume,' she said. She took a deep breath. 'And the eau de toilette.' Oh well, she had now spent so much that she might as well splash out properly. 'And the bath oil if you have it.'

'Sorry, we're out of bath oil.'

Well, thank goodness for that: she had spent over a hundred pounds already, and Liam's eyebrows went up as she started counting out twenty-pound notes. The pharmacist's expression softened and Kate hoped she had purchased the right to ask him some intrusive questions. They were still the only customers in the shop, but Kate had to think of a way to get the conversation on to something more personal.

'It is extravagant of me to buy all that *Ivoire*, but I wear it because it fits in with my name,' she said with her best coaxing voice. 'Ivory, you see.' She batted the eyelashes again, but the pharmacist was presumably not a reader of historical romances, for he didn't give his opinion of her books.

'Your name's unusual, too,' put in Liam, helping her out. 'But as it happens, we do know some Baights in Oxford.'

'We go running together,' said Kate. 'We're quite close.'

'Then I suppose you know all about the tragedy.' His face changed so that he looked old and sad. 'You'd better come in,' he said, unexpectedly. 'Marianne!' he called into the door behind the counter. 'Finish up your tea and come and look after the shop for a minute.'

A girl in a blue nylon overall and a lot of long curly brown hair appeared and started to rearrange the display of shampoos. 'Tea?' the pharmacist offered. 'Coffee?'

'Herb tea, please,' said Kate.

'I expect you know more about the tragedy than I do,' said Mr Baight. 'And after something like this, you need to talk, don't you? Find out if there was anything you could have done to prevent it. Sophie doesn't speak to me, of course.'

'I don't know that we can tell you much: the police have been asking a lot of questions, but no one has been arrested.'

They were handed china cups of apple and cinnamon infusion. Kate was glad to see that Liam didn't turn his nose up at it or make a rude comment about compost heaps, the way Andrew would have done.

'Of course, she would be running, she was always keen on fitness,' said the pharmacist.

'I suppose so,' said Kate. 'She was so slim and elegant. So well co-ordinated.'

'Not Yvonne,' said the pharmacist. 'I was talking about Sophie. I still think of her as my little girl, but you could hardly call her slim and elegant, I'm afraid. But she was so keen on getting strong. She could have been a really fast runner, county standard at least, if only she could have taken some of her excess weight off. It was costing her several seconds in her times, and that's no good at that standard. Here, look at these,' and he pulled some framed photographs down from the mantelpiece.

'I never wanted Yvonne to take her away, but I was given

no choice in the matter. When did you last see her? How is she?'

'She's fine,' said Kate. 'She's coping well with her mother's . . . death. I'm afraid we didn't know of your existence, though, or we'd have been in touch sooner.'

'Yvonne liked to pretend that I was dead. She found it easier than admitting that she'd run off with that man. But I'm afraid that Sophie never understood. She always blamed me, and took her mother's side.'

'They did seem to have a very close relationship,' said Kate, and thought how to frame her next question without sounding crass. 'What happened to the . . . man?'

'Her lover? She was obsessed with him. That's why she moved to Oxford: to be near him. But he left her after five years or so. She never forgave him, and she never forgave me for finding someone else while she was gone. Difficult woman, she was. But she didn't deserve this to happen.'

'Nobody does.'

'Who was he?' asked Kate. 'Do you know his name?'

'Tom Grant.'

'Ah. Yes, it would be.'

'I don't like to say it now that she's dead, but I think she took it out on poor old Sophie. I was never happy about it,' said Mr Baight. 'Sophie should have had her independence. She should have moved out of that house and lived her own life. I blame myself partly: maybe I should have stayed around and made sure that she got free of her mother. Still, with a woman like Yvonne, what can you do?'

They each took in the implications of what had just been said. Then Kate looked at the photographs, and she stopped smiling.

'Look at these,' she said to Liam.

'But if this is your Sophie, I recognize her,' he said, pointing. 'Didn't I tell you about the dedicated runners I see out training most lunch hours in the University Parks, with countdown timers that go off every thirty seconds and expensive running shoes? And this one does a couple of dozen press-ups on the wet grass during her recovery periods.'

'Then I wonder why she isn't fitter and faster than the rest of us?'

'Tell me more about Yvonne these last few years,' said Mr Baight. 'I need to fill in the gaps. And was it my fault, do you think? Should I have kept in touch?'

'I'm starting to see how it could have been done,' said Kate to Liam, as they drove back to Oxford later in the afternoon. 'The timing still isn't right, though. Gavin and Penny could have worked it out between them and murdered her. And Camilla might have done everything she said, but omitted to tell me that she hit Yvonne over the head hard enough to kill her.'

'What with?' asked Liam. 'What did she use? And where is it now?'

'I don't know. And what about Carey? He could have done it, too. I saw him in the right place at the right time. And what was he doing with Rose's mourning box?'

'You're low on motive for Carey,' said Liam. 'And you're not absolutely sure that it was the Oxford box you saw for that instant when he was juggling: from what you've said, he's quite capable of fooling you about it just for fun. And is he really a violent type? It doesn't sound like it. And watch out for the next turning to the right.'

'I can almost believe that he'd kill her for kicks. Or perhaps as part of some weird sexual game.'

'Not one that I've come across,' said Liam. 'Oh, and there was another of your group that I've seen out training for speed.'

'Which one?'

'A bloke with a beard and green shorts and a T-shirt with some sort of Save the World message on it.'

'Gavin. The beard's gone, and I'm not sure I believe the message on the T-shirt. And why are these people putting all this extra effort in, do you think?'

'They're probably much more competitive than you imagine. People get like that in club races: there's real needle there.'

'There's something else I've seen or heard recently that's sitting waiting in the back of my mind for me to make a connection.'

'The trick is,' said Liam, 'to concentrate on something else and then the thing you wanted to remember will come unbidden into your conscious mind.'

'Has that ever worked for you?'

'I don't think so. But it beats worrying about it.'

'Gavin. That's it. Another piece of the jigsaw has just dropped into place. The windlass. That's what I fell over when I ran out of his room when the phone rang.'

'Should I ask what you were doing in his room?'

'Better not. But that makes him the flooder of houses, doesn't it?'

'A strong candidate, certainly.'

'I think we may have solved it,' she said triumphantly.

'Why don't I concentrate on the road now, while you tell me the story of your life?'

Chapter Twenty-One

They were running early in the morning on Tuesday, though there wasn't perhaps quite the same spirit among the members of the group. Were people not meeting each others' eyes? Had it occurred to some of them that the murderer was perhaps one of them rather than some vague and faceless outsider?

But there were only five days until the club race and this was their last serious run before it.

'We'll take an easy pace,' said Penny. 'I think the water has subsided enough to take the track by the canal and into Oxford. Five miles is enough.' That was the theory of it, you tapered your training so that on the actual day you could put all your effort into the race. Any training that hadn't been done by now would never be made up.

It wasn't actually raining, but the dawn light was struggling to make an impression through the thick clouds that hung low over Fridesley. They set off in the yellow light of the streetlamps rather than the encouraging light of the sun.

They were all subdued and conversation was desultory.

'Have you heard about Barbara?' came Penny's clear tones.

'What now?' Kate said to Camilla.

'They're moving,' replied Camilla. 'They're taking the girls away from the Amy Robsart – too blue-stocking – and sending them to somewhere that costs three times as much.'

'I've never really come to terms with the fact that you work in the private sector,' said Kate.

'Well, leave that old argument for the moment,' said Camilla, who seemed to have grown a lot fitter and chattier over the past few weeks. 'And listen to the gossip about Barbara and Nick.'

'Where are they moving to?' called Kate to Penny.

'Some mansion out in the expensive Oxfordshire countryside,' replied Penny. 'Paddocks for the ponies. The sort of garden you open to the public. A house with separate wings for the children on the occasions when they're not off at school or skiing. Heaven.'

Kate thought of her small, warm, womb-like house and felt no envy. 'If you didn't want to share your life with your children, you shouldn't have them,' she said.

'You are a pain when you're in your puritanical mood,' said Camilla. 'Where do you think they got the money from? We're talking something really serious here, aren't we?'

'Yes, and he's been off looking at cottages in France, too, according to Barbara. It sounds like the sort of money that someone would come into if they had pulled off a multi-million pound deal for a man like Grant,' said Kate. 'I think he's going to get his expensive development and his access road, and probably an acre or two of red-brick executive housing as well, all within a mile of Carfax.'

'What about Gavin? Didn't he help? Why isn't Penny

sporting expensive new trainers, at least?' Penny was wearing her usual tracksuit and her scarlet trainers had been through the washing machine several times. 'And where is Gavin, anyway?'

'Feeding the children. He's doing his bit as a new man.'

'And you know my opinions on that.'

The miserable sun was still skulking behind the clouds and the dawn light was hardly brighter than the night. They padded on for a while by the side of the canal, in silence.

'And what about this new man of yours?' asked Camilla suddenly.

Kate growled something about *New man, what new man?*

'You don't think you keep it quiet in a town like Oxford, do you? You've been seen, noted, gossiped about. He's tall, dark, thin, they say. Not particularly handsome. Looks like an academic.'

'They know it all then, don't they?'

'What does Andrew think about it?'

'We haven't talked about it. Why should we? And anyway, Andrew and I are just friends these days.'

'I think, Kate, you're going to have to face up to a little messy emotion, instead of side-stepping it all the time.'

'You're exaggerating, Millie. We're just talking about a couple of men who are friends of mine. Nothing emotional. Nothing messy.'

'Huh!' said Camilla.

'What is that supposed to mean?'

'It's about time you got yourself properly involved with someone rather than carrying on the semi-detached relationship you've always had with Andrew. No danger of getting hurt there, have you? And you may disapprove of Carey and me, but at least I'm taking risks, and having some fun along the way. I'm living my life from the inside rather than sitting back and observing it.'

'Is that what I do?'

'Of course it is. Haven't you noticed?'

Kate was silent for the next twenty minutes.

It was when they were getting back towards Fridesley, running through the soggy grass of the recreation field, with the lights of the Baight house shining like a beacon in one corner, that it started to rain. Not a light, friendly drizzle to cool off a runner and refresh the skin, but a heavy, painful, cold, drenching shower that had the sting of hail in it. Sophie was leaving them, plodding away to their left towards the yellow lights of her studio, overhanging the recreation field.

'This way,' called Penny. 'We'll take the short cut.'

'Short cut? Why did no one ever tell me about it before?' said Kate.

'Because we thought you needed the extra distance and because you never asked,' said Camilla, unkindly. 'These streets are all built the same, with a lane running between the back gardens.'

It looked as though they were running straight into someone's garage, but no, it was a separate passageway leading, as Camilla had said, into the lane that ran between the back gardens of Redbourne Road and Wheatfield Road. They were passing along the side of the Binns's garden, Kate saw, nearly brushing the sides of their garden shed. Now what was it that that child had said about the shed on the night of the murder? She couldn't think with the rain in her face and dripping down the neck of her tracksuit. All she could think about was her coffee maker and a pile of toast and marmalade and a hot bath and dry clothes. She would think about it all later. Her brain needed food and warmth before it could work at full strength. They turned left and crossed Wheatfield Road and then were running in single file up another path into the lane that led into Rosamund Road.

'Who knows about this short cut?' Kate asked Camilla as they raced back over the pelican crossing on the Fridesley Road, ignoring the glares of the commuting motorists as they brought the traffic to a halt.

'I thought everyone did,' said Camilla. 'Anyone who's ever lived in a Victorian or Edwardian house knows that they were built back to back like that, with a lane running between the ends of the gardens.'

Everyone, thought Kate. Everyone except me.

After her bath and her breakfast Kate went and worked for an hour on her book. She managed to get her hero and heroine into the same room and at splendid loggerheads. Then her hero departed under a cloud of suspicion and her heroine, whose name changed daily, but was currently Alice, was left in deepest danger in war-torn France.

At this point she pressed Exit, copied her file on to a backup floppy disk, and climbed the stairs out of her workroom to face her own murder mystery. It was a lot easier to make it up as you went along and only present your heroine with problems to which you already had a solution.

She knew now who had killed Yvonne, and why, and she knew how he had done it. But she still needed a piece of concrete evidence before she could go and tell Detective

Sergeant Taylor all about it. She had the feeling that the irritating Binns children held the key, but wasn't sure how to squeeze the information out of them.

'Oh no,' said Valerie Binns, when she opened the door of the house in Wheatfield Road. 'Of course they're not here this morning, Kate. They're at school.'

'Aren't they a bit young?' asked Kate who was ignorant about these things.

'They go to Meadowland,' said Valerie. 'It's so important for them to learn the right way to relate to their peer group, don't you think?'

Kate, who still had a small white scar on her arm where she had been bitten by some anti-social infant in their reception class, could only agree. She could see that Valerie was about to close the door, but at that moment the phone started ringing in the tiny hall behind her, and instead of leaving Kate slipped inside the front door and waited for Valerie to finish.

Valerie was making 'tut tut,' and 'oh dear,' remarks into the phone. 'I'll see what I can manage,' she said, and put the phone down.

'Trouble?' asked Kate, hopefully.

'Elma's leg's playing up again,' said Valerie. 'And Betty wants me to give them a lift up to the Nuffield Orthopaedic to see the physiotherapist. But I have to pick the girls up in just over an hour and I don't think I'd be back in time.'

Gotcha, thought Kate. 'Please let me pick the girls up,' she said with great sincerity. 'I think the three of us get on rather well, and they can come to my place until you get back. You can come and collect them when you've delivered Elma and Betty back to Mr Gatlock.'

'They do seem to like you,' said Valerie, with just a touch of suspicion. 'And it would solve a problem.' She obviously hated not to be helpful to a neighbour. It was all part of being a real member of the old, authentic community, though the Gatlocks probably saw her only as a free and convenient taxi service, and she doubted whether Valerie took it as far as patronizing the old and authentic pub, the Cobblers, with its kippered ceilings and loud computer games.

'Where do I find this Disneyland place?' asked Kate.

'Meadowland. It's off the Banbury Road,' said Valerie. 'I'll ring Mrs Cook to let her know you're coming instead of me. You have to be there by twelve-ten, and please don't park on the wavy lines by the school gate.'

Twelve-ten gave Kate time to stock up on all the unhealthy goodies that Valerie hoped her children never touched. 'Would you like me to give them their lunch?' she asked. But Valerie didn't trust her to that extent and promised to be back soon after one o'clock.

Smarties, thought Kate. Choc ices. Some of the lurid red and black sticky things that Mrs Flack had on the counter and that she watched the schoolchildren buying. Fatty, salty things in packets. She went off happily to Mrs Flack's shop.

'Off the diet, I see,' said Mrs Flack.

'In training for the club race,' said Kate, and smiled blandly back at her.

At twelve eight she was sitting in her car outside Meadowland, ten feet south of the wavy lines, watching in horror as middle-class mothers swooped up at reckless speeds in their expensive cars and parked on pavements and across driveways and slammed car doors behind on the

Justins and Emilys, the Ariadnes and Oscars bickering in the back seats of their Volvos and Peugeots while they went to scoop up their Henriettas and Karls as they tottered out of the big front door of Meadowland, clutching poster-painted pictures and egg-box models.

She saw Amelia and Dorrit come out in their identical flower-printed dresses with the lace collars and climbed out of the car and went towards them with her best child-conning smile.

'Are you going to ask us some more questions?' asked Amelia when she had strapped them into the back seat and let the female Nigel Mansells screech away from Meadowland. Kate pulled gently out and turned left into the Banbury Road.

'Why don't we wait till we get back to my place,' she said, and let Amelia and Dorrit wonder what was in the large paper bag on the front seat for just a little longer.

When she had silently taken all the sweets and snacks out of the bag and displayed them on her kitchen table, she turned again to Amelia. 'Now, you were going to tell me what Dorrit saw in the woodshed.'

Amelia frowned. 'That's not a woodshed. That's where we keep our bikes and our big toys.'

'Sorry,' said Kate. 'Wrong book. I wasn't thinking. Well?'

Dorrit made excited and incomprehensible noises. Kate handed them both a glutinous scarlet sweet, then hastily tucked paper napkins round their lace collars. She would have to scrub their faces thoroughly before Valerie turned up.

'She found two things,' said Amelia. Kate handed them both a sticky black and green striped sweet.

'Thanks,' said Amelia. 'First of all she found a hat.'

'What sort of hat?' asked Kate, handing over a salty snack in the shape of a space monster. She was glad she had bought so much: this child knew how to time her answers all right.

'It had pictures round it,' said Amelia, accepting three monsters and handing more to Dorrit.

'Yellow pictures.' She took a couple of fizzy white sweets and listened to Dorrit's nonsense-talk for a moment more. Kate handed over the choc ices and waited while they ate the ice cream and spread most of the chocolate over their faces.

'There were flowers on the hat,' said Amelia, while Kate opened a small packet of salted peanuts. 'Pictures of flowers.'

Kate realized that that was all she was going to get about the hat. 'What else did she find?' she asked, while the Binnses scrunched on their peanuts.

'Have you got any Coke?' asked Amelia. Kate went to the fridge and fetched a couple of cans.

'It was a piece of plastic,' said Amelia. 'The see-through stuff.'

'How big?' asked Kate, but the Binns children looked genuinely puzzled, and drank their Cokes. Kate looked at her watch: it was time to remove all evidence of her wickedness. She swept all the debris into her rubbish bin and wiped down the table top, then took the girls into her bathroom. The cleaning operation took nearly ten minutes but was effective and completed just in time. As they went back into the kitchen, Kate saw Valerie's Morris Minor drawing up outside.

'Where are they now?' she asked rapidly and desperately. 'The hat and the plastic, I mean?'

'They've gone again,' said Amelia just before the doorbell rang.

'Hello, darlings!' cried Valerie. 'Have you missed Mummy?'

'I'm sure they have,' said Kate. 'But they've been very good.'

'Don't you look clean!' said Valerie. 'What have you been playing with Katie?'

'She's been telling us stories,' said Amelia. 'It's what she's best at, she says.'

Valerie shepherded them out to the car, but Dorrit turned back to Kate. 'Thank you for having me,' she said, quietly but clearly.

Kate was left wondering who had conned whom. And what had happened to the evidence Gavin had left in the toyshed?

Chapter Twenty-Two

Kate was in her element, organizing the club race. She knew she should be worried about the possibility of a murderer still being at large and creeping up on her, axe in hand, in some isolated spot, but with the frost melting in the bright morning sunlight and the promise of spring in the woods, she could only feel exhilarated and excited and glad that she was alive and in the open air, wearing a pair of running shoes and with ten miles of woodland and riverside paths ahead of her.

She had asked a couple of friends to turn up to time people in and out and to help with the working out of times and places. The runners started in the recreation ground, with a small crowd of the curious and the sceptical to give them a half-hearted cheer when they started off. They left in groups: first the slowest of the women, including Sophie, then the main group of Kate and Camilla, Penny and Rose, then Gavin some twenty minutes after them. Gavin still had a good chance of winning though, thought Kate. And he's looking pretty confident, too, in his black and white Lycra muscle tights. All the group members were present, even the two women who shirked the dark early winter mornings and joined them in the spring and summer when the weather and the countryside were more welcoming.

They stretched and bounced and jogged round in circles as they waited for their turn to leave. Gavin was drinking from a bottle of spring water and telling anyone who would listen to him that the main problem with distance running was dehydration and how important it was to make sure that you were fully hydrated before setting off.

'And we had a meal full of complex carbohydrates last night,' Penny was saying.

'Super,' said Camilla. 'I'm chewing some refined sugar, glucose, ascorbic acid, and assorted E numbers. Have one?'

Kate shook her head. The combination of food and nerves were bound to make her sick. 'And you shouldn't be eating that, either. You know what it does to your guts.'

'It's just one small biscuit, Kate. It won't do me any harm.'

The first part of the run took them through the streets of Fridesley before they turned west towards the bypass and the wrought-iron entrance to Wytham Woods. All except Gavin had exchanged their usual long trousers for shorts, mostly pale or dark blue, but Sophie's were red satin like a boxer's. Penny had been brave enough to wear a running vest, but the rest of them wore T-shirts with short sleeves. White winter legs gleamed between shorts and bright-coloured running shoes: turquoise blue and white, scarlet and green. Like parrots, thought Kate. And then it was her turn to leave. She and Camilla left their tracksuits behind with the marshals and set off in T-shirts and shorts. After the winter months in long trousers, her legs felt exposed and pale in the early March sunshine. There were twelve miles to go, some of it uphill, some of it muddy.

They took the first couple of miles steadily, though Rose soon fell back, and they quickly overtook Sophie. Penny ran just behind the two of them, next to Barbara and a woman who only ran in the spring and summer and whose name Kate had forgotten.

'You are unusually silent this morning,' said Camilla, eventually.

'I'm saving myself for the running,' replied Kate. 'I remember that hill just after we turn left in Wytham Woods. It goes on for ever and I hate every yard of it.'

'That's more like it,' said Camilla. 'I don't recognize you unless you grumble all through the first three miles of a run. After that you're so cheerful that the rest of us want to throttle you.'

And there was an awkward silence as they both wished Camilla hadn't said it. Behind them the footsteps and chatting voices were fading as Rose and Barbara fell further behind with the summer runner, whose stamina was apparently fading already.

'On the subject of throttling,' said Kate, 'or beating about the head with a heavy blunt object or whatever, I do believe that I may know who did it. Though I hate to think it's one of us, and I'm probably wrong.'

'Well done. That seems to have covered all the possibilities,' said Camilla.

'I've been going over our suspects,' said Kate, and then stopped again, because one of the suspects was running at her side up a path in a large and underpopulated wood. No, she reminded herself, there was no danger from Camilla or anyone else: Rose and Penny, Barbara, the nameless woman, Sophie and Gavin were on the path behind them. No one would risk another murder in such company. Would they? She was really quite safe. Really.

'And their motives,' she added. 'It must be to do with the Fridesley Fields development. Yvonne was blackmailing someone and they, or one of the other developers, saw her as a threat to their profit, so they eliminated her.'

'But that left the rest of the Friends,' objected Camilla. 'Why haven't we been killed off one by one, like in that Agatha Christie story?'

'How effective are we compared with Yvonne?' asked Kate. 'Not very,' she said, answering her own question. 'It was an obsession with her.'

'Did you find out why?'

'The old story: Tom Grant was her lover until he dropped her. She never forgave him. But, oddly enough, he and Sophie seem to have got on well, at least when she was a teenager.'

'You should still watch it, Kate,' said Camilla. 'I reckon you were at risk with that high-profile clipboard and list of questions of yours. It doesn't matter whether the murderer thought you were on his trail or whether he thought you really were a Friends activist, either would have put you at risk if you believe that motive. I think you should watch out for yourself, Kate.'

Was it a threat or a warning? How much did she know about Camilla? She herself had changed immeasurably since she was twelve years old, so what made her think that Camilla was the same colourless, good little girl? She

thought of the swish of pink sequins in Millie's wardrobe.
Not Millie, she reminded herself: Camilla, a new and
strange person. Someone who took a young and irrespon-
sible lover, who did unimaginably naughty things with him
and had her photograph taken doing them. And then got
herself blackmailed by the local dentist. No, she didn't
know this Camilla person who was padding doggedly and
silently at her side, any more than she had understood
Yvonne. Or Gavin, if it came to that. Or Barbara. She had
known them for several years, she had categorized them
and pigeonholed them and made assumptions about them.
And every time she had been wrong. And about Theo, now
she came to think about her list of recent failures. The only
people who had acted according to her preconceptions had
been Rose and Penny, and as a matter of fact she wasn't
completely sure about Penny.

'My money's on Gavin,' said Camilla. 'To tell the truth I
never really believed in all that saintly New Man stuff, and
it seems to me that he has got the strongest motive.'

'He flooded the houses on the Postle to get the people
to leave,' said Kate. 'I think he's made money from the
development scheme so far and stands to make a lot more
if Grant's complex is actually built. I think he's taken bribes
to help other applications through the Planning Committee. He was being blackmailed by Yvonne and he was
missing for part of the evening she was killed. I don't think
much of his morals, and I think he's a hypocrite, but I still
haven't got any real evidence that he killed Yvonne.'

'But he could have done,' persisted Camilla. 'The timing's a bit tight, but he's a pretty fast runner, you know, and
he's been out practising on his own these past few weeks. I

bet he could win this race if he wanted to: he's probably holding back on purpose so that we don't know how fast he is. He could have made up several minutes on the Fridesley circuit that night.'

'Especially,' said Kate slowly, 'if he took the short cut past the Binns's shed.'

'Talking of speed,' said Camilla, 'shouldn't we be picking up a few seconds on this downhill section?'

'And talking of Gavin,' said Kate, 'you were right about his speed. The man's a flyer. I've just caught sight of a pair of black and white harlequin legs at the bottom of the hill. He's less than a quarter of a mile behind us at this moment and he's going to finish a good twenty minutes in front of us if he goes on like this.'

Gavin's feet soon became audible on the path behind them, and though they took the hill past the sawmill and down to Wytham village at a speed that probably did permanent damage to their knees, Gavin overtook them with a smug smile and a cheery wave long before they got to the bottom.

It wasn't until they were on the level stretch of road leading up to Wolvercote that they started talking again. Cars were taking the narrow road at fifty and they had to hug the right-hand edge to keep out of their way.

'And what about Penny? Maybe she could have done it for him?'

'Oh come on, you can't possibly suspect her: you're just being ridiculous now.'

'I was right about Gavin and how fast he'd got, though, wasn't I?'

'You weren't right about Carey,' said Kate, unfairly. 'He's

a complete disaster and so is your relationship. I can't think
why you stick with him now that you know about Lynda
and Yvonne. And what about the way you got yourself
blackmailed? If you hadn't done that, none of this would
have happened.'

'Oh yes it would. We would all have stolen back Rose's
boxes and someone would have murdered Yvonne, just the
same. The difference is that you would have been less wary
of me.'

Kate couldn't disagree with that.

'I don't think you're being so clever over men yourself at
the moment,' continued Camilla. 'It's no good falling for
some ambitious young academic, you know, they haven't
got time for serious relationships. They concentrate on
their careers until they're in their mid-forties and then they
settle down with some sweet twenty-five-year-old. Along
the way they may amuse themselves with the likes of you,
but it never lasts long, you know.'

'Stop being so cynical. You haven't even met Liam yet.
And anyway neither of us is serious. We haven't had time.'

'They never do have time, I'm told.'

'Did we think about the possibility of Barbara murdering
Yvonne?' asked Kate.

'You're just trying to avoid the subject of your immature
emotional life.'

'Yes, that's right. Or perhaps Nick went off to France on
the Tuesday, leaving instructions with Barbara, and she
crept out into the storm . . .'

'Wearing Rose's knitted hat and Lynda's duvet coat, and
then unlocked Yvonne's door with a spare key that she
happened to have about her person . . .'

'Well, you come up with a better suggestion, then.'

'Actually, I am going to come up with something.' Camilla sounded odd. 'Do you mind stopping for a moment, only I feel I'm going to be sick.'

They had run along by the river and had nearly reached the point where the path swung right to pass behind the willows and cross the Postle.

'Sorry,' she said. 'But I'm—' and she disappeared behind a bush. For a moment, still in her suspicious mood, Kate wondered whether this was some sort of trick. Was she about to beat Kate over the head with one of the blunt instruments with which these fields seemed liberally provided? But her face was a nasty whitish colour and there was a sheen of sweat on her forehead that seemed to having nothing to do with the miles they had just covered.

'I told you you shouldn't have eaten those revolting biscuits. You should have stuck to Gavin's spring water,' said Kate unsympathetically when Camilla reappeared.

'I had some of Gavin's water as well as one of Sophie's oatmeal biscuits.'

'Idiot! You know what happens to you when you eat just before a run.'

'I thought I'd accustomed my system to it gradually.'

They must have run faster than the other women without noticing it, because she could see no one behind them on the path, and Gavin had long disappeared in front of them. They might have come joint second if Camilla hadn't been taken ill. Oh well, thought Kate, so who wants to come second, anyway?

Camilla disappeared behind her bush again and there were more retching noises.

When she emerged, she said, 'Leave me here, Kate. It isn't far to walk back to Fridesley; the other women will be through soon and I'm sure I'll be better in a few minutes. But it's a shame for both of us to drop out. Go on, go and give Gavin a run for his money.'

There was really nothing she could do for Camilla except look sympathetic, and she could achieve more by completing the race and alerting the others to the situation. It would be some time before Penny and Barbara, let alone Sophie came past, so she might as well get on. 'Are you sure?' she asked half-heartedly.

'I'm sure.'

'We'll come back and find you when the race is over,' said Kate. 'I'll make sure that the flying Gavin comes sprinting back to see how you are.'

She set off down the path by the river and then took the sharp right turn that took her out of Camilla's sight and down to the Postle. Some part of her mind was aware of the figure that moved away from the low group of willows and alders and came running at speed towards her. The footsteps were quiet and rapid and the hand that caught hold of her wrist and forced her arm up behind her back and the arm that half-throttled her were very strong indeed. All Kate could see was the sky through a light grey haze, but she recognized the voice that said, 'We're going for a short walk, Kate dear. Down to the Postle. Don't bother to cry out, because no one is there now. The place is deserted and no one can hear you.'

Sophie.

Chapter Twenty-Three

Parrots, thought Kate. Red and green parrots. Somnolent grey parrot at one end of the room; lively green and red parrot swinging on its perch at the other.

Today she isn't wearing the grey parrots, the plain grey shoes that clump down on to the pavement as though they were full of lead weights. You fool, Kate, you saw it on the chart on her wall: she's been training with weights, not just in that studio of hers, but out on our runs, too. No wonder her legs always looked like tree trunks: she was wearing a couple of kilos of lead sewn into blue canvas and fixed with Velcro round her ankles.

Kate stumbled over a tussock of grass, and Sophie jerked her upright again, so that she grunted with pain. She saw the hairs on the woman's arm, black and downy on the sweat-filmed skin. She thought about sinking her teeth into that arm, but it would be like biting on a metal bar. The grip round her throat and on her wrists made her realize that Sophie had the muscles of an Arnold Schwarzenegger underneath their layer of fat. She must have been using weights on her wrists, too, she thought. We wouldn't have noticed anything odd under those baggy tracksuits of hers.

Sophie was pushing her towards the houses she had visited that day on the Postle. She hoped that Jude and Beck were still there, or even the crazy old woman in the end house. But there were no unkempt dogs coming out to investigate, no noise of barking, no unfriendly voices. If she was going to escape from Sophie she was going to have to do it by herself. She remembered the moves she had learned ten years ago in a self-defence class, and wished that she had kept practising them. But even if she had, she knew that she would not be able to break free from this grip: Sophie was far too strong for her. If she saw her chance, she could start sprinting, but even there she thought that Sophie would easily outstrip her. She tried relaxing and co-operating for a few steps, to put Sophie off her guard, but Sophie merely increased the pressure, and the result was painful.

'Fuck you, Sophie!' she croaked into the suffocating, sweaty arm. She tried kicking at the woman's shins with her trainers, but Sophie just grunted, and Kate felt a hard blow in her lower back that propelled her towards the abandoned houses. Her guts were cramping, the blood was rushing away from her face and neck, leaving her skin cold and clammy, and in a detached way she recognized the symptoms of fear: she didn't like being hurt. But if she was no match for the woman physically, she would have to put her mind to the problem instead, because she didn't think that Sophie meant her to leave this place alive, and brainpower was all that she had to fight her with.

They had reached Jude and Beck's house, with the boarded-up windows. Today the door was swinging open, its wood splintered where someone had hacked out the lock.

'They've vandalized the place to leave nothing of value for Mr Grant and his developers,' said Sophie, as she pushed Kate inside. Kate remembered that Jude had said something similar. The house smelled of mould and stagnant water with overtones of dog excrement. The only light came from the half-open front door.

'What happens now?' asked Kate, hearing the fear in her own voice. Sophie still had her in a painful grip with her arm twisted high behind her back.

'We have some waiting to do. I turned right before I got to the Five Sisters and ran down through the sheep pasture. It's a lot shorter,' said Sophie, sounding as phlegmatic as ever. 'You and Camilla had drawn some way in front of the others, especially Barbara. She hasn't been training much recently, you know. I didn't think she'd enter the group race, but since she has, we have to wait for her to go past, and then I shall cut round by the other bridge and run past Camilla. I shall stay with her, I think, and be wonderfully sympathetic about her little tummy upset. She really shouldn't have eaten my oatcakes: we all know how food before a run makes her feel sick.'

Listening to her, thought Kate, you'd think this was nothing out of the ordinary, all part of a normal training run. She's planned this, and she's going to kill me like she killed Yvonne unless I can stop her. She's in control of this scene so far, but I've got to start fighting back. She took a couple of quiet, deep breaths and made sure she had plenty of air supporting her diaphragm before she spoke again.

'Did I tell you that I drove down to Denington last Saturday and met your father,' she said, and was pleased to hear that her voice sounded much firmer.

'What?' She had startled Sophie. 'Why did you do that?'

'He showed me photographs of you when you were young and athletic,' said Kate. 'It made me wonder about you, but obviously not enough.'

Sophie was expelling breath with a hissing sound. 'You shouldn't have done that,' she said. 'We don't talk about him, not since he betrayed Mother.' Kate's wrist was jerked higher up behind her back until she thought that her shoulder would be dislocated. She forced herself not to cry out with the pain.

Change the subject fast, she thought. That one was not a good idea. But she had won back a small corner of self-confidence by making Sophie respond to her at all.

'I thought Yvonne left your father for another man?' she said. 'Not much betrayal there.'

'Tom Grant,' said Sophie. 'That was only natural. Anyone would fall for a man like him. But Father should have waited for her. She needed him when Tom left.'

'This explains a lot,' said Kate. 'No wonder Yvonne had it in for the man.'

'She was wrong there,' said Sophie. 'He was really kind to me when we first came to Oxford. I liked him, and he was going to build us that wonderful sports complex.'

'Do you think you could release your grip a bit?' Kate tried. 'You're hurting me like this.'

'You don't deserve it.' But Sophie crouched down so that Kate had to follow suit. She was exuding a dangerous, feral odour that turned Kate's stomach over. Sophie undid the laces of Kate's running shoes and loosened them.

'You can't run anywhere unless I want you to,' she said. 'And remember that I'm faster and stronger than you. You have to stay close beside me here. And if I think you're trying to escape, I'll make you sorry.'

The froglike green eyes were quite expressionless and Kate believed every word. At least it was a relief not to be jammed up against that damp, stocky body. They sat in the gloom, facing the half-open door, with their backs against the wall: figuratively in her case, thought Kate, as well as literally. Sophie seemed content to wait in silence.

'That was a very clever scheme of yours,' started Kate, hoping that she wasn't overdoing the flattery. 'Killing Yvonne, I mean. But I still don't understand why you did it.'

The silence stretched on. Then Sophie said: 'I knew about the photographs in her filing cabinet. I thought that if I destroyed them, she'd be powerless. I thought I could set fire to them, maybe. She wouldn't be able to make people do what she wanted then. But she was shouting at me and trying to stop me.'

'It was an accident, then?' asked Kate, tentatively. 'You hit out at her on the spur of the moment?'

'No,' Sophie's voice was wooden. 'I knew I had to kill her. It was there on the box: *Live to die.* Do you remember when we talked about what it meant? You all got it wrong, I could see that. The meaning was plain to me: Yvonne had to die so that I could live. *Die to live.* I knew the message was meant for me.'

'How do you mean?'

'She kept me in a prison. There were all these things I wanted to do, but she wouldn't let me.'

Kate wanted to argue, but she felt that if she stayed silent herself, Sophie might open up. And as long as Sophie was talking, Kate could plan how to stay alive. Live to live, as Carey had misquoted.

'You saw the photos at Dad's house,' said Sophie. 'I could

have been good – well, County standard at least. But I couldn't get thin. You have to be thin if you want to run fast. I expect you know that. It seemed to give her pleasure, watching me get fat and staying thin herself. And it's true what they say: there is someone else inside, trying to get out. I could feel this other person in there, hear her. At first she was just a child, crying for her missing father. But I knew he was bad and so I forced her to grow up. She had to be strong. I made her practise, not just with the running and the weights, but at all sorts of things. And one day she'd be free, and then she'd set us both free. But it all went together, didn't it? I had to get thin and strong and fast, and then I'd be different, and I could walk away from Yvonne.'

'Why couldn't you just move out?' Kate risked.

There was another long silence before Sophie answered, and Kate thought she had misjudged her again. But then Sophie said: 'Have you ever been to talk to someone? A professional listener?'

Kate shook her head, but didn't risk another comment.

'I have. My doctor told me that I should. She was like you, this psychiatrist, she asked me questions and sat there listening with that expression, half judging, half frightened, that you've got on your face. "Why don't you just leave, Sophie?" she said, in that sweetly reasonable voice of hers. As though I could! I told her that Yvonne had to understand, had to see it my way. If only she would admit that I was right, I could go. "Have you spoken to her about these feelings of yours, Sophie?" she said. "Have you tried speaking to Yvonne at all?" I answered. "She twists your words and laughs at you and . . ." Her voice trailed off into another silence.

'I wanted to kill *her*, sometimes, too,' she went on, eventually. 'The woman at the Littlemore. If I killed her, I could walk away, I'd be free. And they'd all understand at last about what's happening inside my head. They'd have to understand then, wouldn't they? And they'd have made Yvonne understand too. I could have left. But she sat there, looking frightened, and saying these soothing things, and suggesting that I could come and stay in the hospital for a time and see more doctors. But I couldn't do that. When I told them – she brought in another doctor this time, a man – they said that the relationship between Yvonne and me was not a healthy one. What did they mean by that? They said that it would lead to tragedy if it was allowed to continue. What did they know about it? Nothing! I couldn't leave her. What would Yvonne do while I was away?'

'Didn't you think she'd cope?' asked Kate, tentatively, trying not to sound as frightened as the woman at the Littlemore.

'That's not what I meant!' snapped Sophie. 'She was going to sabotage the Fridesley development scheme. She'd do anything to oppose Tom Grant. She never forgave him for leaving her. As soon as my back was turned, she had people signing petitions, and organizing public meetings.'

'Why did you want the scheme to go through?'

'Don't you know about it? Don't you know what he's going to build there? A swimming pool and a gymnasium full of the latest equipment, with trained instructors, and advice on diet.'

'It sounds expensive, though.' However she had envisaged the last minutes of her life, it hadn't been in talking about slimming diets and fitness regimes.

'Do you think I'd mind about that? It doesn't matter what it cost, as long as I could walk out of there feeling beautiful and free. She said it was my fault that Tom left us, and I had to show her that it wasn't true. She never listened to me, not properly: she just laughed. I used to sit up in my room while she was downstairs in her studio, and go over all the arguments, but she never saw it my way.'

Kate wanted to say that it was difficult for Yvonne to understand Sophie's arguments if she kept them locked up inside her head.

'She's gone now, though,' said Sophie in her matter-of-fact voice. 'And I can be beautiful and do whatever I want.'

'Oh, I don't know,' said Kate, without thinking, 'I'm not sure that anyone ever has things all their own way, however beautiful they are.'

Sophie's index finger jabbed into Kate's thigh. It felt the way Kate imagined a karate expert's finger would feel. And her thigh was not, after all, made of spongy white rubber, but of flesh and blood and nerves. It bruised. It hurt. It was real. It brought her back to the fact that if she didn't start talking herself out of it, she was in a very nasty position indeed.

'I can do anything now,' hissed Sophie. 'Anything at all.'

Ivory skull, Kate thought, that's what I'll be, like the one inside Rose's mourning box.

'What did you do with Rose's enamel Radcliffe Camera?' she asked, curiosity getting the better of her again.

'The dark blue mourning box?' Sophie's voice was still indifferent. 'Nothing. I haven't seen it.'

'Lynda was supposed to have left it on top of the glass-topped case full of casts of people's teeth.'

'Yes, maybe it was there when I let myself in. But some-one must have taken it afterwards.' Sophie's attention was on the segment of the Fields visible through the door.

Live to die, thought Kate, and shivered. But I don't want to die. Not yet. *Die to live.* And I can't believe that. It was all very well if there was no alternative, but she was still sure that something would occur to her. Nervous sweat was trickling down her back, underneath her T-shirt, though she felt quite cold.

'You'd better tell me how you did it,' said Kate, thinking it would give her a bit more time to play with. 'After all, I'm the only person you *can* tell, and it's a pity not to share it with someone.'

'It seemed a waste to use that plan of ours just on stealing those stupid boxes back for dreary Rose,' said Sophie, obediently. 'I thought that by the time everyone had lied to the police about their part in the theft, then there would be a real chance for someone to get away with a worthwhile crime. And did you see how Yvonne was manipulating everyone? She enjoyed that, and she always won. I could pretend to argue against the plan, but I knew I'd lose.'

'And on the Wednesday night?'

'I borrowed a wig from the drama club at the Amy Robsart and cut it to match Lynda's, just the way Barbara did for Rose. And I found a jacket that looked enough like that red one of Lynda's to be mistaken for it in the dark. You taught me all this: it's the general effect that matters, and people see what they expect to see. Oh, and Mother gave me that awful hat that someone had knitted for her:

it looked enough like one of Rose's hats in the dark to fool people.'

'As a matter of fact, Mr Gatlock, being a keen gardener, did notice it,' said Kate.

'None of you realized how fit I was, how fast I had got, and how strong. I was wearing my racing shoes, too, and none of you noticed that, either.'

'The red and green parrots,' said Kate, forgetting for a moment that this was not a normal conversation. 'No, but I should have done, you're right.'

'And I took the short cut, through the lane that runs between the gardens, and down between the houses. That gave me several minutes extra, too. It really didn't take me long. I went up to my room and fetched down a three-kilogram weight. I'd wrapped it in a sheet of that thick polythene she used. And I wore plastic gloves. She was in her studio, with the drawer to her filing cabinet open. She was looking at some photographs and laughing over them. I took the photos and tried to screw them up and throw them away. I told her they had to be destroyed. But she wouldn't listen to me. I knew she wouldn't, really. So I hit her.'

They were both silent. Kate tried not to imagine the scene in detail, but Camilla's description of it filled her head. She swallowed down bile and willed herself not to be sick.

'It's surprising how little blood there was. I suppose she died at once. I'm glad about that.'

'Then you ran back through the lanes?' Kate wanted to move the story forward, away from that scene in Yvonne's studio.

'I hid the hat and the plastic in the shed in the Binns's garden. I picked them up later and dropped them in a skip in North Oxford. It was good luck that it was such a wild night. Practically no one was about and those that were weren't interested in anyone else.'

'You were lucky not to be seen and recognized at any stage.'

'Not lucky, clever. Cleverer than you, anyway, Kate Ivory.'

How much time had passed? They were both watching the narrow segment of light outside the door, and they both saw the figure of Barbara thudding past. As they watched, she got a tissue out of her shorts pocket and blew her nose.

'It's early for hay fever,' said Kate.

'Exercise-induced rhinitis,' said Sophie, the pharmacist's daughter. 'Now we need to watch for Rose. I shouldn't think she'll be far behind Barbara.'

Kate was praying that Rose had got a blister, had been sick behind a bush like Camilla, had even given up and gone home. But on cue another figure plodded slowly across the lighted stage: Rose, talking to the summer runner, with Penny just behind her.

'That's it,' said Sophie. 'Come on.'

'Just a moment,' said Kate, her voice high with fear. 'Think what you're doing, Sophie. Surely you don't want two murders on your conscience? The first could have been in self-defence, or down to diminished responsibility, couldn't it? But you won't get away with it twice.'

'You talk too much,' said Sophie. 'You always have. Get up.'

Kate's wrists were grabbed again, and jerked upwards.

267

She stumbled to her feet, her right leg numb with the prolonged cramped position on the floor. Sophie pulled her towards the kitchen and the door down to the cellar. It was awkward in her running shoes with the laces undone and loosened, but Kate fought against her all the way. She could get no purchase on the dusty cork tiles, and she slid across the floor, her wrists painfully clamped in Sophie's steel grip. She shouted at Sophie, screamed at her and tried to jerk her wrists out of her grip, but the woman took no notice of her at all.

'You know what Gavin did, don't you?' said Sophie, pausing by the cellar door. 'He took that big switch for the weir gates and he stopped the water from being taken off into Peter's stream. It overflowed and it flooded the ground floor of these houses up to a height of one foot. And that means, I'm sure you realize, that the cellars were full of water. And they still are. Several feet deep. And that's where you're going, Kate, face down and unconscious, until you drown. It will all be over in less than five minutes.'

She pulled open the door to the cellar. It was quite dark at this end of the house, away from the open door, and beneath them the cellar yawned even darker. Sophie tugged viciously at Kate's wrist and stepped backwards on to the top step.

Then the pressure on her wrists was abruptly released as Sophie reached out for a support that she failed to find and let out a scream that ended suddenly in the splash of water and the darker sound of a body hitting a concrete floor.

It was a moment before Kate scrambled to her feet and realized what had happened. Then she remembered what Jude had said: he was going to leave a few surprises for the developers. And he had left one for Sophie, too. When, much later, they came with their ropes and ladders and strong torches, she saw that not only was the cellar flooded, but Jude had taken his axe and he had removed the staircase that led down from the kitchen. He must have done it just before leaving, after Sophie had checked the place out. The water in the cellar wasn't deep, only a foot or so, but Sophie was unconscious, and lying on her side with her nose and mouth beneath the surface.

Kate couldn't, on her own and without equipment, get Sophie out of that cellar, out of the stinking, stagnant water. When she went outside and shouted, she found that Sophie was right: there was no one around to hear her and to help, not in the four or five minutes that was all they had to get her out alive.

Chapter Twenty-Four

'Why do I have to come to Leicester?' asked Kate.

'Because you want to learn the end of the story,' said Liam. 'Because it will give you useful copy for another book. Because it's time you stopped being overwhelmed by people with letters after their names. And because all they want to do is offer you a cup of tea and talk to you.'

'I thought it would be sherry.'

'You dislike sherry, you told me, so settle for tea, OK?'

Since they were now approaching the Parks Road entrance to Leicester College, it was obvious to anyone but Kate that she had already lost the argument, particularly since she had dressed in neat black and white, was wearing respectable shoes, and had left her oversized, scuffed leather handbag at home. Camilla would have told her that she was feeling inadequate and undereducated, and was overcompensating. But luckily for Kate, Camilla was busy at the Amy Robsart, impressing parents, charming governors, turning herself into the sort of headmistress they all wanted, while she tried to forget about Carey.

'Accept it, Kate, this is the way it's done,' Liam was saying.

'The University looks after its own, and sod the rest of us.'

'But where do our interests differ?'

'Not this time, maybe, but they will.'

'And then you'll be out there, fighting the system?'

'Then I'll be at home, typing fantastical stories on my word processor, pretending it isn't happening, hoping it will just go away.'

There was a navy-uniformed porter in the lodge who ignored them as they walked through the archway and turned left, skirting a square of the green velvet that in Oxford takes the place of grass. Kate saw a façade with pillars and niches and heroic figures with self-satisfied expressions offering each other scrolls. A gargoyle that grinned down at her from the corner of a gutter was more to her taste, and she winked at it in return. They passed through another small archway, walked under the copper beech tree where she and Liam had met that first time, turned another corner, and stopped at a sturdy door, pedimented and pilastered and surrounded by woody stems that would doubtless soon turn into something leafy and blossoming and completely charming. For the moment, Kate was refusing to be charmed by any of it.

Liam had a key, and they walked into a small eighteenth-century hallway with a polished floor and an expensive-looking Eastern rug. The door on their right opened and they entered a well-proportioned room, with walls and floor in the soothing shades of blue and green that are recommended by psychologists for calming down potentially violent visitors. Through the window Kate could see the garden they had just crossed.

'Warden, meet Kate Ivory,' Liam was saying.

Kate shook hands with a white-haired man who so well fitted every preconception she had about Oxford colleges and dons and heads of houses, that she thought he must have been hired for the day from a theatrical agency.

'You write those amusing books, Miss Ivory, don't you?'

'Historical thrillers,' muttered Kate, wishing that she didn't blush.

'And this,' said the Warden, 'is Hallam Russell, from the Ministry.'

Another powerful man, thought Kate, taking in the dark expensive suit, the thick neck, the pouches under the assessing eyes. 'Leicester, 1955,' added the Warden. 'Tea, Miss Ivory?'

He's actually going to ring that bell and order it, thought Kate. The Warden rang, watching Kate and smiling slightly as he did so. I suppose I'm as predictable as he is, she thought.

A young woman in a white overall brought in the tea, and the Warden waited until she had left before continuing. To Kate's relief he poured the tea himself. For a moment she had wondered whether she would be expected to be mother. He handed her a perfectly ordinary cup filled with undistinguished tea.

'I gather that you've been concerned about the fate of Fridesley Fields, Miss Ivory,' said Hallam Russell.

Kate swallowed hot tea, nodded and said, 'And how it is that rich and powerful people get their own way, and make even more money, in spite of the wishes of the rest of us.'

'Yes. Well, your concern is of course shared by the Ministry,' he said. 'And I can tell you that the matter has even been discussed in Cabinet.'

'While the Cambridge men sat back and looked amused?'

'Surely the important thing is that the development scheme and its associated road have both been turned down. We do share your concern for the environment and for preserving the unique character of our city.'

Beside her, Liam was looking embarrassed. This was his home ground and she shouldn't be fighting here. 'You're right,' she said, and experimented with a smile: it didn't kill her. 'The result is the main thing, and the preservation of the Fields and the Postle.'

'I'm not so sure about the Postle,' said the Warden. 'Didn't you say those houses would have to come down, Hallam? But they'll be replaced with something entirely in keeping with the site, Miss Ivory.'

'No final decision has been taken, I believe,' said Hallam Russell, smoothly.

Kate opened her mouth to argue, but her eye was caught by something on the mantelpiece: small, dark blue, familiar.

'You're admiring my Oxford mourning box,' said the Warden, as she stared at it for longer than politeness allowed. He took it down so that Kate could see it close to. She hoped he wasn't going to open it: she didn't want to be reminded of the ivory skull.

'My son picked it up for me,' said the Warden, and suddenly he sent it spinning up in the air before catching it deftly in his left hand, in a gesture that was familiar to Kate. 'He doesn't often live up to my expectations, but this time he knew just what I coveted. *Live to die*,' he quoted, and handed the box to Hallam Russell. 'Thank you, Hallam,' he said. 'For everything.'

Kate wanted to ask where Carey had picked up the box, but she thought she knew: Yvonne's hall table on the evening of her murder. Was she already lying dead upstairs and did he just pocket it and walk out again? It would be in character.

'Stop scowling and finish drinking your tea,' muttered Liam in her left ear. 'Kate and I have to be going,' he said to the Warden. 'It is very kind of you to have seen us like this.'

'Kind!' Kate exclaimed, when they were outside again. 'Kindness had nothing to do with it. It's all short-term advantage and looking after their own interests. And I thought you were one of us.'

'I'm not sure which "us" you mean. But I'm an insider now. Part of the system, as you'd see it. I have to be if I'm to get anywhere in this world. After all, you have to stick with the conventions of your job, so let me belong to my world too.'

'I suppose I was being a bit intolerant.'

'Sometimes it's more effective to let Oxford do things in its own way: you're not, single-handedly, going to change it now.'

'I'll try to come to terms with it. But one more thing, Liam: what's your Warden's name?'

'Bill Stanton. Why?'

'No reason. It doesn't matter.'

They had come out of Leicester the other way and were standing in the Broad, looking across to the emperors' heads and the Clarendon Building. A camera crew were filming someone coming out through the archway and walking down the steps.

'*Inspector Morse*,' said Kate. 'Sometimes I feel as though we're living in the middle of a film set, and what happens in front of the cameras is as real as the rest of our lives.'

'I have to get back, Kate.'

'One always does, I find.'

'I was going to say that full term ended on the fourteenth and I shall have more free time for the next few weeks. So how about that concert?'

Kate found she was singing as she opened her front door, and when the phone started to ring she was irritated that it was in the wrong key. Perhaps she could even learn to love Janáček if she tried.

Her first caller was Penny.

'Kate, I had to tell someone. You'll never guess what's happened.'

'Surprise me.'

'Theo and Rose: they're back together.'

'Silly cow. Why?'

'Theo and Lynda's fling didn't survive the unpleasantness with the police, I'm afraid.'

'And Theo couldn't survive without a woman?'

'At least it's solved the problem of Rose's boxes. I'm sure she would have carried on waiting for the knock at the door and the questions from the police.'

'I wonder how she explained their presence in Rosa- mund Road to Theo? And the disappearance of her Oxford mourning box . . .'

Five minutes later the phone rang again.

'Kate? Andrew here. Look, I was wondering if I could

pop round this evening? There's a little problem come up in one of the libraries, and I thought we might discuss how you could help us to solve it.'

'What sort of problem?'

'Just some minor nastiness. A little criminal activity, perhaps.'

'No, Andrew.'

'Where's your spirit of adventure?'

'Gone, Andrew. I was nearly killed back there on the Postle and I didn't like it. I was terrified, and if it hadn't been for Jude and his booby trap, I'd be dead. I'm just not clever enough at this detecting game, if that's what you want to discuss.' She didn't mention the unpleasant hour she had spent with Detective Sergeant Taylor, when she had had to admit to several large lies.

'This is something entirely different. Right up your street. Not dangerous at all. And it uses all that lovely experience you gained when you worked for us at the Bodleian a couple of years ago. And, Kate . . .'

'Yes?'

'Isn't your publisher's advance running a little low? We'll pay you a reasonable salary. See you six-thirtyish. Goodbye now.'

Kate stood and looked at the telephone receiver in her hand while it purred at her. Why hadn't she said 'no' in a more positive way? The dialling tone changed to a sardonic whine.

Oxford Mourning

Veronica Stallwood

When novelist Kate Ivory first meets Dr Olivia Blacket, an academic at Leicester College, Oxford, the atmosphere is far from amicable. Olivia refuses to show Kate the fascinating material she is researching, even though it concerns the same esteemed literary figure that Kate is writing about. Determined to nose out the scandals that could provide her with a best-seller, Kate discovers a darker side to Dr Blacket. What are the strange obsessions that haunt her? What is her relationship with Kate's boyfriend Liam? And most of all, who would want to murder her . . . ?

Liam's name heads the list of suspects, but Kate knows that several others were in the vicinity of Olivia's rooms at the time of her death, including a bizarre 'family' of civilised squatters – four men guarding a blank-faced girl. As Kate is drawn into their circle, she struggles to understand a complex web of overlapping lives, and realises that, before she can unravel the truth, her own beliefs and values will come into question . . .

'Stallwood is in the top rank of crime writers'
Mike Ripley, *Daily Telegraph*

0 7472 5343 9

HEADLINE

Call the Dead Again

Ann Granger

When Meredith Mitchell picks up a hitchhiker on a lonely road one evening she is left feeling distinctly uneasy. What business can this confident, yet secretive, young woman have at Tudor Lodge, the beautiful old home of Brussels-based lawyer Andrew Penhallow, where she asks to be dropped?

Penhallow is constantly toing and froing from the Continent, but that night, unusually, he is at home, and – with his son away and his wife Carla in bed with a migraine – alone. Which is unfortunate, for the next morning he is found murdered in the garden. In the ensuing revelations about his double life, it becomes clear that Andrew Penhallow certainly had some ghosts in his past – has one come back to claim him?

'A well-plotted and always entertaining tale, told with wit' *Oxford Mail*

0 7472 5642 X

HEADLINE

If you enjoyed this book here is a selection of other bestselling titles from Headline